RUMOUR-FUELLED SOCIETY

By David Hurst

tuesday morning publishing

RUMOUR-FUELLED SOCIETY

© 2000 David Hurst

Without whom... Sarah Lee, Colin, Joe, Jon L, Ben J, Tim M, Pete H, Tony D, Harry, Warren, Ray, Mick, Bill, Norman T, Bernie, Gerry G, Frankie, Martin H, Dave C and Jen, Mark A, Simon E, Mike B, Mark and Ali, Hannah and Allan, Patrick C, Emma E, Georgina B, Smythers, Mark H (both of them), M&D, Gran Chaplin, Beth, John, Jo and all @ Airlift, Douglas G, Christian L @ Orion, Mandy L @ Watson Little, Andrew M, Adam B, and Simon T and Sophie L @ PF&D. Sorry to anyone who I've missed out, but my mind's still at the launch party (most of you were there anyway) ...*the world would stop turning*.

Published in the UK by:
Tuesday Morning Publishing,
PO Box 12608,
London SE14 6ZR.
Tel: 020-8244 0000
Fax: 020-8244 1000
Email: tuesdaymorning@cwcom.net

ALL RIGHTS RESERVED

ISBN 0 9530457 1 4

No part of this publication may be reproduced, stored in a retrieval system, rebound or transmitted in any form or by any means, electronic, mechanical, photocopying, recording or otherwise, without the prior permission of the author, nor be otherwise circulated in any form of binding or cover without a similar condition being imposed on the subsequent purchaser.

All characters and places are fictional. Don't believe what you read in the papers. Nothing is real.

Printed and bound by: WS Bookwell Limited, Finland.
Distributed by: Airlift, London (tel: 020-8804 0400).

'I am unwilling to leave the world worse than I found it' - Timothy Bennet, Hampton Wick shoemaker who beat the establishment in 1754 to gain us the right to walk through royal Bushy Park.

THE JOURNEY

THE DRIVER'S STORY
KNOWING YOU KNOWING ME
A CARJACKER'S LIFE OF CRIME
YOU STILL HERE
CANDLE IN THE WIND
BELOVED WOOD
IN A HAPPY STATE OF MELANCHOLY
LINES AND LINES (LINES AND LINES)
HA HABIDO UN ACCIDENTE
JOURNALIST IS HACKED TO PIECES
THE PASSENGER
THE SOPORIFIC SPLENDOUR OF SOAPBAR
CRACK HOUSE GUN HORROR!
HARD
HERE IS FEAR
THE NEXT BIG THING
PUNCH-DRUNK
LOST IN LUST
KILLER KNIFEMAN GOES ON THE RUN
SEX AND THE LUSH ENGLISH COUNTRYSIDE
MINDLESS VIOLENCE CONTINUES TO RISE
BULLY BOY
PRINCE CHARLES IS 'SAFE AND WELL'
NAMING NAMES
PITTER PATTER PATER BATTER
MEDIA IS HYSTERIA
LISTEN UP
KNOCK KNOCK
VICIOUS LONDON GANGSTERS PLAN MURDER ATTACK
THE MEN WHO WOULD KILL US
FROM USA TO THC
EVIL GANG AND THE 'HILL OF HATE'
GED OR DEAD
STONES IMMACULATE
HOLE
REAR-VIEW
LOVE IS ALL YOU NEED
SYMBOLIC GESTURE
THE WOOD
THE LONERS
LONDON MAN IS TORTURED
GONNA GO MY WAY

David Hurst is a London-based journalist who has written for *GQ*, *The Sunday Times*, *Sky Magazine* and *Time Out* among others. While researching for a feature in Chicago he met the expat who told him this story in a bar called North Side. On discovering he was a journalist the expat suddenly urged Hurst to record what he had to say. As they drank the stranger told him of the most important few days in his entire life, the result of a vicious carjacking. Many hours later, while at the bar, the man disappeared and although his story touched a nerve, there was nothing Hurst could do with it. Until a few weeks later. Researching another story, he discovered a small report in a local London newspaper that matched the expat's story. When Hurst replayed what he'd been told that long Chicago night everything fell into place and after further research he uncovered the full extent and wrote the story, virtually word for word, starting from where the expat – 'the driver' – was carjacked at traffic lights in north London. He wanted his story to be told and in this manner…

THE DRIVER'S STORY

JUST THEN as I waited at the traffic lights in Tottenham High Road, I met him. 'Drive round to the street there fucker or I'll cut your fuckin' head off with this blade, I ain't scared,' he shouted. 'I'll cut your throat to ribbons if you don't do as I say.'

No way man, this guy was really scared, he was trembling. Man, his journey had just started. I stuck my foot down and sped through the red. Put my foot down and sped. This uncool character had yanked my car door open, jumped in. I know I should have locked the passenger door like they tell you to, but I don't want to give no cops more routine. We're going for a ride all right. This guy's going to remember today forever. He's in for a big surprise. I'm gonna make him a star, ho hohumhum.

I can feel the blade by my vein. What a different day and he's really imposed himself upon me. I glance left at him, as my foot goes further down and smirk at his terrified eyes with their pin-dot pupils. 'Geezer,' he hisses in an excessive East End accent. 'I'm gonna jib you. Drive round there and stop the fuckin' car. Don't make me fuckin' jib you.'

We're doing about fifty now, a bit of overtaking. I smile at him. He likes himself too much to stab me. Make yourself comfortable. Check this ride out.

'Ever seen the Pennines?' I ask him.

'Cut the crap you fucker, don't make me do it. Fuck the Pennines and fuck you. I'm gonna do it.'

I was born in the Pennines. I'll show him their forever

beauty. Fasten up, the show of a couple of days in the life of a Tottenham carjacker is about to begin. Sit comfortably. And that goes for you too Cool Cat, I say to him. It's an ironic nickname I've given him considering he's the most frightened he's ever been.

'Woah! There's the fuckin' pigs!' he cries.

'They're the least of your worries,' I say as I put the accelerator down. It looks like we're in this together. Me, you and *him*.

KNOWING YOU KNOWING ME

T HE COPS weren't after us oh no, probably too bothered by other busy baddies. So there's a blade pressing on my neck, pressing to pierce, to slash, to splice my vein and spurt my blood out through a gaping gap. The guy holding it has fear in his eyes, he's so out of control that he's dribbling like a rabid dog. It's eleven years since I've seen the tracksuit top he's wearing. Fila BJs went out of fashion long ago. But it looks good on him, the cream cuff contrasting pleasantly with his pale bluey-white skin.

There's a Union Jack hanging from above a shop window, a relic of remembrance. What would I have done had I been a young man when World War Two started? I couldn't kill a stranger, but I wouldn't have wanted Hitler's system imposed on people. I respect those who stopped the ferocious march of fascism, but why did so many of a generation have to perish? We are animals.

So I'm sat with an uninvited passenger. I'm sat next to a white-boy punk carjacker. He's more scared than I am. Man, those blue eyes of his are darting like he's out of his head. He is out of his head, on fear, rushing, gushing, shitting his pants as we swerve past another car. I have to keep the speed up along these urban high streets, concentrate on doing some skilful steering, through reds, past cars, squeezing in gaps.

I overtake a slow car and slip through a narrow space caused by parked cars on either side and then all of a sudden there's a bright red Routemaster bus coming straight for us. I screech back onto our side of the road just in time and hear the fury of the bus driver's horn fade into the distance as we motor on. We quickly come up behind another car, a black cab, and I swerve round it only to be faced by another bus, two buses in fact as there's another right behind it. I cut in back to our side as I catch the bus driver's angry eyes, but they're nothing compared to the scaredy cat's next to me.

'Typical,' I say to him as we continue our fast route out of the city. 'You wait ages for a bus and then three come along at once.' He's lost his sense of humour though, if he ever had one, and glares back at me, so I put my foot flat down again. It's a decent car, brand-new and fast, so luckily it can move swiftly which is unlucky for this unhappy, skinny white-trash punk. I think about slamming the brakes on and sending him headfirst through the windscreen, but I want him to come on this journey now that he's here. Ha! He's made a vicious situation that he don't like now, and I wonder what is going through his malicious mind.

He's got desert boots on, quite cool, I'd have bet on him wearing nasty cracked trainers like plain-clothes coppers and thieves do. But nah, he's a trendy one. No socks. His ankles are even more pale than his hands and somewhat dry-skinned. Not very hairy, kind of worn smooth by his ankle boots. His army pants are brown, too tight and patchy on the thighs and knees. There's a small square rip on his outer right thigh.

I want to put a cassette on, something ever so slightly loud and angry, so that it encourages my ferocious driving. Manic Street Preachers would be perfect, but the tape's not in this tidy car I've borrowed. There's a cassette with some punk hits though, they'd be just right too, three minutes of energy and then another like bursts of speed. Cool Cat's probably into some punk, I prejudice. Not The Damned and that original lot, but more recent stuff as he's slightly younger than me. I take my left hand slowly from the wheel, watching him eye me up. I push the cassette in and it starts loudly with the Pistols.

I place my hand back on the wheel feeling the heat from where my hands have been gripping and the knife is still pressing, it's so deep, ugh, that if we bump up in the car the blade rises with me, dragging my skin. It feels close to piercing my skin's surface. Turning my head to look at him, I've lost my smirk for the moment, I notice his fear once more. His sharp blade's starting to rub away at my skin. Well, it's not normal to have a sharp three-inch blade under your chin, pressing the jugular and feeling as rough as a bad bear's hairy arse. His grip on it is tight, his nails have turned white. Except for the dirt underneath the ends.

His brow is constantly furrowed, like a dumb dog that's puzzled and his flat, wide light-brown Mohican hairstyle would be covered except that his blue cap with red writing on the front has been knocked backwards. I can't make out the writing, I check in his wing mirror, but can't read it backwards. I could if we stopped, but if we stop I'm dead, my fucking head would get severed from my body. If I keep going fast, I'm in charge of this situation. It's kind of like chess where I'm playing with just a castle and a pawn, but he's retreating into his half of the board with his queen and king. I bet he's never played chess, only violent computer games. I bet he's never played this game before. How he wishes he could press the escape button on this mistake.

Outside the number of shops and cars and houses and people are diminishing as we head out of the city into the balmy fresh country air. They are flashing past. It's summer and we're both still young men and neither of us wants to die, especially in the summertime. I'm twenty-eight and he's got more years to lose than me if the car goes cartwheel.

Even if we were equally fearful, it would put me at the advantage as he is the aggressor, he attacked. It's just that my self-defence is better than his attack. We're hitting sixty, sometimes seventy in the outer-city suburbs. There's a full tank of petrol and this car, a Saab convertible, goes well, looks swell. It can last miles and hours. It's white which makes it look wider and that's fairly handy as I live on a narrow north London street where a lot of cars get scraped by anonymous drivers. Anyway we've got enough juice for a ride, all right. This guy's going to see the Pennines. I'm going to give him a treat and a half.

We pass some pretty girls just outside Enfield as a large roundabout looms and without slowing much we spin round it and out the other side onto the A10. Then we'll connect to the M25 and go round west until we can get on the M1 and start the ride north. Then, when we hit the –

'Fuckin' 'ell!' he abruptly bawls like a baby. 'You wanker, that car back there nearly crashed into the side of me. Look geezer, let me out or I'm gonna fuckin' jib you.'

'Into the side of us,' I reply, glancing at his pasty face turned inside out with fear. 'If the car had gone into your side of the car, it would have gone into the side of us. I saw it. Close, huh?'

He shuts his eyes and leans his head back, letting out a big breath. The knife keeps pressing at my throat and the malodorous smell of his adrenaline sweat is strong and there are sweaty droplets forming on his grimy forehead. He needs teaching right from wrong and he's elected me to do it, so this is what I'm going to do now that he's here. I want to see that it's possible to find the good in everyone. Looking ahead now we speed up onto the straight open three-lanes. I slam my foot down; seventy, eighty, ninety… it's great to miss the rush hour.

'Go ahead,' I drawl. 'Go ahead, stab me.' My eyes are on the road and my grip tightens as I grasp the steering wheel firmly. 'The car would roll at least three or four times, so if you don't quieten down and enjoy the journey, I'll ram it off this road and kill both of us.'

'Is that a threat mate?'

I shake my head carefully. 'No. That's a promise. Man, that is a promise. Do you want to try it?'

A CARJACKER'S LIFE OF CRIME

AS WE SPED northwards, grey buildings gave way to vast fields, round rolling hills and clumps of leafy trees that were green of every shade of green in the world. Blue summer sky was being covered by a white air-mist and heavy clouds appeared like a black-blue bruise on pasty English skin, looking ominous and threatening. Signs for Cambridge flashed by and for the first time there was a silence inside and outside the vehicle.

He was sat there, regretting ever joining me, head hanging, and deep in thought, contemplating his life, probably feeling sorry for the state he was in, for his whole entire messed-up way of living. The knife was not pressing so hard to my throat at this stage. In his wing mirror, his pale face was creased with anxiety, reflecting how much his mind was away from the glorious English countryside and bulging storm clouds that were undoubtedly about to burst. I reckoned he was born about twenty-four years ago. By his sad glaze it looked as though it had been downhill for him ever since.

'Why did you do it?' I asked firmly, making eye contact. He looked up my face, then down. His lower lip slightly twitched and his skinny shoulders rounded. I repeated my question. 'Why did you do it?'

He looked down to the space between his knees. 'Why should I tell you anything, you wanker?' he demanded solemnly without looking up.

'Because you want to. Because you're scared now and you're longing to cry out, let someone hear why you are as you are, how life has been so bad that it's turned you evil.'

He rubbed the end of his big nose with his right index finger, still staring into empty space. His hand dropped into his lap, palm upwards. 'All right mate,' he said, staring at me with hatred. 'Just so you know who you're dealing with here, right?'

'Right.'

'I ran away from a children's home when I was, er, about fourteen,' he mumbled as he looked down into his lap. 'I went to the centre of London where I met this other geezer, young geezer like me. We lived in an, er, lift shaft thing. Well, it wasn't a lift shaft, it was a building, the lift housing on the roof of a warehouse.'

He briefly looked at me with his pin-dots, keeping his head hung and, as he thought of his story, he absent-mindedly pressed the knife harder against the side of my neck. He looked down again and I alternated my gaze between him and the motorway we were tearing along at eighty. I wasn't surprised at all to hear a tale from him, the egotistic git, but I was taken back at the intimacy of this story.

He continued, looking away from me now, staring ahead through the windscreen, but still pressing the knife more firmly to my neck. 'There was a row of things that looked like miniature, sort of, oil-well pumps, always fucking clunking away. We could hear the lift moving up and down. That's where we lived. We worked mostly at night doing whatever we could to get money, robbing tourists down Leicester Square, bit of begging in Covent Garden, bag-snatching in Soho, that sort of thing.'

'And you're still stealing ten years later,' I stated.

He ignored me. 'Me and him lived different lives, but we helped each other out. I tried to look out for him cos I can handle myself all right.' He paused, clenching his eyes tightly shut as though he could clothe these fluorescent rags of memory in black darkness. Or trying to think of what to say next. At this stage I wasn't sure. In the driver's mirror, I glanced at the red BMW that had been sharking behind us for a while.

The carjacker opened his eyes, eyes with purple pools underneath and eyelids to match, to stare at me and then blankly ahead. He carried on speaking, faster now. 'All that mattered was that somehow we survived. I didn't think much about the future then mate. No, nothing about the future. But I woke up one night feeling fuckin' freezin'. I could hear the rattling of the weights going up and down, the electric motors spinning, the belts humming... fuckin' noise it was geezer and the smell of oil was everywhere. So anyway, I pulled the blanket over me a little more and pushed my feet further under the newspaper.' He turned to face to me. 'Then I took his blanket from him to keep me warmer. I tried to keep warm until, it occurred to me that the reason I was cold was because he was cold. He wasn't well. He may have died and I thought if he died accidentally, I wouldn't be prepared. It wasn't part of the plan.'

He wiped his nose with the cream cuff of his jacket and looked at me with a scowling smile. 'So I held his throat in my hands. I squeezed it tightly and I watched as he took a last look at me and struggled weakly. Then I watched his face fall, then his neck slowly bruise when I'd taken my hands away. And that was it.' He shrugged his shoulders and looked out the front of the windscreen once more. 'I enjoyed that feeling, that feeling of power and the helplessness that I caused to another.' He sat there nodding to himself. 'So now you fuckin' know, right. And I'm still gonna fuckin' jib you geezer. Soon as you slow down.'

I pondered his story as we whizzed under a bridge with 'pay no poll tax' crudely painted across it in metre-tall white brush strokes that had dripped at the edges, then the motorway wound to the left and we went up a long, long hill. An embankment grew at either side where the Tarmac had been laid through the green land. The red BMW was just a few cars behind. A couple of large suited chaps were in it, one sat in the back leaving the front passenger seat empty. There was a loud silence.

Then suddenly the smooth Tarmac changes to a rough noisy concrete. 'Shit!' I cry out, instinctively putting my hand to where the knife has cut me, but not slowing down.

'I'm sorry geezer, it slipped. It's the road.' I glare at him. He still keeps the knife at my throat, just above the wound. 'It was an accident. Shit geezer, there's blood.'

'Get me a tissue!' I order. 'In there.' I point at the glove compartment.

'I can't.'

'What do you mean you can't? It's just there in front of you. Hurry up. It's a fucking good job you missed my vein man. Get me a tissue, come on.'

'I can't. I need two hands to open it.'

'Well, go on then, you've got two hands. They're on the end of your arms man.'

'The knife though,' he whined. 'I need to keep it on you. I can't open the glove thing. I can't.' He looked at me with desperate eyes. He was frightened of what the consequences were going to be. He was really scared of me.

'Look,' I say, stabbing a finger at him. 'You cut me, now get the tissues.'

'All right mate, all right. I'll get them. Don't go mental at me.'

I wipe my neck with my left hand and check the blood on my fingers. 'Come on! I'll bleed to death at this rate and remember if I die you die.'

'Okay, but I'll have to move the knife away.'

'Yeah?'

'You might do something.'

'I will if you don't get something to stop me bleeding! Look, I'll slow down. We're doing eighty now. I'll go into the inside lane and slow down to thirty. Just for a few seconds.' I glance at the red BMW. I can almost feel the men inside it breathing down our necks and a shiver runs through me.

'Okay, I'll get ready,' says the carjacker.

So I indicate and slide over to the far left lane, slowing down. He keeps his eyes on me and his trembling hands quickly fumble the glove compartment open and he pulls a wad of tissues out. Then with one hand he dabs my cut while the other holds the knife back up to my throat. He dabs me gently. Sweetly and serenely like a child. It feels good to get the attention. I watch his face soften and then grimace as he tends the wound he's caused. Dab, dab. Dab, dab, dabbedy dab. The red car has come into the inside lane too and slowed to our pace.

'Okay, enough,' I say, watching him and the red car. 'Thanks. Now I'm going to speed up again, so make sure you've got the knife held properly to my throat, okay?'

'Okay.'

And as we swerve over lanes and speed up he presses the knife harder. The red car follows, right behind us now.

'Listen,' I say, noticing that we're approaching the M1 turn-off. 'I think we're being followed

It was, predictably, too late, an never,' he grimaced, looking at m it. You're going to hand me over.

'It's not the police,' I told him

'Who the fuck are they then? to me.'

'It doesn't matter who they a me and this car they want, not

1

I indicated to exit the M25. Seconds later they indicated too, dropping slightly further behind. We smoothed onto the M1 and the red car followed in our trail. Cool Cat watched them in his wing mirror.

'Who the fuck are they mate?' he asked again, sounding scared.

'I told you, it doesn't matter man. Let's just say they want me and to get me they'd kill you. They're sussing us out now. They've been following for quite a while.' I checked them in my driver's mirror. 'What I'm going to do is look as though I'm pulling into that service station up ahead, just to make sure it is us they're following.' I flinched at the very thought.

We stayed in the left lane and indicated to pull into the service station's slip road. Suddenly, the red car went down a gear and pulled out swiftly to the outside lane to speed past us with a roar, like that of a lion setting off after the prey it was bound to catch and rip to pieces. I knocked the indicator off and uncertain what to do, cruised along for a second. Then I saw him, the other one.

He stood there just after the service station's exit road smiling like a jovial giant with his left arm outstretched and thumb thrust skywards. I flicked the indicator on again and slowed up on the hard shoulder. The carjacker looked at me, worried. He knew that he should do something. Like kill me.

'I figured you're not going to kill me,' I said taking my first totally clear view of him. His brow was still furrowed, thickish brown eyebrows arched underneath his creased forehead, and blue bulging eyes with their pinky crow's feet nes at the edges looking panicked. His complexion was dry, y reddish in patches, and his nose had been on the losing fights a few times. He had ears that stuck out slightly ther side of the off-centre flat Mohican haircut that his slim head and his narrow, blueish lips were l and he didn't so much as grin, more like white teeth that gave him the appearance

of a salivating wolf. Somehow this odd mixture o.
when thrown together, made him look roguishly attrac

I found my voice. 'You can go if you want, I won't
you. But those big guys may in that car. They may stop y.
for good. Don't think they didn't take in every bit of your
detail. Especially the fact that you've got a knife to my throat.
They probably think you want what they want.'

'Which is what and what the fuck have we stopped for
then?' he asked, getting irate and blinking at me with those
pink-edged eyes. Waaaah! Suddenly he startled to a jolt and
cried out sharply like a pig squealing as his door was opened
with force.

'Hi, thanks for stopping,' said the huge hitchhiker, looking
at me and then Cool Cat. 'Hey man, I'm sorry, for making you
jump. I'm going home, near to Manchester. Any chance of
ride on way?'

'Get in,' I said. 'We can take you all the way.'

The carjacker stared at me in disbelief, breathed out a
weary sigh and settled back in his seat.

f ugliness,
tive.
stop

YOU STILL HERE

THE HITCHHIKER clambered in the back, putting his massive frame in first followed by his big trekking boots. He wore faded ripped jeans tucked into the boots, and his long sun-streaked blond hair rested gently on broad shoulders which had a tatty scarlet T-shirt covering them. He must have been a fair few inches over six foot and his long powerful-looking thighs cramped up behind the carjacker's seat, his knees pressing deeply into the back of it.

He was a good-looking guy, about my age, maybe a little older, deeply tanned and with a gingery-blond goatee beard. He beamed me one of the most alluring smiles I've seen as I checked him out in the driver's mirror. The Saab reeked of patchouli.

'Thanks lads, I'm on way to see my girl,' he said in a slight Lancashire accent omitting the word 'the', like I would have done, I thought, if my parents hadn't moved south before I could properly talk. 'Can't wait.' I noticed that his sentences went up at the end too, like the Aussies speak, making each sentence sound like a question. He rubbed his hands together and smiled to himself. In fact he didn't stop grinning, not at first anyway.

We pulled off and I cranked up the gears, quickly hitting a ton. Soon enough we passed the red car waiting on the hard shoulder. I thought they would hang around. The hitchhiker stayed silent until I'd fallen into my rhythm. Then he piped up, still smiling, his straight white teeth brightened by his dark sunbaked skin. He had more wrinkles than me and his rounded face looked well lived in.

'What's with knife?' he asked, still grinning.

'Oh, it's a sort of joke, really,' I answered, thinking quickly of how I could challenge the carjacker. 'Old Cool Cat here gets a thrill from doing it, a kind of sexual thing. He fancies me.'

'Piss off!' snapped the carjacker turning to the hippy but directing the insult at me. 'I'm a robber, not a fucking poof! I'm his fuckin' robber.'

'Right,' the hippy nodded, the smile momentarily fading while he worked out what sort of situation he'd arrived in. Then the beam came back.

'I've never tried that,' he slowly grinned. 'I can see how it could turn you on though. Like you pretend to rob him. Ha ha, that's brilliant! Just let me out if you want to have a shag!' He let out a lewd cackle. 'Yeah man, live and let live I say. Sex is great, even though it's root of all evil. I don't mind, whatever turns you on.'

'No,' blurted Cool Cat, getting irritable. 'I *am* a carjacker and I'm robbing him.'

I smiled to myself.

'Well, where did you get in, man?' asked the hippy, grinning at the carjacker. 'We're in middle of nowhere. Don't see many motorway muggers.'

'I got in at Tottenham geezer. Fuckin' Tottenham. All right?'

'Shouldn't you have robbed him by now?'

'Any minute, any minute.' He looked away from the hippy and at me. 'I will you know geezer. I'm bad when I want to be. Fuckin' fuckin' bad.'

'He's telling the truth,' I said to the hippy. 'He's bad and I'm taking him on a journey to try to make him good.'

'Bollocks!' cussed the carjacker looking back over his right shoulder at the hippy. 'I'd rob you as well, but you ain't got anything worth robbin'.'

The hippy kept grinning at him. 'You're right, I haven't got a lot to show, but sure got a lot to tell.'

'Anyway, what's it got to do with you? I'm the fuckin' carjacker. You're just a hitchhiker. I'll turn the knife on you if you don't shut it.' The hippy continued smiling at him, but my next statement caused him to realise that he really had hitched a lift in the wrong car.

'I think you should also know,' I said to the hippy in my mirror, 'that, as well as this knife to my neck, we're being followed. The red car behind us. Both of you need to know that I have something in the boot, too much of something in the boot, that the two large guys in that car want.'

Just then, as my two passengers turned round to look, the red car dropped further back, easing lane by lane into the hard shoulder, where they stopped. God only knows what they were doing there, but for the first time, I'd got close enough to see it was unmistakably Dead Cloutner in the back of the car. I could taste his menace in the back of my throat.

'Well, they've stopped now man,' said the hippy.

'They'll be back,' I stated bluntly. 'And I'm afraid that you two are unwittingly, but intensely involved now. If you left the car they could get you. Maybe torture you as you don't know the whole business.'

'Are you serious?' queried the hippy, sounding alarmed.

'Deadly,' I replied.

'What's deal here then man?' asked the hippy.

'The less you know the better, for your sakes,' I said glancing round at the hippy's concerned face. 'I'm sorry you got involved.'

'So am I!' exclaimed the hippy. 'I'm only going to meet my girl and I've ended up in a car with dark cloud of death floating over it. Strangest lift I got before this one were a bloke who were naked. I soon got out of that car I can tell you! I'll soon get out of this one as well. I try to avoid trouble. Let me off on hard shoulder, I don't mind walking.'

'They'll kill you,' I told him.

'So tell me whole deal here then man,' said the hippy, edging to lean close to me between the seats. 'Better see if I can help out in any way.'

I wiped a blemish on the inside of the windscreen with the back of my knuckle as I thought where to begin.

CANDLE IN THE WIND

'THEY CALL HIM DEAD,' I started. 'He's the main man among a London firm and he's the one sat in the back of that red BMW on our tails. He's a complete nutter, real name's Johnny Cloutner, but most people call him Dead. He's a violent piece of work. Worst of all, he's smart with it. Understands the psychology of violence and if that doesn't work he misses out the psychology bit.'

'Why's he called Dead?' asked the carjacker anxiously.

'From a time when he'd gone to have a chat,' I answered, 'in the gangster manner that is, with a rival gang member, from a group of young villains who'd just come onto his manor and foolishly got one of their lads to have a pop at Cloutner. Finish him off. When Cloutner walks into this boozer where the young villains are drinking with some of their women, the top young upstart who's ordered the pop at Cloutner looks at him, then double-looks. He notices Cloutner's left arm is in a sling and behind his shades that his face has some bruises. He's shocked to see Cloutner because his lads told him they'd given him such a bare-fisted hiding that they'd killed him. Rumour has it that it'd taken six of these younger guys to get him down and they'd had to spend half an hour battering him before he finally stopped throwing punches back.'

'This is bloke on our tail, one in back?' asked the hippy.

'Yeah, that's him,' I nodded. 'Dead Cloutner.' His name hung in the air.

'So what happened in pub man?' asked the hippy.

'Trying to hide his shock,' I said, attempting to move my neck from the knife that was still held to it, but without success, 'and keep his bravado in front of his lads and the girls, the young villain says to Cloutner: "I thought you was dead.' He looks at his lads for an explanation, but none is forthcoming, so he looks back at Cloutner. "Just like a Spacehopper, Johnny, you've come bouncing back."

'"Take a good look at me," replies Cloutner in a Bow Bells' accent, as cool as an ice cube. "I'm not dead, and you won't be callin' me that again."

'The young pretender just smirks and laughs at his gathering of lads who try to laugh with him. "I'm the one you listen to round 'ere," menaces Cloutner taking a step towards the young upstart. Then the villain does something that he shouldn't do – he ignores Cloutner and carries on laughing.

'"D'you and your fuckin' peabrains hear me?" demands Cloutner, looking angry enough to charge through barbed wire. Suddenly, Cloutner whips a brass knuckleduster out from the sling with his free hand, slips it on and says: "I call this my brass hearing aid. D'you know why?" The young rogue freezes and his lads lean their bodies away from Cloutner's clenched fist.

'"Okay Johnny, not now," says the young one, obviously fearful. "Not with the birds around."

'"Yeah, that's right," continues Cloutner with raised voice. "Soon as I get the brass hearing aid on everyone always fuckin' hears." Then he raises his fist and without even leaving a blur the knuckleduster crunches into the young villain's face. The women are screaming and the lads know what they should do, but they also know who's the real boss of the manor. Rumour has it that Cloutner got in twenty right-handers in five seconds. When he goes to leave everyone knows they've just seen him murder the young gangster.

'Just as Cloutner puts his hand on the door handle to leave

he turns to the young villains, his coolness returned, and says: "Nothin' personal to you boys. You can call me Dead any time you want. But it suits him more." Well, the crooks like that sort of tale. So the name stuck.'

The carjacker put his head back and groaned. 'Shit. This is like something from a fuckin' film,' he mumbled. 'Or like something really bad happening on a TV programme. I can't believe it.' He was not at all happy in his work; he was having a very poor day at the office.

'Dead Cloutner's got a huge family,' I continued. 'They come from Stepney Green but half of them live on the east side of Stoke Newington now. A long way from the area's charming Church Street though. Much closer to its charmless crack-cocaine centre. According to Ged, Cloutner's firm is by far the major firm in London.'

'Who's Ged?' asked the hippy.

'My best friend,' I answered. 'I'll come to him.'

'Great,' groaned the carjacker, 'not just any firm on the tail of the car I pick to jump, but the tastiest firm in the fuckin' city. Fuck me mate, why didn't you tell me this when I got in?'

I just looked to him and unsympathetically smiled. 'Usually Dead's the organiser, the instigator, laying low as the Old Bill know of him only too well. Of course they do; if he wasn't a criminal he'd be a top cop. Cloutner himself has moved up from Stoke Newington and lives in Enfield now where he can be seen conspicuously driving around in his red Bentley dressed in white velvet Versace, chunky gold jewellery, open silk shirts, and with that tidy crew-cut showing scars in places we don't even have. Even in winter he's got a tan either from the Costa del Sol where he maintains some 'business interests' with the north Africans or the Stoke Newington self-tan shop where he carries out 'business interests' with the north Londoners.'

'Why's he after *you* exactly?' asked the carjacker, looking at me with disdain.

I decided to spare him my full tale of woe. The only pity he was capable of was self-pity.

'I used to run a flower stall in Farringdon, but a year ago I opened a flower shop over the road.' I paused to watch their eyebrows raise at the incongruity of my appearance and my profession. 'It wasn't doing very well though. A new Metro supermarket had taken most of my business. One of the strange things about being a florist is that rather like being a hairdresser, everyone seems to want to confide in you. I could make a fortune by blackmailing the City guys I know who used to buy a bunch of daffs for the missus and a big bouquet for their mistress.' They were both bemused and intrigued as they listened intently.

'Anyway,' I continued, 'Ged's club, Penelope, is close to the flower shop and one of the guys who regularly comes in is this guy called Stan I've seen a few times down Ged's place. He always likes to tell me about how off his face he's got during the weekend. He's a bit of a pratt really, but he looks after his mum with flowers a couple of times a week, so I've got some time for him. I call him Stan the Man because he's a bit of a ducker and diver, a lad of the manor, but not as much as he thinks he is.'

The BMW didn't seem to be following for the moment, so I eased off the speeding and continued telling them what events had led to us being in the car together.

'The other morning I'd finally admitted to myself that my business was over. I couldn't even afford to pay the phone bill that had arrived in the morning's post let alone the rent or order any new stock. Then Stan the Man bounds in, a pale stick insect in baggy hip-hop gear and wisps of fluff on his pointed chin looking like the real-life version of Shaggy from *Scooby Doo*.

'"All right fella!" he exclaims, offering me his hand to soul shake. "What's up fella, you look like I feel," he continues, talking fifteen to the dozen as usual. "Got right off my tits this weekend. Six pills one night, three grams the next. Plus the weed. Rockin' it was fella, I'm tellin' ya. So what's up with you Flowerpot Man?"

'I don't normally give customers as much information as they give me,' I said to the hippy and the carjacker, 'but I needed to get this one off my chest. I looked at his wasted expression and realised he wouldn't recall what we were talking about the moment he left the shop. So I told him about the rent rise. I showed him the landlord's final demand that had arrived that morning. My bastard landlord wanted six grand there and then or me out. Six grand? No way. And so that's what Stan the Man read and that's what I told him.

'Stan shuffles a bit on his feet, before speaking, more slowly than usual. "I may be able to help you here fella," he says, looking over his shoulder to check the shop door's shut and that we're alone. "I need something and I know you know that Ged fella who owns Penelope down the road. I know you know him well, school and all that. Thing is," he says as he glances over his shoulder again and lowers his voice, "I met this fella a couple of months ago, South African fella he is, and he's fuckin' minted. He works round here, banker or something, wears a suit and that for work. Thing is, he wants a bit of the old C, know what I mean. If I can get hold of some, he'll pay me a top price, guaranteed. Money's no problem to him, spending it fast enough's the problem. Now I can always get the weed and pills, but a large amount of coke like he wants is a problem for me. It's an easy earner and I reckon you, fella, might be able to help me."

'So I tell him I'd do anything to save my business, but that dealing drugs is not my scene. He puts his hands up defensively. "You won't be dealing fella. Just passing it on. All you got to do is get your mate Ged to get one of his bouncers to sort it out – and I know they're onto it. Perk of the job, innit. And all you have to do is drop it off at my place. I could ask them, but they don't know me and anyway I don't want those fellas finding out where I live. But I trust you fella."

'He can see me wobbling, so he comes in with the killer punch.

'"You won't even have to touch the stuff, just do a bit of driving from A to B and B is only about twenty minutes from Ged's club. Go on fella, it's easy money, sort you out. It's just like delivering plants in a way. Look, I'll charge the South African suit six grand over, so I can give you six grand – then and there – and you take the rest of the cash back to the bouncers. Yeah, that should work out if I cut the Charlie with something. What do you say? Go on fella. Six grand and you're back in business, give you time to sort a new shop out. It'd be a shame for all your hard work to go down the pan."

'And I'm standing there picturing the future, me at the door of a new shop full of flowers and the pavement outside this shop is brimming with fresh sweet-smelling blooms, all colours and the sun's shining and an endless stream of customers are cheerily buying bouquets from me. I almost feel like giving Stan the Man a bunch of red roses. But I find myself shaking my head.

'"I'll do anything to save this shop," I say to him, "but that doesn't include risking my liberty. Sorry."

'Stan the Man grabs my shoulder, his Scooby stubble twitching. "Come on, think about it fella. All you need to do is sort out thirty."

'"Thirty what?" I ask him.

'He clocks over his shoulder and lowers his voice again. "Thirty big ones." Then he takes his hand from my shoulder, folds his arms and stands there in front of me nodding his head, encouraging me to do the same. I shake mine. "Sorry. What do you want for your mum today? Got a couple of nice sunflowers from the south of France."

'"Think about it fella," he says. "It would sort us both out."

'I shake my head again, this time firmly. "Shall I wrap the sunflowers?"

'He nods now and as he's paying, he scrawls his mobile number on the corner of the landlord's letter. "Thanks for the flowers," he says. "They don't offer this service down the supermarket. It'll be a shame fella... seeya later." And with that he's off.

'Go on then,' urged the hippy as we motored on down the motorway. 'What happened?' I noticed both he and the carjacker were still listening intently and both were frowning.

'The next day,' I continued, 'I get the bastard landlord barking at me on the phone. He threatens to send some of his mates round to get the money or get me out. The shop's really quiet and as empty of customers as flowers. When Dead Cloutner's man came in mid-afternoon for Dead's daily bouquet he was the first customer of the day. He's a massive fella in a dark suit with long grey hair. And I mean massive. They call him Big Big Don, not to be confused with Dead's other man Big Don, who's a bit smaller.'

My two passengers both edged nearer to me, breathing loudly towards my face.

'This is bullshit!' exclaimed the carjacker in disgust. 'What's this gangster geezer getting a bunch of fuckin' flowers for every day?'

'Ever since Dead Cloutner heard that this massive international star has a fresh bunch of flowers delivered every day he'd sent one of his men in to get him a bunch,' I continued. 'I've never had the heart to tell him it's Elton John. Anyway, Big Big Don came in and he's a boastful sort, so he's straight into it.

'"Dead's flowers have had to wait today and I'll tell you why," he says to me in a north London accent and rubbing his hands in glee. He looks over his shoulder to check the shop door's shut and that there's no-one else with us. "We got a massive shipment through last night." I nod my head politely as I always do when Big Big Don boasts, even though I never really know what he's boasting about.

'"We got a fuckin' shipload of the purest cocaine in the northern hemisphere," he continues. "And do you know the best bit – shall I tell you my son?" I nod while wrapping Dead's big bouquet of pansies, green foliage and whatever red flowers I have in the shop. Big Big Don glances over his shoulder once more and in a hushed voice says to me: "We've shifted all the fuckin' lot, money's in our pockets, the lot. Deal of the fuckin' century my son." I don't really know the magnitude of what he's talking about, but I look suitably impressed. After all, Dead paid good money for his bouquets.

'"Well," Big Big Don continues, "all except a little bit, but you know how Dead likes his pennies, so we're working on gettin' shift of that now. The guv won't be happy 'til he's squeezed every last grain out of that shipment. Dead's a fuckin' perfectionist if I ever saw one. So as soon as we get rid of the final thirty we're celebrating."

'I hand him the bouquet. "Thirty what?"

'He raises his eyebrows to me and lowers his voice to a whisper. "Thirty big ones." With that he drops me a fifty quid note and as he turns to leave the shop, he adds with a wink: "Keep the change my son."

By now you could have heard the hole in the eye of a needle drop, such was the silence in that Saab.

'So I'm left there in my shop,' I continued telling these two who, like you, are just starting to grasp what's happened here, 'with the biggest coincidence since God gave us and the monkeys ten fingers and toes each. It's fate now that's intervened, made it all too easy for me to get one over on that landlord. So before I know it I'm on the phone to Stan the Man to see if he still wants thirty big ones, then I'm onto Big Big Don whose mobile number I have from months ago to see if I can purchase thirty big ones from him, and then I call Ged to tell him what's what and to borrow his car, this car, as I don't want thirty big ones around in my shop.' As I spoke it through it was starting to become clearer in my mind. I wish it hadn't.

'Two of the people I call are happy about it,' I explained to the hippy and the carjacker, who seemed to have stopped breathing, 'but Ged's not happy.'

'"It's not your scene," he says to me. "You don't know who you've got yourself involved with. Dead's at the top of the ladder and that slippery guy you call Stan the Man's just an amateur. You shouldn't mix with either, and you definitely shouldn't mix the two together."

'But when I explain it all to him, he says that it's too late for me to pull out now, so he comes round with this Saab, great car except for his personalised number plate: G3D 1. It's the one thing Ged and I have fallen out about.'

'Yeah,' agreed the hippy. 'If I hadn't been in such a rush I wouldn't have got in with you when you pulled up. I thought you were going to be a right tosser.

'It's the main reason I got in,' mumbled the carjacker. 'Thought you were loaded. So how come they haven't got the coke then geezer? You trying to get away with it all?'

I shook my head before continuing. 'As Ged leaves he tells me he's going to make a few calls so that Dead knows the deal's nothing to do with him and to find out more. So I call Big Big Don next who is clear about the arrangements.

'"You park the car round the side of your shop," he tells me. "Leave the boot slightly open. A couple of the men will stop off two minutes later in a white transit. They'll unload the stuff, that will be packed in weedkiller bags as though they're doing a delivery, then slam the boot shut. You drive to deliver, don't even look in the boot, the thirty big ones will be there, don't worry my son. I'll come to your shop at five o'clock, collect the cash wrapped in Dead's bouquet. That's it. By this evening we'll all be celebrating. One thing, we have to make sure we get the right fuckin' car. Give us the number plate."

'"Easy," I tell him. "The registration plate is G3D 1."

'"Sweet," he says, before his tone suddenly changes. "One more thing my son. Even though I know you, fuck me about and I'll get fucked by Dead and that will mean you'll end up dead, not by Dead but by me, cos if you fuck us about Dead'll want one of us dead, so I'll make sure you're dead because having you dead by me is better than me being dead by Dead. Got that? Actually that's not a question – you got that."

'So I told him that I had, the mentions of dead and Dead had delivered it home to me, and it was at that very point that I realised just how fantastic cocaine must taste to those who take it.

'So now,' I carry on to my two passengers, 'we're up to this morning, a few hours ago. As agreed I park the car round the side of my shop, boot slightly open. Sure enough, a couple of minutes later I watch a van park outside. I try watching what's going on, but one of the PAs from a nearby office comes in for a bunch of Dutch tulips. It's the middle-aged woman who's always telling me about her lonely nights when her husband's away on business. So as I wrap her pink tulips, I can't see a thing outside because she's thrusting her vast boobs in front of my face. As she leaves, I see the van pulling off, so I turn over the "Closed" sign on the front door and lock up. I'm nervous now and do exactly as Big Big Don instructed. Half an hour later I'm at Stan the Man's.

'You must be doing a runner with it,' says the hippy, looking at me with a mixture of excitement and worry. I carry on with my story.

'At Stan's flat I throw him the keys and lean over as he opens the boot. "Where is it then fella?" he asks, trying to move one of the heavy weedkiller bags out of the way.

'"In there," I tell him. "You've got your hand on it. It's in all of those. Do you want a hand carrying a couple?"

'That was when I knew there was something up. Stan the Man slams the boot shut and places the keys firmly back in my palm.

'"No way fella!" he says, terrified and crossing his arms backwards and forwards to show he'll have nothing to do with it. "*No fuckin' way!* You got this lot off Dead Cloutner, right?"

'I nod at him, feeling his anxiety. "Yeah, just like we agreed."

'"And they're all packed with Dead's cocaine?"

'I nod again. "Well, it'll be yours when you give me the cash. Thirty big ones, like you wanted."

'"Yeah," he says, breathing in and out deeply. "But this is thirty fuckin' *kilos*." He pauses. "I wanted ounces. Thirty *ounce*s. I'm having nothing to do with this. Nothing. That's fuckin' way over my head."

'"What can I do with it then?"

'"I don't know. Bury it, anything. Just get it way from my house. Get it out of Finsbury Park. I don't want nothing to do with it. Try taking it back to Dead Cloutner. Tell him there's some mistake. Don't mention me though. You haven't told him who it's for have you?"

'"No, of course not."

'"Good – I'm not have anything to do with this. I'm disappearing for a couple of days." Then before I can grab him he's off, bolting into his flat, leaving me stood there.'

I looked at the hippy, then the carjacker as we motored along.

'When I get back to my shop I call Ged whose first reaction is: "What an idiot that Stan is. What a fucking idiot." And his second reaction is: "Right, I've already done some checking and this is the situation. Dead wants his money, and he wants it now. He won't want the coke back unless it's with your dead body because those weedkiller bags weren't vacuum-sealed. You could have tampered with it. Plus he's already laid most of the cash you owe them out on something else. They don't usually operate like that, but he said he trusted you, which puts you deep in the shit. And forget your six grand debt to your landlord, we're talking half a million quid here."'

Two deep breaths were exhaled beside me. Neither of my passengers seemed comfortable as we hit a ton-twenty. In fact, now they were as still as two dead boys.

'Anyway, I can hear from Ged's voice that this is very bad. "Unless," Ged carries on. "You can hold onto the gear for a few more days until a guy I know returns from Amsterdam. He should pay the going rate plus a bit more as he's had some trouble in Amsterdam and really needs to get hold of some as soon as he lands. He sells it to firms that run the doors in the north-west. So there's plenty of demand. I've heard from a good source that he's arriving on a KLM flight in Manchester in a couple of days. I'll get someone to get in touch with him, so we can greet him on arrival."

'"Okay, I'll drive it out of town," I say to Ged, thinking of Stan the Man's advice. "Take a spade from the shop and bury it somewhere. Then I can stay at my Gran's or something."

'"Whatever," Ged tells me, the urgency clear in his voice. "Just fucking stay out of sight. Call me in a couple of days and tell me where you are."

'Unfortunately,' I said to the carjacker and the hippy, 'as I'd pulled off in the car, Dead himself and a different guy to Big Big Don arrive at the flower shop to collect the billionaire's bouquet they're expecting. The driver in the BMW is an upper-class Eton-educated bloke who wanted the crook's life. He met Dead and got it. Moustache, black hair greased back, stylish dresser. He doesn't look mad. Double-barrelled Dan they call him.'

'Why, has he got one of those posh surnames?' asked the hippy.

'No,' I replied. 'He's called Daniel and he blasts people's head off with shotguns. They've been on my tail ever since, although I wasn't positive it was them until I slowed to pick you up hitchhiking. I'm sorry, that's the only reason I was slowing down. I've only got the London traffic to thank for them not catching up so far because this car must be the fucking easiest car inside the M25 to follow. So that's where we are now which is here.'

I paused to see what the reaction was, but there was none so

I carried on talking. 'If it hadn't have been for that fucking Reg,' I said, shaking my head.

'Yeah,' the hippy nodded, 'it's a bit of an easy reg to follow.'

'No, I mean Reg as in Reg Dwight – Elton fucking John. If it hadn't been for him getting those fresh bouquets every day we'd never have been in this mess.'

'We'd better go like a rocket man,' said the hippy.

'That's enough Elton John now,' I said, not realising at the time that the hippy wasn't talking about the Elton song. 'Anyway, we're more like a candle in the wind. One little gust and we'll be snuffed out for good.'

'Why hasn't this Dead character made a move on us yet then?' asked the hippy.

'Probably because he can't figure out who you are with the knife,' I replied, turning to face the carjacker who stared straight back at me, a sheer look of horror on his face. 'Fear tactics. We can only imagine what he'll do to us. That's often worse than the physical pain if he did do something to us. Why should he lift a finger if he can get what he wants without doing anything? Enough of this, we'll crack. He knows that. If, on the other hand, we can keep away from Dead Cloutner for a few days, he'll get his cash and I'll get to pay my debt. I don't think I'll ever be able to step foot in London again. I'd rather that happened than giving another florist the job of making three wreaths.'

'What about your mate Ged?' asked the hippy.

'He'll be all right, I think,' I answered. 'They know he was only involved with the loan of his car. Plus they do a lot of business at Ged's club, so there's no need for them to upset the balance there. What I know though is that we're dealing with ruthless people here. If people is the right word. This knife at my throat, particularly with you holding it, is no match for their guns.'

'Guns! Oh shit, guns!' screeched the carjacker, his flat

Mohican virtually standing on end with fear. 'You wanker, you never said anything about guns. They'll kill me! Guns! What the fuck are am I gonna do?'

I ignored the panicking carjacker, looking down to check his blade wasn't going to slip again. Sheffield, England it said on the shiny blade and I wondered if the person who made it in Yorkshire could ever have imagined it would end up in the situation we found ourselves in.

'Where do you want to go?' I calmly asked the hippy. Remaining calm was all I could do in this situation. It was my one strength and, luckily, I was good at it.

Then, bizarrely, the hippy handed me a tape. 'I'm not into punk,' he explained. 'Can you play this? It's a bit more chilled.' I put it on.

As the soothing sounds came on, the hippy spoke again. 'We should conserve our energy for when it's needed,' he said. 'Try to overcome our imaginations with reality.'

There was still no sign of Dead and the red car. The hippy was right, it was time to take it easy, enjoy the ride, and I slowed back down to seventy, as we didn't want the cops sniffing around us for speeding.

'I'm heading for some old stones, a sort of mini-Stonehenge that hardly anyone knows about, to meet my girlfriend,' the hippy grinned as his music swirled around. 'That's if I can remember where they are. Should do. I drew this little map. Look.'

The hippy lifted up his arse and pulled out a neatly folded and slightly frayed piece of paper from his back pocket. On it, drawn roughly in dark thick pencil lines, was a childlike lake, a hill with a clump of trees marked and a big arrow pointing to the clump. The words 'Beloved Wood' were written below the map in neat handwriting and twice underlined. He turned the paper round and overleaf was an intricate set of left twists and right turns showing an arrowed route through a thick maze of trees, at the centre of which was a small circle of stones. 'It's not to scale or anything, but this is where I remember it was. Been there thousands of years, shouldn't have moved.'

'Why are you meeting her there?' I enquired.

'It's a bit of a story,' he said.

'That's all right,' I soothed. 'It's why I'm here.'

BELOVED WOOD

'OKAY THEN, IF YOU WANT IT, here goes. It starts when I were about eighteen or so and I'd just started to see who I were,' explained the hitchhiker, drifting off into another world, aided by his ambient sounds. 'I'd started to be able to create my own history, just realised who I'd been as that little boy. What others thought of me. Once, it were raining, really pouring man, and just to step out into it gave me solitude. No-one was out. It was as though I was only one in world. I walked without worry, drops of rain drenching me and running down face so much that my vision become blurred. So I walked from my family's old house in Pennines, near to a place called Hollingworth Lake –'

'I was born in the Pennines,' I butted in. 'I know that Hollingworth Lake.'

'No way man!' exclaimed the hippy.

'Every way man! My family moved when I was small. That's why I didn't pick up an accent. But I'm from Todmorden.'

'Half Lancs, half Yorkshire.'

'That's it. They used to reckon the cricket pitch was where the county boundaries were. You could bowl from Lancashire to someone batting in Yorkshire.'

'I've been there a couple of times, but can't remember where exactly.'

'Well, I can't remember much about it to be honest.'

'So you know hills around Hollingworth Lake then?'

'Not been up them, but I know they're there.'

The carjacker couldn't be doing with being left out, so he bared his bitterness once more. 'Fuckin' northerners,' he mumbled.

'That's right,' replied the hippy, gently nudging the back of the carjacker's seat.

'Least I talk fuckin' proper English mate,' sneered the carjacker as he looked round at the hippy who was grinning at him, but staring without blinking..

'Don't bother about him,' I said, feeling the knife press tightly into my neck as the carjacker tensed up. 'I'm looking after him. Tell us about what happened up on the Pennines.' The carjacker shot a shocked look at me and for a moment I felt the blade slightly pull away, then press hard against my jugular again.

'Yeah, you're right man,' said the hippy as he stopped smiling for a moment. 'I shouldn't let him bother me. But I can help you look after him.' He looked at me watching him in the mirror and quizzically raised his golden eyebrows.

'I'll fuckin' knock you out if you have a go at me geezer,' said the carjacker, as menacingly as he could muster.

'Go on, go on,' I urged the hippy. 'You're walking near the lake.'

'Okay man,' said the hippy while the carjacker just sat there scowling, snarling at life. 'I walked and walked, up and up, until I got so high that grass started to become rock. Then I came across a wood, a small clump of trees all of about same age. They were old, really old man. When I saw clumped trees I felt a feeling like never before. It was "Beloved Wood", one of my childhood. I was pulled to them trees, walking now so fast that my feet slipped from under me on wet ground. Man, shall I go on?'

I nodded.

'Okay.' He drifted off again, sinking into his seat, his music taking us all there. 'I walked through dense wood and a slight light filtering through leaves allowed me to tread. I'd been walking for hours now and needed to sit and was thinking about turning back when I came to it: most beautiful sight I'd ever seen. It's a small clearing like one we'd called "Paradise" when I'd been on a picnic with my auntie years ago on one of those summer days that seem to last forever when you're young. It were heaven on earth. It's a place with red and purple and yellow flowers, a smell of pure freshness, soft bumps of grass, almost like green cushions to sit on, and there, right in middle of clearing, are stones. Waist-high and stood into ground in a small circle, just about a pace across, as though they've always been there. Branches of an old dark green tree dangle towards them keeping it shaded. I'd heard about stones years ago, an old man had told –'

'That they're from Glastonbury, the stones I mean,' I butted in again. He nodded excitedly, eyes wide open. 'That they're supposed to hide Christ's bowl from the Last Supper,' I continued, excited too. 'But they're supposed to be even older. Even older than Christ.'

'Far out man!' said the hippy, beaming. 'That's amazing. Karma. That's what this is man. Good karma.'

'Hippy shit,' smirked the carjacker, offering his profound wisdom.

The hippy pointed at him as his smile was replaced with a stern look. 'I'm warning you. Shut it or I'll smack you one, right in fucking gob.'

'Leave it,' I said to the hippy, concerned as much as anything that if the carjacker received a good whack from behind he might accidentally cut my throat. In any case, as I'd said, he was mine to look after now. 'Carry on,' I said to the hippy, who still pointed at the carjacker. 'This is something special. How come I picked you up and we're virtually from the same place?'

'Amazing,' said the hippy, dropping his pointing finger and looking at me in the rear-view mirror.

'What happened up there anyway?' I asked him.

'I just lay there feeling energy,' continued the hippy, giving the carjacker a warning eye, 'and memories flowed through me, like I'd been plugged in. Tingles were running up my spine. I'm rushing tits off like nothing ever before. Then I opened my eyes.' He closed his eyes now. 'And she was there. My soulmate, my dream and we were together for an endless time. She were my rock at stones, seeing her held me together.'

He paused, snatched a look out of the window, then continued, speaking rapidly. 'And although we tried we could never bring ourselves to find if magic of that place would be repeated. Then, even though I ached with love for her, I had to wander to find more of myself, so I travelled. Have done for more than ten years now. All over world, from China to Calcutta. And I've shagged myself senseless.'

He opened wide his blue eyes and grinned. 'And all grass I've smoked has made me a bit loopy too,' he chuckled. 'Mind if I skin up in bit as it goes?'

I didn't move. 'Great,' the hippy said, taking no reaction as a yes.

'Anyway,' he started again, looking ahead, 'from that day we first met we agreed to meet back there in fifteen years, wherever we were, whatever we were doing. I'm going back there now. Come from Vietnam to be there in a couple of days. Stones are perfect to go back to because they'll never move. They'll always be here on earth, long after we've gone. Even when we're dead and buried, a stone – our headstone – is all that will remain of us on earth.'

'The only thing you've got connected to stones is that you're a fuckin' stoned loser!' smugly interrupted the carjacker, laughing to himself at the hippy.

The hippy looked to him. 'Yeah, you're right. That's all I

am. That's why I'm going back because I don't want to be loser. I still ache with love.'

'Are you sure it's good idea to go back?' I asked, doubting for a moment. 'It was a long time ago. And, you know, love can make you blind.'

'That's right. And lust can make you squint,' smiled the hippy, squinting as he smiled to himself. 'Thing is, I've found plenty of answers out there in world, but she's the one. She's my soulmate. There's no choice is there?' he asked to no-one in particular, without wanting an answer and continuing without waiting for one. 'If I don't I'll spend rest of my life wondering what would have happened. Some people get like that on Lottery and do it week in, week out. Just in case they didn't do it one week and their numbers came up. Like that, if I don't go back I'll live a life of regret. When I lay on my deathbed I'll wish I could live my life over again. So I'm going to stones.' He stabbed his index finger in the air. 'And no-one, no-one, is going to stop me doing that. Not even those blokes in that car that's following.'

'We'll take you there,' I said solidly. 'We'll find it. There's vibes there aren't there?'

'Ley lines,' the hippy nodded. 'Strongest in world. Britain's known for ley lines, for power surges. It's a magical place. Think of history. Why here? Why here? This pissy little island. I'll tell you why. Because of ley lines.'

'You're both fuckin' mad!' exclaimed the carjacker. 'Off your rockers! Schizo.'

'We'll take you there,' I repeated, ignoring the rude remarks. 'It'll be safer. I want to see the place, and it'll be perfect to hide the cocaine. Anyway I want to see if you meet her. You might need a shoulder to cry on if she doesn't show up.'

'She will,' nodded the hippy.

'So when can I get off?' asked the carjacker.

'Take the knife down and I'll tell you.'

He hesitated.

'It will help me drive better,' I explained. 'We can get rid of those guys in that red car once and for all. Then you can get out.'

He pulled the knife away, but still kept hold of it. 'I've still got it though. Just remember that,' he snarled, curling his upper lip in a moody Sid Vicious style. 'I'm still holding the knife, see.' He showed it to me and then to the hippy in the back.

'Or,' I said to the lowlife with a knife, 'you can help me carry the coke, bury it and I'll count you in. I'll give you ten grand's worth of cocaine when we've buried the rest. Don't worry, there's enough.'

'Ten grand?' asked the carjacker, perking up. 'Where exactly are we going to bury it again?'

'At the ley lines. We shall lay lines at the ley lines.' I smiled at him.

He buried his head in his hands, the knife he gripped glinting beside his cap, then he suddenly looked up, smiling for the first time. 'I thought this carjacking had gone wrong, but it could end up sweet as a nut.'

'Nuts aren't sweet,' I said. 'Are you in or not?'

'Course I am geezer. So long as you steer clear of Dead Cloutner,' he replied, looking like he was about to puke from his fear of the gangster. 'Course I'm fuckin' up to it. Just no more fucking about though, eh? Eh, no more stopping and that?'

'Course we're stopping,' I said. 'We've got to take a slight detour to pick up my gran.'

'Your gran!' laughed the hippy. 'Nice one, I like old people.'

I glanced sideways at the carjacker. He'd just been sick.

IN A HAPPY STATE OF MELANCHOLY

YOU MAY PICTURE ME driving that car for all it was worth along the slinking motorway on that August evening; glancing back at first over my shoulder, and looking anxiously to the next turning; then driving with eyes wide to spot if the red BMW was again creeping up beside us for I was thinking freely of what an exhilarating day this had turned out to be.

The carjacker had told me a pack of lies – carjackanory. All his yarns about living in the lift and murdering the boy was scum bullshit, I think, and so was the London accent. I could hear the Home Counties in the way he spoke, a few country curls wrapped his tongue as he tried to sound more of an eastie Cock-er-ny than those born by Bow Bells. On top of that was the smoothness, and almost richness, underneath of a public schoolboy or at least a grammar school lad who had mixed with well-spoken people as he formed his accent. His use of language when telling the story of being a killer had been too elaborated for someone who'd had to skive and dive in the East End. Also, his desert boots were, I'm sure, from Hackett's, not the markets. So what kick was that Cat on? Perhaps he'd had so much order in his life that he craved disorder. Well, now he was getting some.

As my mind span so my tummy turned from the smell of

sick piled on the floor between his legs. I used the electronic button by the gears to move fully down all the windows, letting in a fresh whoosh of cool air as he coughed and spat yukky yellow foul-smelling bile from his vile mouth. It smelled like dead bodies, in the car. He smelled like dead meat to me. I'd been getting hungry, but not now; not for food anyways. Hungry for honour, ravenous to do the right thing, but my appetite for food had subsided, and as my insides turned over so did the tape; ambient smooth sounds replaced by robotic Techno beats.

'Sven Vath!' the happy hippy chirpily announced rustling Rizlas and seemingly oblivious to the terrible wretch in front of him as he displaced the acrid smell of vomit with sweet-smelling smoke from roasted hashish. He asked me to put the windows up slightly so his rolling operation wouldn't get blown away. I obliged, just leaving a small gap.

Now it's me, you, *him* and the hippy travelling along. As your host on this onward journey it would have caused confusion if you'd headed home already, without knowing why you ever started. But, thankfully, we're in this together. All the way, all ways, always.

'Get the tissues,' I told the carjacker for the second time, causing me to recall the nick he'd put in my neck. I glanced at it in the rear-view mirror. Crispy claret-brown blood surrounded the pinky small slash, but it didn't sting. It was nothing done by a zero. 'Scoop your sick up in some tissues, then chuck it out the window,' I politely asked him as I lowered his window. 'Get some fresh air too.'

In a strange way I cared for him while he was in the car, or not so much cared, but felt that it was my duty to put him right. His face transformed from that pale white Englishness to a pale blue deathliness, his guts must have been as fragile as an egg shell as he breathed in some gulps of fresh countryside air. Slowly some colour came back into his pasty smooth complexion.

'My gran's all right,' I said to him. 'She's eighty-four an͟
has barely been outside her village. But that doesn't make her
narrow-minded. At all. In fact she's totally open-minded. My
great-grandparents brought her over from Ireland's west coast
when she was a few months old. They went to Liverpool
before her dad got a job on a farm in the Pennines. He loved
it there. Gran's still very fond of Ireland even though she's
never been back. But then Ireland's that sort of country, the
sort where people don't want to leave their roots behind.'

I turned to the 'jacker as I shifted gears. He was turned to
me and I looked into his blue eyes and at those tiny eyelashes
that fluttered with both defiance and fear.

The hippy leaned forward, coming into view of both of us
in front. 'We should spend more time with oldest generation,'
he declared, his deep voice commanding attention. 'They are
wisest people on earth. Yet here in Western world we shove
them away to die. No wonder this side of the world is soaked
in sadness. We are vexed generation, but our irritability can go
nowhere so we are sad everywhere and our sadness is
epidemic. We are Prozac population popping pills to keep
away mental ills. All so that we can exist in a happy state of
melancholy.'

The carjacker still looked at me and couldn't without
scowling. *He* couldn't look at *me* without scowling. Did he
think this, his position, where he was right now in life, was
down to me? He looked away and out the windscreen, and I
glanced at the fuel. We were okay, for now at any rate. I eyed
him as we sped by a gigantic Sainsbury's lorry. I wanted to get
something out of him and find out who he was before we
sought to correct his ill manners.

'So it's good,' added the hippy, 'that we're going to pick up
your gran. You don't think it's a bit dangerous though?'

'She's madder than anyone I know,' I said, continuing to
eye the carjacker. 'All she wants is some adventure in her
twilight years. She'd love to go to America. My grandad is

buried out there. He died eighteen years ago while he was visiting some friends. Sudden heart attack. It was his first time abroad. Only he could afford to go. They won the pools. Just a bit. He had always wanted to go. Gran told him to go. She always put my grandad first. It was their first time apart in years. It turned out to be their last too. When Gran heard he'd passed away it was Valentine's Day.' There was no reaction on the carjacker's sullen face. 'She couldn't afford to bring his body back,' I continued, talking quietly. 'My stepfather didn't give a damn and mum was broke as usual. So Grandad lays near Chicago.

I paused, sad at the memory and I thought some more about Gran, trying to find something to say that might spark a speckle of humanity from the 'jacker. I remembered what happened to her during the war.

'She already thought she'd lost him during the war,' I said to him, watching his every twitch. 'He'd been shot down over Germany, but parachuted to the ground where he was picked up by a German family opposed to the war. They got in touch with the French Resistance who smuggled him to Paris. As Paris was occupied, he had to pretend to be a deaf and dumb gardener called Pierre.'

'Occupied by who?' asked the carjacker indignantly. I stared at him. Surely he was winding me up.

I decided to ignore his question. 'By this time Gran had been told he was "Missing, presumed dead". But my grandad had been smuggled back to Britain on a boat. Eight months after she'd been told he was dead he turned up, unannounced, knocking on her door. Imagine the feeling she had then.'

'She must have been happiest person alive,' said the hippy.

I looked at the carjacker. He shrugged his shoulders and snarled at me. He didn't give a damn.

I looked at him in despair.

'Piss off cunt,' he responded, eyeballing me back while wiping the corners of his lips with a tissue. I noticed his knife lay where he'd dropped it when he'd been sick; down the side of his seat, by the gears, within easy reach of all three of us. It had a blade, sharpened on both sides with a point that looked like it could slip into someone easily. Its handle was khaki-green with some sort of silver emblem on; it looked like an army issue. It was really too shiny to have been used. Unless that is, Cool Cat spent hours and days wiping blood from it, then polishing it like some sort of assiduous, crazed serial killer who has great pride in his murder weapon. Murder weapon.

The big, long-haired dude leaned back now, quite contentedly in his own world in the back making a 'tschh-tschh' noise to accompany the hi-hat that was underneath the booming bass on his Sven Vath cassette. He'd sparked up an enormous spliff. I suspected that he smoked so much dope that he'd feel strange if he *wasn't* stoned. His eyeballs displayed tiny red veins beyond the whites which stood out against his handsome tanned face.

I don't touch dope; I don't touch any drugs, not even aspirin; I don't eat red meat, white meat, cheese or any dairy products; I don't drink, or at least I didn't at this time; I have a black belt in Shotokan karate; I swim most every day for two kilometres: that's two thousand strokes as it takes me one stroke to move a metre; I don't smoke; I fast once a week; I tend to avoid confrontation, if I can; I am in control of my mind and body. I am in control.

Spiralling ever downward, the unwitting instigator of this journey completed wiping the sick-stained carpet. I closed his window. It was so dim outside now that it enabled our reflections to appear inside and I noticed his forlorn face reflected and slightly distorted by the curve of the glass.

Beyond the window the expanse of landscape and sky was massive, almost too much for my urban eyes to take in. Thick, dark clouds had formed with wispy grey vapour below them drifting in the high heavenly winds. This part of England's land was coated in cloud, the hilltops marinated in mist. Some wisps hung lower than others like spectres floating to survey their old stomping ground below and watch how we, their ancestors, went. The bright light of the sun, too bright, momentarily lightened everything, not quite making it, but nevertheless showing its brilliant incandescent presence.

Now large drops of rain start to plop on the window and run down the side mirror. The sun gives up its brief battle and we feel cold as the dim dreariness returns. Listen – the music stops at the end of the tape for a minute: all we can hear is the noise of air rushing past and the low hum of the car, groaning like an old lover. Black-blue clouds hang heavy as though something is pushing them down, as though they want to burst and cover the ground, which they do soon enough with torrents of rain. Giant electricity pylons stride the land and ragged hedges play host to raggedy plastic bags, both strangers straining to escape with the steady wind.

As we flashed by, cars, vans and lorries swiftly switched lanes and I noticed the name places and phone numbers painted on the lorries change as we travelled further from London. Occasionally, there'd be a London number and I'd think of the start of the journey, back there at the shop, then back there at Tottenham High Road. Occasionally a powerful motorbike smoothly sped by, and was soon off, off, off into the far distance to become a tiny dot.

When we really moved fast along it felt not that we were moving forward but that the shiny road was being pulled back underneath us and the scenery was being sucked up by London, which it slowly is.

'Look at this!' declared the hippy, as though reading my mind. 'Four lanes here. Where will we stop? With a Tarmacced Britain, enough lanes for everyone who's going from one place to another, except all places will be Tarmacced and look same.'

I checked him out in the passenger's side mirror, through

the yellow spliff fog he was creating. Both passengers w
contemplative mood. Cool Cat looked resigned and a littl
relaxed for my comfort. I had to think quickly. After all
wasn't exactly invited on this journey, like you or
hitchhiker, so while I wanted him to enjoy the ride all right
also wanted to keep him on his toes, discourage him from
living his pathetic life of cruel imposition, find out who he
was.

'The word "host" derives from Latin,' I stated while staring
straight ahead, forehead low down with my eyes quite in the
top of my head, my jaw clenching and unclenching, my dry
grip tight on the steering wheel.

'Originally it meant stranger. It also meant guest.' I paused
and swallowed, for the first time my throat feeling a little
parched. 'And it also translated as victim.' Keeping my look
straight on the white lines ahead I could tell that I'd acquired
attentions and you should more often than not go with your
first instinct, so I paused again, still clenching, still gripping
tightly. I spoke in a flat emotionless tone. 'Look at your
reflection in the window and ask yourself which am I;
stranger, guest... or victim?'

I licked my lips before continuing. 'Look deeply into the
eyes staring back at you, this applies to all of you, and say
which you think you are. Watch your lips mouth the words. Be
aware of all noises about you, all you can feel, the noise of
your breath, the movement of your chest as you breathe, how
your hands lay, how your feet rest, all sounds, smells and the
noise of your own voice as you speak your answer. Hear your
heart beat.'

Mine was thumping, pumping with adrenaline.

LINES AND LINES (LINES AND LINES)

H E FELT HIS HEART pump erratically with excitement as his reflection stared back at him, its dilated pupils looking at the dark rings under his eyes and studying the lines that were starting to carve deeply into his otherwise boyish face.

Ged Nealson didn't mind snorting a bit of cocaine, but as a club owner who had lived the nightlife highlife for fifteen years he had to do it a lot more often than he really wanted. If a dealer or another club owner or a crook or a celebrity or, in this case, a girl he'd fancied for a few months, came into the club's back office, it was only polite that he got the mirror out and chopped out a couple of fat ones. You could hardly offer people a cup of tea in a nightclub, especially one known for its hedonism. In any case, for the situation he was in now, when it came to having an inhibition-loosening, aphrodisiac effect, Charlie beat char. Hands down.

He ran his hands down her back as they finally kissed. It was frenzied, all tongues and saliva. Her tongue was firm too, pushing and swirling his around like she was having the first or last French kiss of her life. He could taste the chemical in his mouth and the numbness around their faces allowed them to kiss hard, their first passionate kiss lasting for an age.

He'd been with her all day, just passing the time from the night before when they'd bumped into each other, still

52

chatting as it became light in the morning. Ged had seen this girl in his club loads of times and he really fancied her. Now they'd spent several hours together, he fancied her even more and was nearly bursting with the urge. His nightclub was opening soon and Ged knew that he'd had to make the move now or it'd have had to wait until another time. He felt her hands rub his muscular back, then move round to his hip, dropping to the front of his thigh where she kneaded his leg slowly as their kiss became more sensual with little darting bites to each other's lips, then as they worked up again and the full effect of the drug kicked in, her hand slid down to his inner thigh.

He moved his hands round to her front and he pushed them onto her breasts. He felt a Wonderbra – he'd thought so – and he went to where her white Lycra top plunged and unclipped the bra so he could slip his hand in. God, her nipples were erect and as he caressed them she rubbed his erection which was throbbing with his heartbeat's every pump. She slipped a finger through the space between two buttons in his Nicole Farhi jeans. He felt her pointed fingernails claw at his erect penis. She stopped kissing for a second and pulled back, looking into his brown eyes. 'No pants,' she stated with a smile.

'Would you like to join me?' he asked, almost cringing at the poorness of that line. But before he could dwell on it much longer, she'd stood before him, lifted her top and bra off to reveal the firmest pair of breasts with perfectly symmetrical dark pink pointed nipples. While keeping her gaze on him and with utter confidence she unzipped the side of her tight, short skirt and wriggled her hips causing it to fall down to the floor, revealing a small pair of black cotton g-strings which she cupped at the sides with her thumbs and slid down.

Ged looked at her, taking in her beautiful, almost perfect figure paying particular attention to the parts he'd spent many a night imagining. It was no disappointment and her shaved-at-the-sides little mound was about the colour of light brown that he thought it would be. He'd done the 'eyebrow test' and it had yet to fail him, unless they were completely shaved of course. A perk of his job was that he more often than not got to know the answer to the 'eyebrow test'.

He watched her sexily glide away from him in the room until she reached the red velvet chaise longue which she slowly and tantalisingly spread herself on.

'Now, would you like to join *me*?' she asked, and Ged thought that he would.

HA HABIDO UN ACCIDENTE

WE WERE STILL MOVING FAST at about eighty. Beyond our reflections and raindrops the verges and trees flashed by in a blur creating a vast kaleidoscope of ever-altering pictures. Further, we could see the earth curving away to a horizon that goes on forever, stretching to other cultures, to different places, passing love and hate on the way, joy and pain, tears and smiles, wealth and poverty, gluttony and hunger, life and death.

The hippy chuckled back at his laughing reflection which was gradually revealing more detail like a developing Polaroid picture as the long day started to pass into night. The brow of the other one furrowed further and further as his reflection furrowed back. Then our man in the back looked forward and chuckled again to himself.

'They reckon eyes are windows to soul, but in your case,' he said to the carjacker in between hefty huh-huhs. 'I reckon they're windows to your asshole. You look shit scared!' The hippy laughed, but *he* didn't reply. He tried not to let it show, but it was obvious he was really regretting and ruing. He hadn't expected any of this when he'd gone about his bad business earlier today.

'I see a guest,' said the hitchhiker, matter-of-factly, regarding his reflected face. 'I am everybody's guest, nobody's stranger and never a victim. Who are you?'

'I am the host,' I replied. I hadn't looked at my reflection; I was driving looking ahead, glancing at the other two. I had to probe for answers from the carjacker, point out his behaviour and fathom his answers. 'It's strange how life is so desperate to survive that it will unknowingly kill its host in its endeavour to live and grow. Like the HIV virus. It finds a host where it can live and grow and in doing so kills its host. When the host dies, so does the virus.'

'That's exactly what we're doing on earth,' said the hitchhiker. 'We're smaller living thing on larger living thing and like HIV virus we're slowly ravaging our host: the earth. Anyway, scientists reckon next big Aids-like illness will be airborne – so there won't be much chance of avoiding it. It'll spread like fire on dry hay, so we'll all snuff it and as I see it what's point of worrying? We may as well enjoy each day as it comes.'

He took a deep drag on his spliff before leaning back and offering it to me. He looked back at his reflection studying what seemed like every pore and hair on his handsome bronzed face. I shook my head to the spliff, so the hippy offered the wrapped burning resin to the scowling face in front, from which there was no response so he took it back for a long lone toke.

'Check this out,' said the hippy, blowing a billow of smoke out into the car while staring into the glowing embers of the spliff he held out in front of his face. 'I've got this mad tale. I was hitching from San Sebastion to small village near Pamplona, deep in Basque country. All Basque people I've ever met have been mad. Lorry driver who picked me up was mad, ugliest man I ever saw and most pissed driver I've ever been driven by. He was Basque. They're very tolerant of drunks, Basques, and they speak Europe's oldest language, so nobody but Basques knows what they're on about even when they're not pissed!'

He took another drag and flipped the ash into the door's ashtray. 'Anyways, he told me this tale after we stopped at a lorry driver's cafe for *tapas* and *cerveza*. He refuelled with some more San Miguels leaving place even more hammered than when he went in. Back in cab I couldn't stop him singing and clapping with hands off wheel unless I got him to tell stories. It was *adios amigos* if I didn't keep him jabbering. So I got him to keep telling stories. Every so often he'd break back into song, as happy as could be, so I'd show such interest in his tales that he kept on. They were toss mostly, but there's one that lives with me.'

'What's it about?' I asked.

'I'll tell it if you want.'

'Yeah, go on,' I encouraged.

'So it goes that a couple of hundred years since, there was a young lad who lived in a Spanish Catholic church. Late teenager now, he'd been abandoned as few days old baby. Unwanted and left to die in a bag by a church.' He turned to look at the image of himself in the side window, then carried on talking. 'But priest of this tiny hot little mountain village found him and took him as his own. Priest lived very virtuously, you see, probably only priest in history of world who has.'

The hippy stopped, to check something on his face he'd seen in his reflection. He mumbled to himself, tucked some strands of loose hair behind his ear, brushed his cheek, then continued. 'Never had priest seen such a beautiful baby with his dark fluffy hair, big brown eyes and an aura of innocence that could only create compassion. And so it were that h brought up boy. But as boy grew, lad felt abandonment in l guts and throughout his bones. He was afraid. Afraid that would be alone again, afraid to leave church where he safe.'

'Fear of the unknown is often the greatest fear,' I said, scanning the road ahead and behind for any sign of the red BMW.

The hippy nodded. 'Dead right, that's what this were. Anyway, by time he were teenager, he'd never left church, spending his days reading in shaded courtyard and nights in his room studying Bible. Priest was not concerned for he felt that lad, who he'd named Juan, was a good boy and was happy for him to lead a lonely life away from growing vices he saw outside church: drunkards, brawlers and whores.'

'Sounds like Bethnal Green on a Saturday night,' I joked.

'Yeah, I'm sure it does,' said the hippy quite seriously. 'So, only time Juan saw others was in congregation and one time when scary awakenings were stirring in him – you know, like I say, sex is root of all evil – he spotted a lovely lass who used to come in every week. She always stood facing him, two rows back and always with same man who was her father, so Juan presumed, close by her side. But when she prayed and sang, she did it to Juan. She just stood there shimmering and staring at him, without even blinking. Like this.' The hippy took a long drag on his joint and, making his eyes wide open, slipped on a serene look over his entire face. The carjacker didn't even bother looking. He was listening all right, but he didn't want to acknowledge that he was interested in hearing the hippy's tale.

'Juan looked on at her long brown locks,' continued the big one in the back, shaking his face back to normal, 'cascading about her, and he felt guilty because he slowly fell in love. He had thoughts he didn't think he should be thinking. His religion made him feel bad about some natural things. It put upon him an unbreakable lock and threw away key. For years looked at her and she at him, but still he didn't leave church find out who she were. He were scared to leave for fear of he may find. He knew that he couldn't miss what he know…'

'Fear of the unknown again.'

'Like the fear we have for this Dead Cloutner,' said the hippy. 'We know he'll do something if he catches up with us. But we don't know what.'

The carjacker looked to me, alarmed, as though I was going to tell him what Cloutner would do. I didn't know either. 'And like the fear you have in meeting your girl,' I said to the hippy as the carjacker looked away and out the front again.

'Yeah, shall I carry on with the tale?' asked the hippy, and it was then that I sensed he was a little uncomfortable about something, something to do with meeting his girl. What was it? What didn't fit together?

'Yeah, carry on,' I said to him in my rear-view mirror.

'Okay. So with Juan's heart still consumed with love, and lust, one day priest asked him to clean bell up tower. Juan was keen, as bell were important to town; it would ring for service – God's calling to one and all, but only if you're Catholic.'

The hippy was chuckling to himself and took another couple of long drags. 'Only other time it would ring,' he continued, 'was when there was a marriage, or when something equally terrible was going to happen like French invading or Martians. Or worst of all, bloody hippies.'

I smiled to myself, then to the hippy in the mirror. He was engrossed in his Basque tale.

'This bell tower rose high and mighty above small town,' continued the hippy, his mind in that Spanish village now, 'from where Juan, as he cleaned, could survey life about which he knew nothing and dusty red mountains beyond. So he went about his duty like a good Catholic boy. He polished bronze bell so much that it shone like summer sun. Then he had a thought: what if girl looked to him because she liked him? Maybe, now that he were a young man, he were handsome, like some men he'd read about in Bible. He coul feel things changing on his face, but he'd never seen himse He touched his square jaw and soft stubble on his chin. H been taught that looking at a reflection of yourself was wrong, that you should only look to others. Only devil admires itself.'

'What do you think the devil looks like?' I asked the hippy.

'Fuck knows!' he replied. 'But I don't think he's a red man with horns. Maybe we all look like the devil at times, you know like there's the devil inside all of us.'

'Well I never cause trouble,' I said.

'No man, but there's the potential in everyone. You must have felt the devil clawing you at times. What about when punky lad here jumped in and stuck that knife to your throat. Didn't the devil grab you then and tell you to kill him?'

The carjacker quickly looked at me and I back at him.

'Maybe he did,' I said. 'Maybe the devil did claw me, but to me it felt more like God brushing by.'

'Fuckin' hell!' blurted the carjacker. 'You two don't half talk a load of shit. I thought his tale about the Spanish wanker was bad enough, but… fuckin' hell. Let me out of here. Get me away from this shit.'

'Finish your tale,' I said calmly to the hippy and all the while looking at the carjacker. For a while he stared back at me, but then he looked away, something in my expression appearing to disturb him.

'Juan was by now so in love with this girl,' continued the hippy, 'who was out there in town he surveyed that he broke rules and went to polished bell in which he'd look at his reflection.' The hitchhiker looked up and he saw that we were listening to his yarn and listening we were because he told the story with such emotion and expression that I felt as though I could feel the Spanish sun beating down on me and the pungent smell of garlic was in the air. He carried on. 'Maybe he'd grown to look like a prince, he thought, and he could marry that girl and bells would ring and they'd be happy forever. So he looked.'

I watched in my mirror as the hippy held what was an imaginary bell in front of him and looked into it, his face aghast at what he saw. 'When Juan saw his face looking back at him he was horrified,' said the hippy excitedly. 'He nearly fell from tower. He saw a face looking back at him that resembled more a grotesque fish than a young man. His eyes were little and too close, his chin too round and small, his face an ugly oval shape. Worst of all his nose was bulbous like a pig's. What a hideous sight, he thought. Nobody can ever love me, he thought.'

I snatched a look at the hippy once again in my rear-view mirror. He took a few final swift successive drags of his joint, then flicked it out of the gap at the top of his window while forlornly staring at himself through the smoke into his reflection and moving his head side to side as he did so as though he was shadowboxing. Suddenly he stopped, and looked at us two in front, then to his reflection again. The carjacker stared solemnly ahead appearing not to listen, but in our confined space we had to listen to each other. The hippy regarded his reflected lips mouthing the words as he spoke again.

'That evening, priest heard bell ring, as did rest of town dwellers. Fearing an invasion, entire townsfolk hurried to church. There they assembled outside, a frenzy of bobbing black hair, wailing to know what was to be their destiny. But from among wails one stood out. It were priest. His only son Juan had had a terrible accident, he wailed to crowd. "*Ha habido un accidente. No puedo respirar!*" cried the priest. Juan was dead, he told them and he told them how it had happened, even though he hadn't seen it.

'"Juan," he murmured,' said the hippy in a mournful high-pitched Spanish accent, "Juan, he slip against bell, trying to hang onto rope that swung bell, before falling to his death." And he lay at bottom of tower by shaded courtyard for all to see. Whole hushed village stared at Juan's twisted lifeless body, then slowly a murmur broke out as those that hadn't heard priest's explanation asked what had happened and then murmur became a huge gasp and air was filled with sobs as everyone understood what a terrible accident had happened.' Even the carjacker seemed to be listening now.

'Soon, murmur was rumour and rumour was fact,' continued the hippy, 'and whole village knew how poor Juan had died. They looked up and down, and down and up, down at Juan's jelly body and up to shiny bell that still swayed slightly. "Why?" wailed the priest. "Why *Padre*, did this terrible accident happen?"

'Good story man,' I said, and see how I remember this story to tell you now.

'It's not finished yet,' the hippy said to me. 'Only one person left crowd assembled by church that night. She'd always been taken everywhere by her guider. Her parents had abandoned her because she was born blind. But that night, blind girl felt her way back to her house, and it was first time in her life she'd been truly alone. She had a sixth sense that'd developed without sight, one we all have, but we tend to go for what we can see rather than what we feel. In church she'd felt Juan's love reaching her like rays of warm sunlight. She went off alone because she knew what had happened. She was only one in town who knew that Juan had jumped. She could see that.'

The hippy stopped looking at his reflection looking back at him and it did likewise. He regarded us in front, his bloodshot blue eyes shifting from me to the carjacker and back. 'They still tell that tale in village and a bronze plaque, made from old bell, marks spot where Juan plunged. But,' he added with a lopsided smile, and a swift change of mood as he turned his attention to the carjacker's reflection, 'if you ask me his surname must have been Kerr: he was a right Juan Kerr, ha ha! Sorry, I know that's bad, but mood in car is terrible.'

The carjacker was staring at his reflection now. 'What do you see inside your reflection then?' I asked him, but it was the hippy who answered with a question.

'Do you know what else I see in reflection?'

'Nope,' I replied, shaking my head subtly.

'I see someone I used to know. Not in my window, like. But in his window,' he said indicating to the carjacker with a casual toss of his head. The carjacker startled. He didn't know where to look, so settled with a downward gaze. 'I see a face in your window that I know,' the hitchhiker continued. 'It's been a long time, but I remember you and your mates ripping piss out of me.'

The carjacker frowned even more and looked like he was going to throw up again.

'You don't remember me do you? But I definitely remember you. I was gardener at your school for a term. Remember now? You and your mates taking piss out of me.'

The carjacker shook his head. He spoke for the first time in a while. 'Nah, not me geezer.'

'Definitely you. Sussex public schoolboy, it's you,' the hippy said, pointing. 'So what're you doing now?' He paused for a reply with an all-knowing white grin within his fair beard. 'I thought I recognised you when I got in. Are you enjoying yourself, creating a meaning for your easy life? We all create a meaning for life, be it an investor investing to get rich, a traveller wanting to notch up another culture, a single person looking for their life-partner, a stamp collector looking for a rarity, a mad person who wants to climb a great big cold mountain, a Cancer Relief collector collecting because her husband died from that disease, a gigolo looking for a rare one, a birdwatcher looking for a perfect beauty, a property developer wanting to make a million before he's middle-aged.'

The hippy's voice was quickening now and increasing in volume as he wound himself up with each word. 'A Muslim lady learning the words of her religion on the tube, an artist seeking recognition, a stoned hippy looking for his soul in place that he can't even remember is real or not, a divorce man looking for sex and so angry that he hasn't found it for a few days that *he feels like smashing someone's fucking skull in!*' The hippy punched the headrest in front of him with such ferocity that he sent the carjacker's entire upper body forward with a mighty jolt.

'Fuck off you idiot!' snapped the carjacker, spinning round to face the angry hippy.

The once mellow hippy let out a hideous elongated guttural growl and shook his head from side to side, shaking his brain, and then moving it more ferociously like a Pitbull dog tearing at a piece of fresh red flesh. He looked with eyes wide at the carjacker who was cowering away as far as he could from the hitchhiker, his hands held open and in front of him, frozen now in terror and fear and horror and all of them combined and with good reason – a temper like that on a big guy can be very, very dangerous.

'What's got into you?' asked the carjacker, acting as though he wasn't scared.

The hippy looked up and down his face without giving away his thoughts. 'We all create meanings,' he said, his voice and pace calming back down as quickly as it had gone off. 'A religious salesman dishing out Bibles to convert world to the Word of Jesus, an environmentalist wanting GM crops banned, a mentalist wanting to pop a pill and lose their head while dancing all night, a Buddhist seeking enlightenment, a football fan wanting his team to win cup, another fan of same team wanting his firm to run another team's firm, a company director wanting his firm to run another firm, someone in their twenties wanting to earn more than their age, a dictator ordering genocide of a different people, a clown wanting to make different people laugh.'

The hippy glared at the 'jacker who glared back. 'Is that what you are doing, making your life nasty so that you can ~~ake~~ away bitter taste of a privileged upbringing? You were a ~~~tle~~ something in your small town – but small town deserves you because you're a big nothing everywhere in rest of world, so why don't you go back to your small town and stay there. Perhaps you feel guilty, maybe all your posh school mates have gone on to do something of which they can become proud, while you were too self-centred to...' the hitchhiker paused. He stopped. He stared out of his window. 'Oh shit! Shit man! Do you know what I see out of my window now?' He didn't wait for an answer. 'I see a red car with four big blokes in it – two from before and now two more big tossers.

'And one's staring right back at me. Pointing a gun.'

JOURNALIST IS HACKED TO PIECES

T HE DOOR of Zülfü's Cafe opened and a man in a cheap, creased grey suit came in. He sat down at a table and peered at the menu above the cook who was frying some eggs. There was only one other customer in Zülfü's that evening, an old man, and he was smoking a roll-up so furiously that the smell of nicotine and grease filled Nick Clark's stomach. He just wanted a coffee.

'Just a coffee,' he told the bald Turkish cook in a white apron who stood behind the counter. Outside on the High Road, among the constant flow of traffic, a bus prowled by casting a shadow in the already dim cafe. He thought about how many hours he must have sat staring at the traffic on that road, although most days he was late for work and running along the packed pavements faster than the traffic moved.

'What else?' asked the Turk.

'Nothing else. Just a coffee. Strong one.'

'You can't get just a coffee.'

'What's it up on the menu for then?'

'You can't get a coffee on its own until nine o'clock, during quiet period.'

Clark looked at the solitary old man smoking and then at the clock on the wall behind the counter.

'It's ten to nine.'

'It's five minutes fast.'

'Forget the clock. I just want a coffee. Strong one.'

'I can give you chips with it. Or a fried egg. I have lots of eggs.'

'Just a coffee.'

'Baked beans, sausages, liver.'

'Just a coffee.'

The old man stopped smoking for a moment. Another bus cast a shadow on the café and Clark's grey face. He was tired. The hostel bed where he was staying was as lumpy as hell.

'Cheese omelette, mushroom, pizza.'

'Give me a coffee and baked beans then.'

'Ten minutes and you can get just a coffee.'

'I want baked beans.'

'Just baked beans?'

'With a strong coffee.'

The Turkish cook tutted and turned away to prepare the beans and drink. The old man made another roll-up.

Nick Clark pulled out a newspaper from his jacket pocket and looked at the title, *Wood Green and Edmonton Independent Journal*, and then at the headline below in block capitals: 'ELDERLY VICTIM GETS BATTERED TO DEATH'. It was a great story. He stared at the byline of his colleague that appeared boldly there on the front page: 'By Sue MacDougall'.

He'd been at the paper for three years now hacking away at useless little nothing stories about nobody and his name had not yet made it there to the front page. He was for the chop soon if he didn't get his byline on the front and the editor had said as much to him this morning. He turned a few pages as a black hairy hand slopped down a mug of milky coffee in from of him. 'That's one pound and fifty pence.'

'It says a pound on the board,' protested Clark.

'And fifty pence for beans. They're coming.'

Clark fished out some coins, counted a bundle of five

and ten pences and handed a fistful to the open hairy hand. He looked back to the page in front of him. Page seven, bottom left of a right-hand page. There it was, his byline, small point size. 'Carjacker strikes again' it read. It should have been at least page five, at the top, thought Clark. His editor had thought differently.

'Old news,' he'd said. 'It's about the tenth carjacking this month. Old news and so will you be if you don't get something juicier on that carjacker.' Clark remembered his very words.

He thought about the shabby hostel he'd been staying in down in Euston since Jill had told him she wanted a divorce. He didn't want to go back there, couldn't go back there without a drink. He thought of little Joe, their son. He was starting school soon and Clark had always imagined the day he'd pick him up after his first day. He remembered his first day at school. Perhaps he wasn't very good at his job, not tough enough for this reporting lark. He had to lay off the booze. That's what had caused this mess in the first place, but he wasn't a violent drunk, he thought. Just a drunk.

He took a mouthful of coffee. It was cold. He drank half the cup. Right, starting the day after his day off tomorrow, let's go to work Nick Clark he said to himself: find that carjacker, get a story on the front page, avoid the sack, get promoted. He'd get off the booze, patch it up with Jill and have little Joe back. That's all there was to it. He looked at the clock on the wall behind the counter. It said five past nine. He took another look at his carjacking story. God, he needed a drink.

A hairy hand came across the page. 'Beans.'

Nick Clark pushed the plate away and left the cafe.

THE PASSENGER

IT WAS A NINE MILLIMETRE BERETTA that was being pointed by the gang. That surprised me. I thought they would have got one of the new handguns being smuggled from Russia which are made from plastic, making them virtually impossible to detect when being smuggled. They're quite neat and much more fashionable to your image-conscious crook. Still, this lot were part of an established East End gang and a gun was a gun. A Beretta could kill as well – or as badly if its owner was a poor shot – as any handgun. Let's face it, a hole in the head is a hole in the head.

'Listen geezer,' panicked the carjacker. 'I know this… oh fuck it, I just wanna get out. Let me fuckin' get out. I'll run for it. If they catch me I'll discuss it with them.'

'What!' exclaimed the hitchhiker loudly. 'You want to discuss it with a bloke called Dead?'

I eyed the 'jacker's knife, rubbing my chin with my left hand, and quickly checked my mirrors – Dead and the gang were close enough for discomfort – and set off, toe down and tongue wagging. I'd learned a fair bit about the gang through Ged and figured it was time I spread some knowledge.

'Let me tell you how that cocaine ended up in our boot an you make up your mind,' I said to the carjacker, talking fa my rhythm with my heart. The hitchhiker listened up too.

ing a ton now, so I had to keep an eye out for
ozzers as well. I rubbed some dust from the dial on
ro and stopped the cassette from banging on and then
th hands on the steering wheel.

silence was huge until I spoke again. 'This gang got a
ive amount of cocaine over during Euro 2000 in Holland
ng thirteen brick-shithouse chaps with thirteen assorted
hicles packed to the brim. They picked it up in Amsterdam
while the England fans who were up for it kicked it off. Then,
when England were done with the tournament and thousands
of supporters were steaming back home, the thirteen joined
them on the ferryside.' I paused and the silence seemed to
grow, even hum a tune.

'Police were there in numbers,' I continued. 'But for once
they weren't interested in smugglers. They just wanted to see
the backs of the lot who'd been smashing up Europe. So the
thirteen vehicles trundled through with the thirteen and a few
English fans they'd offered lifts to. It was foolproof. If any of
their vehicles were pulled over they'd start a row, clomp a
copper. Thirteen chaps would be joined by a few hundred
beered-up chaps and their route would have been cleared once
again.'

The carjacker was staring at me through his pin-dot pupil
eyes, slack-jawed with both shock and admiration at their
plan. He took his cap off, dropped it where his sick had fallen
and ran both hands slowly along the shaved sides of his head.

'And it did kick off,' I continued, delighting in letting the
carjacker know how small he was in the scheme of criminal
ways. 'Nothing to do with Dead's lot as it goes, but a few of
them still jumped out of their vans to have it with the Old Bill.
Until they remembered what was in their vans and that they
were actually in Dover. So as the England firm had it away so
d Dead's men in their vans. They were even waved on by
er Old Bill who were running to join the row, which by
was really something. They thought they were innocent

fans fleeing the off. First time I've heard of uniformed police encouraging kilos of cocaine to be brought into the country. It made the papers. Not the smuggling. The off. The ferry was wrecked – they even threw a lifeboat at the law. Three Chelsea lads and one from Rotherham got nicked.'

I paused for a moment and noticed a tiny tattoo just at the border of the 'jacker's scalp and hair, a yin-yang symbol: in all things bad there is good and in all good there is bad.

'So that was their brawn with brains way,' I said, keeping an eye on our tail. Dead and his men were looking at us from all angles, working out if they could shoot. 'The brain with brawns way took more money and organisation, but those guys in that car are capable of putting together some slick operations.'

'Go on, tell him,' urged the hippy, sensing that my cocaine tales were scaring the daylights out of the tough urban 'jacker beside me. Whatever evil world he lived in, it wasn't as scary as the one we were taking him into.

'This cocaine probably started on plantations owned by the Columbian cartels,' I said, putting my eyes back on the road that we whizzed along. I knew all this and about the guns from Ged. He wasn't directly involved, but he couldn't help knowing what went on. 'From there it was refined in labs in the jungles of Venezuela, taken by lorry to the port at Puerto La Cruz where it was concealed in various shipments, sealed in containers and shipped to the North Sea; off the coast of Holland it was put into waterproof canisters fitted with hydrostatic valves which operate flotation tanks activated by a coded radio signal; it was abandoned overboard for a while on the ocean bed, then after a few days the valves were reactivated bringing the canisters to the surface to be collected by yacht using a Global Positioning System; the yacht was then sailed to the Cornish coast with the cocaine slung in torpedoes beneath her hull; from Penzance, the cargo went by road to the importer – and that's

Dead Cloutner. Now do you want me to stop the car and let you out?'

He eyed me curiously and then shook his head, before picking up the vomit-smelling blue cap and placing it loosely on top of his Mohican, back to front. As he turned it round I noticed the word on the cap in red letters: Motörhead. I quite liked them too.

THE SOPORIFIC SPLENDOUR OF SOAPBAR

S WEAT TRICKLED from Ged's forehead and rolled down the end of his nose where it dropped onto the joint he was smoking and soaked into its fine paper. He passed it to the head leaning on his chest and looked at her as she took it between her lips, taking a slow suck on the soapbar joint and the two of them felt headily sleepy, eyes flickering from the post-sex feeling combined with the soporific splendour of soapbar.

Not only was she beautiful – long shiny brunette hair, a tiny nose, green eyes with long eyelashes, light brown crescent-shaped eyebrows, gorgeous plump red lips and an oval face with the clear complexion that only a well-brought up girl in her mid-twenties can have – but she was into Ged and she was into having lots of wild sex with Ged. He'd been particularly keen when she'd pulled him in front of the full-length mirror on the back of the door so he could watch her face as she ca when he was taking her from behind. The recollection m him shudder. He liked her, liked her enough to want to se again. He knew that in among the one-night stands what he was really looking for was the love of his life. This could be it.

He picked up a flyer he'd just finished designing from a scatter on the floor and gave it to her. She smiled at it. 'Who's the old granny?' she asked as she stared at it through half-shut eyelids.

'It's my mate Patrick's gran,' replied Ged, taking back the joint she passed him. 'You've met him a couple of times. He comes down here a fair bit. I went to school with him, my oldest friend in fact. I've known him since I was seven, that's him, on that photo over there with the cropped hair. His gran looks the part though doesn't she?'

The girl nodded.

'It's not finished yet,' continued Ged, his accent mostly that of a Londoner, but the odd word showing some Caribbean influence from his family. 'I'm going to make her hair bright purple.'

'How are you going to do that?'

'On the laptop over there. I'm getting into computer design now. In fact, I'm getting into that Mac a bit too much – I seem to spend half my life down here in this windowless cell, communicating by email and surfing the net to feed myself with information. I can create anything on there and scan in any pictures I want on that scanner there. Then it can fold up so small that I can just slip it away and it's out of sight, not like those old computers that were the size of Canary Wharf!'

He stopped himself, he knew he was into the computer too much and he didn't want to sound like a nerd. So he got back to a subject he knew she loved. 'Anyway, the flyers are for the new Friday nights down here, starting next month. Purple Rinsed I'm going to call them. They're going to be bossing it. You should come down.'

'Yeah I'd like to come down here quite a bit Ged.'

He looked at her and felt something that he didn't quite

know, it was like the rush of coke without the drug. He took the flyer back from her and looked at it, as much as anything to try to lose the unusual feelings. It was so easy to get on with her. He hardly ever felt this relaxed in someone's company.

'Shit!' exclaimed Ged as the phone rang. The girl sat up abruptly too and he went to grab his mobile from a ledge in the old dressing room that was his office. 'Shit!' said Ged again. 'I always do that. The mobile doesn't even work down here.' He looked at her looking at him as he picked up the phone.

'Hello.'

'It's Northern Wilf up on main door Ged. Sorry to bother you, but there's someone who won't go away. Says he knows you, but won't say your name. I just wanted you to come and have a look at him in case you do know him. I don't want to rough him up if he does know you. But he's been here for twenty minutes, it'll be only way to get rid of him.'

'Northern Wilf, I'll come up, but I'll tell you again: roughing someone up is not the only way to ask someone to leave. Use some manners. I haven't had a fight in my life and always get people to go politely. Even those Leeds fans from your part of the country when they were down here for the night.'

'Sorry Ged. See you in a minute.'

Ged turned to the girl and scooped his jeans from the floor. 'Sorry, won't be a minute. Security camera is broken up there tonight, so I'll have to go up for a second. Got to check a punter out otherwise Northern Wilf the meathead will find some beef with him.'

He'd been locked in the office with the girl since the club opened an hour or so ago anyway, so he supposed as manager he should do a little bit. It was only fair. As he buttoned himself up and slipped his shirt back on, he pointed at a purple sofa along a wall facing the chaise longue. 'Sofa bed. Make yourself comfortable if you want. Or shall I call you a cab?'

'Is it easy to set up?' the girl asked, smiling sexily. Ged nodded and grinned to himself as he unlocked the office door and headed into the club to get upstairs. He knew the least crowded way round the club, but already tonight even that route was an obstacle course of blissed-out clubbers, wide-eyed casualties and stoned heads in the darkest corners. It was as hot as noon in a desert in there and Ged was glad that he'd have an excuse for his sweaty appearance when he got to the door.

He eased himself through the dancing masses and felt pretty good about all things. There were some decent DJs in tonight and they had everyone going, the music was pumping with some Nu-filtered disco mixed in with classic tracks and new bubblers. He looked at the party people sexily shaking their arses at each other; Ged called it 'rumping'. There was a good party going on and he was pleased that there had never been any trouble down there. Hc glanced up to the VIP bar and saw a few older, stockier chaps in suits sat around a table with some blonde stunnas. The chaps were some of Dead Cloutner's crowd and Ged let them in for free, and that was one of the main reasons there'd never been any trouble in the club.

He brushed past a blonde girl leaning on her boyfriend at the fire door leading to the steps up to the main entrance. At the top of the flight he could see the man-mountain that was Northern Wilf. Ged bounded up the steps.

'What's up?' he asked Northern Wilf at the top. Northern Wilf, a blond crop-haired heavyweight, looked down at Ged's shaven scalp and then opened the thick main door to beckon a skinny lightweight dressed in a white sweaty T-shirt to come through to the front of the blaggers and wannabe guests outside. A few people shouted Ged's name out. He ignored them for the moment. He knew they'd only be on the blag and he had to sort some business out before he got chatting to anyone. It was one reason he hid himself away in the downstairs office so often these days. Ged took one look at the skinny blagger before him and thought thing: speed.

'You the manager I know you but didn't remember you was black or remember your name I lived with a couple of blacks once and I met you once down at the thingy club you know the thingy club in south I was up there with you remember and I was off me tits and we was dancing all night together and you said I could come down here and I would should be on the guest list VIP whatever just that I didn't get my I didn't couldn't find a cash I lost got robbed my wallet everything money drugs bus pass comb even though I've got this crew cut neat uh huh huh what's it like go on mate let me in your bouncer said you would what's it like down there can't wait to dance you don't remember me yet do you I can't wait to get in there go on mate I'm only after a bit of pussy go on you know what it's like I can't go walking around all night not when I are you sure I'm not on the guest list are you sure you're the real manager I didn't remember you was black and that but I met you at my sister's party remember you went out with her it's Julie or Samantha. No what about Theresa, Sharon I've got loads of sisters. Oh go on mate, let us in, please I'll... I'll... just let me in.'

'I'm really sorry mate, I can't do that,' said Ged patiently. 'Ten out of ten for trying, but I don't know you and if I let you in, what about all these other people who are waiting?'

'Yeah but they ain't been here as much as me I'm here every week you must recognise me see it's just that I had my hair cut and that it used to be long until last week dreads and that cos I'm really into that vibe man that black ting you know what I'm saying man and I thought I've got to come down here and get in and do some dancing and all that and oh come on mate just let me in it'll be a lot easier if you let me in and then I can go –' Ged put an arm out to gently stop him.

'Okay, enough's enough for you,' he said quietly and w̵ utterly impeccable manners. Ged had built his club busir̵ on being pleasant which was another reason he never had the hassle that many clubs had. 'I'd go home if I were you and prepare for the come-down. Go home, get comfortable and put your feet in a bowl of warm water. You mentioned drugs as well mate. We don't allow anyone in who has drugs.'

'No I haven't got any search me you won't find them on me I haven't got any drugs mate.' The loon stood there staring at Ged, his eyes bulging like a frog's with a twig up its arse.

Northern Wilf nudged Ged and pointed to his feet. 'I told him he couldn't come in with those anyway Ged.' Ged stared down at the skinny blagger's footwear. Ged had been looking at his pop-out eyes so much that he hadn't noticed the slippers: big fluffy, yellow teddy bear ones. 'I told him,' said Northern Wilf as Ged smiled at him.

'Nothing wrong with these mate I came down here earlier with trainers on fucking hundred quid ones as well and you told me,' he said pointing at Northern Wilf, 'that I couldn't come in with trainers so I've come back and these aren't trainers these are fucking slippers and slippers aren't trainers so if you don't let me in I'll have you for false pretences or something fraud that's what it is.'

'Sorry,' repeated Ged, noticing that some of the other punters were getting restless. 'I think you've had a good run. You look like you've had enough. Why don't you call it a day? We can't let you in tonight I'm afraid.'

'What so you're not letting me in if you don't let me in I'll come back with some of the lads and blow you away and your thick fucking bouncers here and I'll personally kick your arse. Go on mate let us in.'

'There's no need,' said Ged, starting to turn away and walk back inside, 'for that. Come back another time when you're not so wrecked and without slippers on and I'll let you in.'

'Yeah but what about now let us in now ain't going nowhere til you let me in you black cunt and that northern fucking illa ape who on the door got no brains between you.'

Ged turned and walked through the door ignoring shouts from others on the guest list and the continuing insults of the skinny speedster man. He shut the door and a second later Northern Wilf opened it and came through before shutting it again. The pair of them stood at the top of the stairs leading down to the club and listened to the speeding guy shouting even louder insults now. A couple of people waiting in the queue started to take further offence to him and Northern Wilf looked to Ged for instructions before it started to turn ugly.

'Do you know what Northern Wilf?'

'What Ged?'

'I'm really worried about Patrick.'

'How's that?'

'I told you what went wrong with that Dead deal?'

Northern Wilf nodded. 'It wasn't Patrick's fault though,' continued Ged. 'And Dead's men seem a bit quiet in there, like there's some stormy wave run through Dead's firm.'

'Well, if Dead's pissed off about something we all know about it.'

'Yeah, and I felt like a couple of them gave me dirty looks.' Just then there was a loud bang at the door. Immediately Northern Wilf peeped through the spyhole. 'Someone's holding that skinny twat up against door,' Northern Wilf shouted, excited that he had the chance to use his large muscles rather than his small brain. 'I'll sort it.'

'Hang on Northern Wilf. This is what to do. Sort the hassle out first, no aggression, just talk to the guy holding him up. Then let everyone in. It's busy down there, but there's no need to leave anyone standing outside. There's room for everyone, so get them in as quickly as possible.'

'What, even let that skinny twat in?'

'No, when you've let everyone else in, beat him up.'

CRACK HOUSE GUN HORROR!

DEAD AND HIS MEN were ruthless enough to kill us any time they wanted without feeling any remorse. In fact our deaths at their violent hands would hardly even warrant a break in their conversation. But they weren't going to shoot at us, not right now. At least I didn't think they would.

With the level of sophistication they had they didn't need to bang away in front of a moving motorway audience. Dead was intrigued and that's why he kept after us rather than send some of his henchmen to finish us off: the punk holding the knife at my throat, the hippy in the back threatening the punk – he wasn't quite sure what was happening in our car. Of course he wasn't scared, but he was angry, for if all had gone to plan for the 'perfectionist' he would have been celebrating by now.

As rain fell, I noted how much we'd plunged into darkness, that is pitch-blackness as there were no lights on this stretch of motorway. It was so dark outside that for all we knew we could be underwater. Maybe now we'll get it, I thought, maybe now as we swim further and further into the deep end, maybe now we'll get our heads pushed under, maybe now 'll be gasping for air. Then we'll drown. I felt as though I

was in the infants, just about standing on tip-toe, face turne
fully upwards gasping for breath and one step away from
disappearing forever.

Pairs of dazzling white lights streamed towards us and then
flashed by leaving a luminescent trail and we'd come up
swiftly behind pairs of red lights, a flick of full beam causing
them to pull over and we'd be past them. Windscreen wipers
whooshed hypnotically to momentarily wipe the screen clear
of dribbling rain droplets, while spray from lorries and other
cars made driving among the pack dicey-dangerous.

I had no very clear purpose in our escape journey, but I'd
steered north as the last of the day's distant light had dipped
away to our left a while ago. As soon as I could I would get
off the motorway and rally out of sight through the
Nottinghamshire countryside. I put my foot down, we had a
chance to get clear and lose this fearsome foursome once and
for all. Their red BMW was out of sight now and I told the
other two.

'Thank fuck for that! Just keep those bastards away from
me – I've had a gun pointed at me before,' announced the
carjacker, breathing out the relief that we all felt. The hippy
nodded, but he was so stoned that, awww... it doesn't
matter... just to say that he was pretty happy and relaxed with
life and that's good.

'I went round to, to this geezers to score,' continued the
carjacker. I turned my head slightly facing Cool Cat and
quizzically raised my eyebrows at him. 'Crack-cocaine,' he
sneered. 'That's what I made *my* meaning of life and why I
started carjacking.'

That was possible, I thought: rich kids do it all the time,
everyone does some drug all the time. I rubbed my fingers on
a rough piece on the steering wheel.

'Either of you two see that cop programme on TV la
week, this was just like that?' asked the carjacker, but neith
of us uttered a word. 'Anyway,' he carried on, 'this was o

estate down Bermondsey, where I went to the crack house. The dealers been there a few weeks doing the usual – a rap on the fortified door, they'd check you through the peephole, you push your cash through the letterbox and back out comes the rocks. Only this time, as I went to rap, the next door opened, but was kept chained. Pointing at me was a gun. A big fuck-off gun, like a sawn-off that you see on TV. It would have put my stomach lining into the next tower block.'

He looked to see he had an audience and of course in our small confines he did, so he carried on, getting quite excited at this particular tale. 'What had happened, yeah, was this other lot had squatted the empty flat next door to rob all the crackheads who'd come to get their licks. So the gun's pointing at me and a voice from behind the door orders me to throw my cash on the floor, and jewellery, slide it over to their door and then fuck off. But I didn't have any jewellery on and I'd come to get my rocks on tick this day as I was skint. So I'm facing a gun with nothing to lose. I think quick, turn my back on the shooter and start to walk away. As I do I immediately say out very loudly: "You shoot Bernie Hackman in the back and see what happens to you." I can almost hear their minds working as I take my steps down the stairs.'

There was a moment's silence as we took this tale in, until the hippy spoke up. 'A cunning use in psychology of violence from Cloutner's College For Crooks,' he said, with sarcasm. 'So hello Bernie Hackman.'

'No, that's not my name,' laughed the carjacker. 'Don't be a fucking idiot all your life. I made it up on the spot, thought it sounded gangster-like.'

'What is it then?' I asked.

'What's what?' the carjacker answered, looking puzzled now.

'Your name.'

'It doesn't matter.'

'No, it doesn't,' I said, shrugging. 'Not really.'

We continued apace, my foot flat down on the floor as we made some more space between us and the BMW. He told the story well and I had few doubts that he'd been a crackhead. I had no doubts that it wasn't his story he'd just told.

'I knew someone at school called Nicholas Soul,' announced the hippy, trying to stifle his laughs and when he laughed, his whole giant body shook, his whole giant body laughed with him. 'Nickle-arse-sole. We called him Silver Bum. And I spoke to an environmental health officer at council once called Mister Meener.'

As endless darkness whooshed past I grinned. We needed a junction quick. In the back, the hippy was laughing loudly.

'We had an Alan Bateman at school too,' he carried on. 'Master Bateman. And I heard of a Seymour Butt!' The hippy erupted in fits of laughter at this. 'And another one. Mike Hock!'

He was roaring now, a great, friendly infectious laugh. Even Cool Cat tweaked a smirk.

'That's not as bad as this geezer I met inside,' snorted the carjacker, regarding me with a scowl and not for the first time. 'His nickname was Viagra because no-one could say his name without laughing in his face. Last name Dick, first name Everard!'

The hippy was laughing so much now that he slapped his thigh a couple of times to try to calm himself down. He gathered himself. 'Then there's those,' the hippy grinned, just stifling his maniacal cackle for a moment to talk, while I thought that if the carjacker had been in prison it was fairly recently... 'famous people's kids like Zowie Bowie,' ... because Viagra hadn't been around for very long at this time... 'or Frank Zappa's kid. What's he called? Something mental like Yappa Flappa Bappa Zappa-doo! What a bunch of Juan Kerrs!'

I think the carjacker was lying again just to up his bravado like he was trying to scare us. I stared at him – him in the passenger seat, him next to me, him who I wished I'd never met, *him* who no-one should ever meet.

'Start silly rumours,' I said to him and he looked over at me.

'You talking to me geezer?'

'Yeah, I am talking to you. Are you listening?'

He shrugged.

'Are you fucking listening?'

He nodded, startled at me shouting at him.

'Good, because this is important,' I said, showing calm again. 'Start silly rumours and you cause all sorts of trouble, trouble that wasn't there in the first place, you know what I mean?' He looked away while I stared at him and kindly thought about the trouble he was in. Something about him was really disturbing me now, more than ever, and I don't think he knew what I meant at all.

'There was another bloke at my school whose parents named him Karen,' said the hippy, breaking up the icy atmosphere. 'But everyone called him Kar unless you wanted to receive a right kick-in. He were hardest in school. So you stuck to Kar man. He ended up hanging himself on New Year's Day, in girlfriend's bathroom, dressing gown cord tied to cistern and... she found him and he was dangling opposite mirror.'

We were passing three cars that had been in a smash with temporary emergency lights brightly illuminating them, and which had been moved onto the hard shoulder. They were splintered open and the roofs sagged in.

'Look,' I said. 'There's been a smash.'

The hippy looked and saw the last car. 'I was afraid of just that all day,' he said. 'I have feelings about things sometimes. I'll never jump in a Saab again. There must be other comfortable cars that don't go so fast.' The carjacker continued staring out of his side window, mentally falling more and more into the darkness that lay beyond the yellow road lights that flared up this part of the motorway.

Things were beginning to look desperate – the car in front, an old black Jaguar was holding the outside lane at seventy and we were hemmed in by cars in the inside lanes, also sticking firmly to seventy. It could only mean one thing: the police were about. Then, closer and bigger and closer and bigger and bigger… and closer… and… closer, the BMW and its occupants reappeared and, slinking past cars on the inside and outside, they finally settled down a couple of cars behind us.

'Gordon Bennett!' startled the hippy. 'I mean I knew someone called Gordon Bennett once. But worst name to have that I've ever heard is bloke whose surname's Sprout and his parents christened poor tosser Russell. Russell Sprout! Ha ha ha!!'

I wanted to laugh too, but there was more on my mind. Behind us the BMW and crawling in front on the inside lane a patrol car.

'They're back,' I announced. 'And they're not looking very pretty. Help me keep an eye on them while I drive.' I really didn't need to have bothered as our two passengers both shot fearful glances over their shoulders

I could see Dead leaning back in his seat, arms folded and his entire tanned face creased in anger, green-blue veins straining with the pressure inside his powerful head. Here sat a man who was used to being in control. The cops up ahead were cruising along at slightly under the speed limit. Suddenly as we drew level with the police car, all eyes ahead, its lights started to flash. I noticed the lights first of all for what seemed like ages. In reality it was perhaps two bluish white flashes in the corner of my eye and then the wail came on. Woo-wooo, woo-wooo – well you know what a siren sounds like.

Then, I hear the carjacker curse. 'Shit!' he says. He really i a worrier. He sinks in his seat, but the cops, two of them in th car, speed past us on the inside and careen round a curve i the fast lane. They're off somewhere else in a hurry an they disappear, our pace on the road moves up: seventy, eighty, ninety then we hit a ton and the BMW stays close on our arses. We start making some distance on them, but not for long, for just as soon as the pace hots up, it cools down again.

Flashing signs overhanging the road tell us <40!> <40!> <40!> <40!>. Three lanes go into two and a coned-off area causes a slow trickle as we filter through. We pass hundreds of orange and white cones, enough to fill the Millennium Dome, but with no-one to be seen working within them. This eerie yellow foggish streetlight, makes like, I imagine, the smog of London that the Ripper did his ripping under disguise in.

My thoughts flitted. I was being bombarded from inside all parts of my skull. The start of our journey seemed days ago, when I'd set off from the shop wondering how to get this cocaine cock-up under wraps. Then I'd gone along Upper Street, driven up Blackstock Road after Highbury Corner, into Seven Sister's Road, left at Manor House tube into Green Lanes and up to Turnpike Lane where the Arsenal/Spurs border blurs. A right at Turnpike Lane tube and along tatty Tottenham High Road. I don't even remember one sight as I crawled down that ugly road, except for a guy in a suit running down the street, obviously late for his office job.

Abruptly the traffic halts and in the distance, round a slow bend, we see the police car's flashing bluey lights cutting through the yellow illumination and shooting into the night's sky like a wartime searchlight. The river of red lights slow to a trickle. There's been another prang up ahead. I look at the shadowy faces in other cars to our left side as they crawl past us or we crawl back past them. Some faces are contorted, screwed up, full of seething, others resigned. There's an Indian family peering ahead, a West Indian guy nodding his head to some music that's silent to us, a white middle-class couple in their tall shiny new car for a big family, white trash

families tearing each other's hair out, a white van driv_
impatiently puffing on a ciggie, and an old couple sit
passively even though the time running out is more precious
to them.

I check my mirror. We're stationary and the BMW is much
too close now. I freeze and sense the figure next to me tense
too. Only the stoned one reacts with any sort of sense.

'Lock fucking doors!' the hippy exclaims, so quickly I
press my door's lever and they all click shut.

'Are... are they getting out?' whispers the carjacker,
looking terrified. I shake my head, while twisting my neck to
look behind. I turn back quickly. Although Dead has on a bold
pair of black and gold CK shades I know his eyes are on mine
in the mirror and he looks mightily pissed off with playing the
pussy.

The carjacker shifts uncomfortably. 'What the fuck are we
going to do?' he asks. 'They'll fuckin' kill me. I'm getting
out.' Then he goes to lift the door lock, so I lean over, keeping
my right hand on the steer and beat his hand away with my
other forearm. At the same time, the hippy grabs the 'jacker's
skinny neck with his big strong hands. 'You're going
nowhere,' he hisses in his ear. 'We're in this together. You're
with us and going nowhere unless it's with us.'

'Okay, okay, let go og me! Fuckin' let go og me! Can't
fuckin' breathe.'

So the hippy releases him, breathing down his neck. 'You
move tosser,' he threatens, 'and I'll slice your windpipe with
this, then you'll have all air you want.' It was quite dark in the
car now, but clear enough to see the hippy holding a Swiss
Army knife to the carjacker's throat and oh man, that cat had
really turned into a squeaking mouse, his little eyelashes
fluttering now like a row of ragged black flags in a lonely
wind.

'Oh shit, there's movement in their car,' I announce, my
voice coming from my throat. 'One from the front looks lik_

he's coming to have a word. Oh... listen, I know what to do. Shit, his door's just opened. Quick!' I said to the carjacker. 'Pick your knife up again. Hold it to my throat. It's our only chance.'

HARD

NICK CLARK STARED in the mirror across the bar at the cut on his throat. God he looked awful, he thought. It was the first time he'd seen himself in days and he noticed the dried blood across his neck from where he must have cut himself shaving that morning. It would have been there all day and yet no-one had mentioned it to him in the office. He took a few large mouthfuls from his pint of Kronenbourg. Oh yes, that tasted bloody fantastic. And another mouthful. May as well finish it now.

'Another one cheers,' he told the barman, an old bald git with greased-across black and grey strands who looked as if he'd start crying if he ever had to smile.

'Thirsty tonight?' solemnly asked the barman.

'You could say,' laughed Nick, masking the sadness within that led him to drink. If people thought he was a drunkard he at least wanted to be seen as happy about it. Perhaps that's why, he mused, perhaps that's why no-one in the office had mentioned the cut on his neck to him. It was the sort of thing alkies do all the time or old men and you don't bother mentioning it because it's, well it's embarrassing to tell someone that they're fucked, so out of it, so passed caring, so gone in the brain that they can't get a simple thing li' shaving right. Bastards! He imagined them talking about h

89

ffice, behind his back. Well, fuck 'em, he'd show

here you go. On the tab?'

Nick nodded. Too fucking right, on the tab. It was his third already, about one every ten minutes. He'd rather drink himself than think himself to sleep. He looked at the clock above the bar. Jesus, if that was the time he'd better make the call. He had enough Dutch courage by now, but little Joe would probably be in bed. He'd better make it now though, then he'd still have time to get another in before last orders.

He dialled the number on the pub's payphone on the bar, his number, his *home* number. It was an old pub, this one: purple velvet seats; the engraved mirror across from the bar; dark, dusty lanterns inside; a dartboard, a pool table, no music and a series of unhappy expletive-heavy conversations. The brown carpets and walls smelled of years of booze and the yellow ceiling stank of a million cigarettes. It deserved its nickname of the Dog and Toilet for that's all it was: a toilet and the only women in there were dogs. In fact so were the blokes, most of them built like pitbulls with faces that made boxer dogs look happy. But it was the nearest to the Euston hostel where he was staying and that'd do him. It sold booze anyway. Suddenly the phone stopped ringing and a voice sounded at the other end. Such a familiar voice.

'Hello,' she said.

'Hello Jill, it's me.'

'Hello?'

'Yeah, hello. It's me. Nick.'

Her voice came across his as he spoke. 'Hello? Who is this?' Burrrrrrrrrrrrrrrrrrrrrr… oh bollocks! Well he'd put the money in. A young lad in his twenties, tapped him.

'Put your coins in there mister, then press that button,' said the lad in an Irish accent pointing at the payphone. Clark stared down at the lad's dusty boots and up to his dusty mop of hair. 'Cheers,' Clark said, looking back to the phone.

'Not a bother,' said the lad as he turned to the barman.

Clark tried again. This time he got in first when the phone was answered.

'Hello Jill,' he blurted enthusiastically. 'It's me. I-'

'I know exactly who it is,' she said coldly. 'You've probably just woken Joe up. Can't you call back another time? I'm busy.'

Clark glugged a couple of mouthfuls of beer. 'Just a quick call. I'm sorry Jill. I just –'

'Can't you call me back another time? I suppose you're in the pub again?'

'There's no phones where I'm staying.'

'I thought you said it was a hotel.'

'It is. Sort of. But it's a hotel without phones and this is the nearest place.'

'Convenient.'

'Sort of.'

'Well, what do you want, now you've disturbed me and Joe and… probably half the street.'

Clark felt like his blood had been drained. He stared at his lager. He just knew, from her voice, from a feeling deep in his gut.

'Who's with you?'

'No-one,' she chuckled, her voice softening to something like how she used to speak to him. 'Don't be so silly. There's just me and Joe here.'

Clark felt his face heat up and saw his vision blur. 'Who's with you Jill?'

'Look, call me back. When you're sober.' Her voice was hard again. As hard as the sound of the phone when she slammed it down.

'*Who?* Who Jill? Who is it? Who is he? *Who's there with you*?' demanded Clark as he screamed down the phone. He screwed his eyes up and without opening them raised the pint glass and poured the booze down his thirsty neck, dropping the phone as he did so. She was seeing someone. He'd never guessed it, but now he knew. Things had been rocky for a few months. But fuck, what about little Joe? What about him? Clark really had to turn around a top story and keep his job. Jill had always wanted him to do better. Perhaps she'd want him more than anyone else then. He just had to get the story that would get his life back on track. He drained the glass and noticed the pub had become as quiet and still as a picture. Not a very pretty one, but it was still and silent as though time had stopped. He looked round and everyone quickly looked away, all the builders and suited-up pissheads and the couple of fat tarts sipping their Malibu, lime and lemonades. Everyone seemed to edge away, as though out of all the pissheads there, he was the one with the worst problem.

All except an older red-faced bloke with a grey crew-cut, a hard-looking bastard with a beer-stained white T-shirt stretching over a fine beer belly and black jogging bottoms that hung way below his arse. He was staring at Clark and wobbled forward. The barman suddenly busied himself and shifted to the other side of the bar.

'Do you think everyone wants to hear that your missus is *shaggin'* someone else mate?' demanded the demented. He spat the word 'shagging', emphasised it like it was a trophy to put up on the mantelpiece, and put it fully into focus in Clark's denying mind. While little Joe slept next door. Clark had never been a fighter but he felt his blood boiling and the room go claret as his blood boiled over into his vision. Before he knew it, without his brain giving his mouth permission to say so he heard himself blurting out: 'What the fuck's it got to do with you? Fuck off ape man! I don't need any more hassle.'

Ape man didn't like that. Oh shit, thought Clark as it registered what he'd said, what challenge he'd put forward and he saw the big bloke before his eyes roll up some imaginary sleeves on his massive hairy, tattooed forearms.

The big bloke nodded at him. 'You want some then?' he

grimaced through gritted teeth. 'Cos you're fuckin' gettin' some.'

'Share your worries mister?' Clark span round to see the young Irish builder stood next to him holding out a pint. 'Ye drink that. I'll see to him.'

HERE IS FEAR

E'S FROSTBITTEN WITH FEAR. 'You heard him!' shouted the hippy. 'Pick your knife up or I'll cut your neck so fast you won't realise until your head's dropped between your knees and you're looking up at a space where it used to be!'

This does the trick and quickly the carjacker grabs his knife and presses it to my neck again. It presses hard and I give a stern eye to the carjacker, but he can only look straight ahead, consumed with one thought: death. His death. The hippy keeps his worn but razor-sharpened red Swiss Army number upwards on the carjacker's protruding Adam's apple, and looks over his shoulder, leaning to one side so that Dead and his men can see what's going on.

'It's working!' I exclaim, looking at the stationary figures in the BMW. 'They haven't got a clue what's going on.' I keep watching as the one who'd been about to get out keeps his hand on his partly opened door but opens it no more.

'But won't they just kill us anyway?' asks the hippy, his blade grazing the carjacker's skin covering his Adam's as it moves up with his terrified gulps.

'No, they want their cocaine back,' I replied, 'and they don't know who you two are, if you've got their stuff, or if you've got their money. They don't even know that their cocaine is still in this car. If I get killed before Dead's had a word, they may never know where it is.'

My eye catches red as I notice a few tiny droplets of blood

slowly grow and form one bigger droplet on the carjacker's cut neck. Now don't go feeling all sweety sorry for the carjacker; remember he made the choice to get in, he knew that there could be consequences for his evil game of life. He grips and ungrips his pale hand on the knife handle that he holds to my throat, turning his filthy nails white where they should have been all nice and pinky. He has a wart that he's picked at on his middle finger, just by the top joint bit, which is scabby. Blood dribbles down his neck.

'I've had enough of him, understand,' explains the hippy and I understand.

'I've had enough of both of you,' mumbles the carjacker, trying but failing to keep up his tough exterior. 'You'll pay for this. I'm bleeding.'

I check my mirror, the carjacker looks straight ahead and the hippy looks at me, then the carjacker and then over his shoulder and repeats these movements, time and time again. The gang are having animated discussions now and Dead Cloutner is leaning forward, and all the time staring straight at me. We start to move slowly again and Dead's crony shuts his door as we crawl along.

Everyone was looking at the horror smash and so no matter, we could have been holding bazookas to each other's heads and no-one on the motorway, except for Dead's observant lot, would have noticed. It had been what looked like a back and then sideways crash between one big powerful car and a small old one. We saw three people being tended to by the big car which lay on the inside lane. Nobody was around the small car which was a twisted wreck. Another person spoke to a rozzer as the flashing blue light blipped around like a scan showing a heartbeat.

Traffic sped up on the other side of the accident, so I put my foot down and reflected that now things were not so simple. Our mellow hippy friend had lost it, and I know that it takes a lot for someone like him to go from passive to aggressive. It may happen just once or twice every few years, but when it happens, get out the way fast for they are far more ferocious than an always angry man.

So he'd lost it and if he spliced the carjacker, the carjacker would cut me and, eighty, ninety, as we were back up to now – and we'd be dead. Or if the carjacker, jumpy as can be, slashed my throat all jagged-like with trembling hand, we'd crash and as we crashed the hippy would split the carjacker's neck from one side to the other, with his strength most nearly taking his head clear off from his spiny bloody neck.

'Shall we put the knives down now,' I tentatively suggested. 'Cloutner's still on our tail, there's a junction coming up and we need to lose them.' The carjacker removed his immediately.

'Drop it!' ordered the hippy. The carjacker dropped it with a soft clanky thud to the black rubber mat under his desert boots and the hippy completed the deal by removing his blade and sliding it down the inside front of his trousers, into his pants I think.

'Sorry,' he said to me as he leaned his huge frame back. 'I'm not a belligerent bloke, but I've learned a bit from travelling into hairy situations to stay cool when it matters, but on other hand to go a bit mental when it's needed.' We were really moving now, making distance and the red BMW, all the while, sharked after us, just a few cars behind.

'I had a machine gun shoved in my back before,' the hippy continued as if to ease our deadly situation. 'In Guatemala. It were just a few days before an election. Soldiers were searching all men who were on move because there'd been several murders a day in lead-up to voting day. I was hauled off this old battered yellow bus with all Guatemalan men while all women looked out of one side. I'm quite big, see, and all Guatemalan blokes were short and they all had jet-black hair while mine was even longer then and even lighter from sun.'

'Fuckin' hippy,' blabbed the carjacker to act up as though he'd not been petrified back then. These two really hated each other. The carjacker's vileness was so complete that it had brought out from somewhere the bad in the hippy like he had to fight fire with fire or take an eye for an eye.

'All of a sudden I felt a sub-machine gun prodded in back by a teenage soldier who's twitching like an eppy,' the hippy continued. 'I'm travelling with this nutty French girl at time and she shouts from coach: "Showdem your Breet-eesh passport, telldem Queen Elizabett sent you! Upfully det shood dooet," before laughing her head off – she thought it were hilarious.'

'So what happened man?' I asked.

'I ditched French tart.'

'No with the gun.'

'Oh that,' replied the hippy. 'Nothing really. But then if he'd killed me I wouldn't be able to tell you story would I? Soldier just gave me a quick search. He even smiled at me as he let me back on coach. Anyway, that was one time when it was best to stay cool. I had half ounce of Mexican grass on me anall.'

'You've travelled a lot then?' I said to him in the dimness of the back.

'On road is best way man,' he answered to his reflection in the side window. 'In fact travelling is best way of life. Once you've done it, there's no way back to a normal life and even if you do you'll always know there's a better life out there. I've tried it, but always come back to travelling. See a place name on a map and point to it and then a while later that name has become somewhere real with buildings and people and personality and maybe a friend.'

He leaned his forehead on the window and sighed. I concentrated back on the lighted road ahead and put my foot flat down.

'Like your map's going to come alive for us when we reach

the Beloved Wood,' I said to him and he nodded, a little uncertainly I thought.

'Make sure you don't crash geezer,' demanded the passenger to my left as he wiped the blood on his neck with his hand, smearing it into a pale brown streak, his full bravado back up and firing on eight cylinders. 'I spent three months in Stoke Mandeville Hospital in a coma and with a damaged spine after a car crash.' We were touching a hundred now and I didn't know whether to believe him. He was a nest of lies. I knew that Stoke Mandeville Hospital was world famous for spinal treatment, but then again so did most of the world.

'I was in hospital for two months,' declared the hippy, 'from a car accident too. Look, I had a pipe put in here to keep me alive.' He stretched his neck so we could see a scar he revealed. We in the front both ogled back and as we looked frontwards again our eyesights collided, for less than half a second, but longer than normal. It was just a moment, but we said something to each other; I'm not sure what, but at last we had communicated. There was something sinister in his sight. I had to do it.

The hippy brought us back. 'I was hit by a fast car on a zebra crossing and dragged down street. Driver never stopped.' He bowed his head for a second allowing his lank hair to dangle down covering his face before looking up with a smirk and flicking the sides back over his ears. 'I asked them to blow some hash smoke down pipe in hospital, but they wouldn't.' He chuckled and I nodded, in appreciation of his optimism as much as anything else. I still felt he was slightly boiling underneath and who could blame him with this thief sat nervously chewing his filthy fingernails next to us. He was dirty scum. I was giving him chances to redeem himself, but so far – as far as I could make out – he was simply the dirtiest scum. The red BMW was still keeping pace, five cars back.

I didn't tell them that I'd been in a crash too, that I'd been driving along a B road in Sussex when suddenly from round a bend a small removal van had come hurtling headfirst towards us. I did my best to avoid it and steered the car into a narrow grass verge. We took off over the hedge and span a couple of times in the field before the side, the passenger side, crunched into a large solid oak tree bringing us to a shattering halt. I'd climbed out immediately and ran round to the passenger door. I tried it with all my might, but it was jammed. I was shaking and panicking and I couldn't open it. I'd looked around for help but there was none, the van driver had sped off, leaving us, so I'd ran back to my door and clambered in.

I'd been giving Mum a lift, just to some shops, close to the town where she lived. I wish every day, every day, that it had been her driving and me in the passenger seat. I wish it had been my blood that I touched. You can't touch your mother's blood, you are her blood, you can't, you fucking can't.

I wish it had been me.

Tears welled in my eyes and goose bumps went up, then down my spine. I wiped the wetness away from my eyes. I didn't tell them about my crash. If only I hadn't gone to visit that day, if only we'd been driving along that road thirty seconds later. Sorry, but, I'm sorry, but why? I lay no blame, but I have no understanding. If that cunt to my left thinks I have any fears about driving fast, then he should know that I can never have a worse crash than that one. I deserve to die, to join her, in a car crash – if we go cartwheel my heart will jump for joy and I'll... 'Psssssst!' I was psssssst-ed out of my sad thoughts.

'Psssssst! Take this junction geezer,' said the carjacker, avoiding eye contact as he pointed ahead. 'I know this part of Nottinghamshire. Spent some years here. You'll have to trust me on this one otherwise I'll never get out of this.'

Trust him, never, but I had no better ideas to get us all away to safety from the four madmen behind. I swerved over the slower lanes and motored into the junction. Less than a quarter of a mile behind, they followed. Spray from cars and especially lorries made it difficult to drive. It was like being at sea in a night storm.

The carjacker started to lead the way telling me to take this turn and that turn and hard left and second right and straight on and past the pillar box under a rare rural street light and sharp right and left swerve.

'How do you know your way around here then?' I asked him.

'My parents moved around a lot,' he replied cockily. 'We lived near here for a little while. I know my way round lots of England.' I wondered, I wondered. He could be telling the truth, but I doubted it. He seemed to know his way around here all right, but I wondered if it was to do with the life of crime, the bad life, he'd chosen.

For miles we ran alongside a high wall, and in a break in the trees I saw a great brightly lit stately building. There were other great old houses around, large and sturdy, mansions with wisteria and ivy clambering to be part of their grand facades, homes of the grand, fortresses of the few. Momentarily appearing between swiftly moving glowing clouds, it looked like it was nearly a full moon which made it easier to negotiate the twists and turns as we swung through little old thatched villages, and over peaceful lowland streams, and past sleeping gardens with hawthorn and yellow laburnum that would blaze with colour in the daytime sunshine. The land was so deep in peace that I could scarcely believe that never far behind were those who sought our lives; and unless we had the almightiest of luck these ruddy country faces round here would be white and pinched from the murders that had smashed their existence into the Twenty-first Century.

The immediate thing to do was to get to the loneliest roads, and fortunately the carjacker was thinking the same. 'Left here!' he bellowed, pointing feverishly at a small virtually concealed turn just after a white-painted and florally-decorated country pub festooned with white bulbs, most of which had blown. I slammed the brakes on, pumping the pedal so we didn't skid, but the smoothed road didn't hold and we skidded a couple of car lengths past the turning, loose stones flicking up at the side of the car, the noise of our tyres resounding in the silent air.

'Quick, you've got to get on that one,' despaired my navigator. For the first time since we'd met I believed him, such was his fear of dying, such was his complete fear. He was desperate for his life and I couldn't for the life of me understand why when it seemed so squandered, but back then I was almost grateful to him for swimming us around those country lanes.

So I act with haste, crunching the Saab into reverse and speeding backwards a few metres before slamming the gear stick into first and spinning off, but behind us – just as our tyres catch hold of the smooth surface – the full beams of the BMW zoom into sight. Ping! Ping, ping! They're shooting at us! Time's up – those gangsters are fed up with our games and out here the bumpkins will think the noise of the shots is pheasant hunters or some other rural-type 'sport'. In any case, the gun's silencers are pretty effective.

In the front we both instinctively hunch our shoulders and put our heads down, while the hippy dives flat on the back seat, occasionally popping his golden eyebrows above the back of the seat to give us a running commentary: 'Yeah, still there, last bend, two hundred metres, guns out both sides, three guns I think, that's…' Ping! Ping, ping, ping! He scrambles down again and I thank the carjacker's knowledge of these winding roads for without the meanderings and curves and his directions the bullets would have been hitting their targets.

'Okay!' the carjacker screeches like our tyres on the Tarmac, grimy sweat dribbling down his hollow temple as we speed along a one-track lane with high untrimmed hedges on either side. 'When I say, and I mean exactly when, hit the brakes full-on. We're looking to spin into a track on the left. You won't see it when I say, but just spin your wheel hard as you fuckin' can. Then there's an immediate right and we'll be out of sight in a field.'

I double-look at him and he stares back at me. It's a chance, and our only chance now and I am prepared to take it. His hand rests on my left biceps, ready to shout and tug at me to turn. Stray hedge twigs slap the car's sides like a race jockey's whip as we speed along the lane, so narrow you can't squeeze a bicycle alongside us. I burn it round blind bends with exhilarated winces as I half expect a tractor or a loose herd of cows or a parked farmer's truck full of hay to stop us dead.

Every time we enter a new turn I see the burning white lights of our pursuers jump round the dark hedges behind, like lasers homing in on us. It's as though we're on a rollercoaster and they're in the car behind, constantly behind, experiencing the same bends and bumps just moments after we have. The carjacker has control for the moment and for all I know he could be steering us into a brick wall. We take a sharp right – Ping! Ping! – another right – Ping! – followed by two winding lefts, then a burst of straight for a hundred metres, into a right and – '*Now!*' I brake hard as the carjacker furiously pulls my arm round to turn the steering wheel and we skid along for what seems like slow-motion ages.

'*Here!*' orders the carjacker and I obey. 'Left, then swing it right *immediately!*' I spin the wheel rapidly to the left, then straightaway to the right and we enter a lane and as the car does the right we smash through a flimsy wooden gate and skid to a halt.

The hippy roars next: '*Lights, engine off!*'

I did as he told me. In the immediate silence we hear the BMW motor past.

The carjacker was in self-congratulatory mood after this, his huge ego feeding its desire to be something. 'Yes, yeeeeees!' he whooped. 'I've done it, I've got away from them. Just like that geezer in that TV programme I watched the other week. I am… I –' He stopped there, abruptly. Just a deep guttural noise came from his throat because the hippy had put his shovel of a hand over his mouth.

'Shut it, like, won't you lad.' The hippy removed his palm and wiped some slobber on the carjacker's velvet skinny shoulder.

'All right,' humble-mumbled the carjacker before bigging it up again. 'Keep your fuckin' long hair on hippy.' He turned to me. 'That gate, haven't been in this field for ten years, didn't know it was there.' I thanked God they hadn't built a new housing estate on the land.

I nodded at the cocky figure on my left as way of saying thanks. It did look like he'd saved us, for now. But now was no time for celebrating, and certainly no time for individual self-congratulation. The hippy and I were sharing thoughts.

'Thanks for getting us out of that one, but we're still in the big one,' the big guy in the back retorted at the carjacker. 'Now I want to get to see my soulmate, or at least see if she shows up, in one piece. That gate made a right racket when we hit it, and we may not be alone for long – so what now?'

'Start up again and we go back the other way,' answered the carjacker, defiantly sticking his chin and skinny chest out.

So we wound back the way we'd just travelled, then back at the white-painted pub turned so that we continued where we would have headed five minutes previously had we not span off up the lane.

'That's a dead-end track where they are,' stated the carjacker. 'They'll be turning around about now, so shift it.'

'We need a place to hide the car and somewhere to hide ourselves for the night,' I said, directing my words at the carjacker. He nodded.

Burning it, we took a few more turns and arrived at a bigger road. A few minutes later we entered a small sleepy town with a typically rural English high street of a few darkened shops named after their owners who would be respected members of the community, as their parents and grandparents and great-grandparents had been. Their children had probably left the town to work for a big city-based multinational company. Two pubs were at either end of the lowly lighted high street: the Red Lion and the Wheatsheaf Arms. Both looked empty. Red poppies placed on a small chained-in war memorial were the only bright colours in the entire street, and the dead of the wars were probably the town's greatest celebration.

I followed the 'jacker's instructions and there was no sign of Dead's firm behind us as he led us up a long dirt track that came to a sudden end in a field of what looked like purplish grey wheat. The air was so still that the wheat stood stiffly upright without so much as a sway.

'We can hide the car here,' said the carjacker, 'and walk back into the town. There's a b'n'b I know that we can book into.'

'What with?' I asked. 'Does anyone have any cash?'

'Well I fuckin' well haven't,' said the carjacker. 'That's why I was robbing you.'

'So it's my fault we haven't got any money is it?'

'Yeah. And his,' he said pointing at the hippy, 'for being a hippy. Fuckin' scroungers, never have any cash on them.'

The hippy laughed. 'Less you've got, less you've got to worry about. Here, how do you know your way round here anyway?'

'I was a knocker.'

'What's that?' asked the hippy, smiling to himself. 'Some sort of tit?'

'No it ain't. I used to rob these rich houses round here.'

'Remind you of home do they?' taunted the hippy.

'No, reminded me of easy money actually.'

'So tell us what a knocker is then?'

'You know nothing in that fuckin' hippy head of yours do you? Half a minute on my streets and you'd be mugged, sawn and slaughtered.'

The heat was rising between those two again. 'A knocker is someone,' I explained to the hippy, 'who knocks on the doors of big houses like we've seen round here. If someone answers they ask them if they have any antiques to sell. Furniture, paintings, jewellery, silver candlesticks, things like that. If they have they try to get it at a cut-down price, usually by using some intimidation.' The hippy flashed a dirty look at the carjacker.

'If no-one's in,' I continued, 'they break in and get the valuables anyway. Take them to the antique shops like in Brighton and flog them at huge profit. Quite often an old relative will get in the way, so they get done over. You hear about quite a few murders of old people out in remote houses like this.'

The 'jacker was nodding, a glint and smile on his face. The hippy glared back at him. 'Thought you'd like that 'ippy. It's like you and your crusty mates are always on about – redistribution of wealth and that.'

'Yeah, well you're still a tit,' scorned the hippy.

As we slammed the doors shut and walked away from the car it was realised that we were broke. At least it had stopped raining.

'So,' I stated, 'it's not safe to kip in the car, and yet we have no money to pay for the b'n'b.'

'Then we shall have to use some ingenuity. Follow me,' the hippy said, before adding to the carjacker, 'and you.'

Unfortunately, I knew we weren't the only ones following.

THE NEXT BIG THING

IN VIRTUAL PITCH-DARKNESS we felt our way along the edge of the field, brushing past the wet bowed wheat stalks that had strayed onto the track on one side and a straggly hawthorn hedge on the other. The hippy pulled out an elastic band from his front pocket and in one swift movement tied his long hair into a long mane.

'Smarten yourself up,' he said mimicking a phrase that must have been said to him by conservatives all his hippy life as he tucked his creased T-shirt into his jeans, 'and get yourself a decent job. It's about time you had bloody hair cut anall!' he added to me chuckling all along as he eyed my crop. He was one carefree character, he really didn't give a toss and every moment of life for him was a moment to savour. Thank God I'd picked him up.

I'd had this crop because I'm thinning a bit, but it suits me; my angular face and that, at least that's what everyone tells me. I don't know if they would say that it didn't suit me, but I should have had it years ago anyway as its low maintenance is a definite bonus and my balding bits don't show so much now. I always thought a crop would make me look too aggressive which is not good for a florist. I like to wear clothes that contrast with it though, opposites of what people would expect, so that, without saying a thing, I can challenge and make them question their prejudices.

So there I was: an athletic six foot-tall guy with a suedehead, as much stubble as hair on top and stinking of blooms, wearing an expensive and tidy bespoke William Hunt light grey three-buttoned suit, boned-collar pastel blue cotton shirt, and creaky spit-polished Paul Smith leather-soled loafers. A tie would have really completed the look, but I haven't worn one since the day I left school. They feel like a noose round the neck.

Sometimes I've worn patchouli, like the hippy, so that people I stand close by, say on the tube or in a bar, grab a whiff of the Indian essence and then spend a few puzzled minutes looking around for the long-haired layabout wearing it. Minor thing really, but minor things like that help me get through the hum-drum normality of life and as a florist I'm quite into smell, it's a sense that we don't use enough. You can tell everything about someone from their smell and as you probably know, smell is the greatest memory jogger: for me, if I smell roses I think of my gorgeous ex Julia; irises are Mrs Sitani, the pleasant middle-aged Indian woman who came in the shop every week; a lily for my old primary schoolfriend Ruth; and sunflowers for my mate Matt. Fuchsias are Mum. But roses are the best memory enhancer, their smell is so delicate and reminds me of so many occasions. The rose really deserves its status as the greatest flower of all and it's no wonder the red rose is the flower of love. Its dark red crimson is like life itself, as though someone has ripped opened their heart and let it drip onto pure white blotting paper.

I suppose the other thing that throws people when they are trying to prejudge me is my tattoos, foolish really, follies on my body. Anyway, I was a lot younger when I had them done. On my right hand, just below the knuckles, a letter on each finger, I have LOVE. Then on the left hand I have four letters, the same: LOVE.

One of my mates did the LOVE/HATE thing on his knuckles, but I didn't want to do that. I don't hate, at least not others; sometimes I wake up with a self-hatred, an immense weight of utter sadness pushing me down into the ground, making my knee-joints ache as the dense gloomy-grey foggy atmosphere gets heavier, blunting colours and taste and smells and sounds, forcing my shoulders down, down, down and shoving my face into a cold solid brick wall in a darkened small room, and repeatedly bashing me, causing headaches and pain and aches and all the suffering I deserve. When these days are over – and they are few but tortuous – I am left with a love of life and a love for anyone who loves it too. Those who try to breed hate through their hating are not worth that knot in the stomach, not worth tearing yourself up for and fighting their hatred with yet more hate – but I wish they weren't here. And so the carjacker disturbed me.

'That's the b'n'b.' He pointed at a symmetrical illuminated yellow-brick building beyond the field's hedge and across a small road. It had castle-like turrets running round the top and was lighted slightly with a couple of old eye-level lamps either side of a heavy-looking dark varnished wooden door which stood in the middle of two large bay windows and, upstairs, three flat windows were equally spread apart above the door, each with faded greenish curtains held back by ties. In the front, a little patch of uncut grass and weeds that matched the colour of the curtains and spreading about two metres away from the house formed a garden and a couple of hanging baskets with violas, flailing impatiens and trailing fuchsias dominated either side of the door, but there were no other flowers or plants around the house apart from some outstanding wisteria that climbed the right side wall, sadly not in flower at this time of the summer, but still magically on show by an occasionally flickering floor spotlight that cast dark, long shadows at the top of the building.

'Where's sign for b'n'b?' questioned the hippy, looking quizzically at the carjacker.

'There ain't one,' he replied. 'This place is word of mouth. Pretty good for me to hide at I thought and no houses that near either.'

'That's if the owner lets us stay without pay,' I commented, wondering if it really was a b'n'b we had before us here. I was supremely suspicious of this little wretch – where could he be taking us now?

'He'll let us stay,' said the hippy taking his colossal trekking boots a couple of huge strides towards a tight space in the hedge. 'You two stay here and appear in a couple of minutes.' He squeezed sideways through the hedge-gap, causing some twigs to flick back and a section of the hedge quiver as he went out the other side and crossed the road to set about his mission. Now what was he going to do? Unhinged as he was, I was fearful.

The carjacker and I didn't say a word as we waited in the dark stillness behind the hedge. It was a little cooler. I buttoned my suit jacket, bent down to wipe my loafers clean with my fingers and then stood back up, with my hands held behind my back, as I would when we went to the house to face the owner. My hushed companion pulled his cap down tightly over his head and chewed some more on his dirty fingernails. As my eyes strained to see anything in the moonlight, I listened out intently for any danger and heard the hippy's voice and another male voice drift in the still warmish night air. I couldn't hear what they were saying, but it was time to get out of sight and hide in that house. For all we knew the BMW and its occupants could be prowling just seconds away. Man, they were angry cats and they would get much angrier if they saw us.

I tugged the carjacker's sleeve and indicated with a nod of my head towards the house. As we walked through the gap in the hedge straight onto and then across the narrow road towards the hippy and the man, the sounds made sense and the man, stood in the doorway with the hall light behind him, gradually came into focus.

'Are you sure? Look, here's other two.'

'Quite sure, sir,' replied a rosy-cheeked tall gentleman in an accent that was a soft upper middle-class Brummy. His hair was cut like Julius Caesar's, only grey going on white. 'There was no record company telephoned here to book in a pop band. I don't get too many bookings, boys, or customers for that matter, so I'd certainly have been anticipating the arrival of three young boys such as yourselves, particularly so late on a summer's night. What did you say you were called again?'

He stood there, hands on hips, slight pot belly squeezed into a lurid yellow shirt and wearing a luscious purple neckerchief tucked underneath the open neck. On his bottom half he wore faded jeans, desert-beige sandals and strapped round his waist was a crisp knee-length white cotton apron with daffodils embroidered around the edge and some writing in what I presumed was Welsh. His large nose was even ruddier than his cheeks, in fact almost deep scarlet against his grey-white hair, and several intricate thin threads of rouge-red veins and a couple of claret boils had forced their way out as though trying to escape the years of alcohol abuse he had undoubtedly put upon his body. What made his nose look even more comical was that it had a sort of dimple at the front thus resembling a rather ugly penis. He breathed heavily from the back of his throat, a breath heavy with alcohol, and as he eyed us one by one with his beady little creased eyes his tongue rolled round the inside of his gums and he made a thoughtful sigh as he surveyed, rockily, from his lofty height.

'We're called the Grateful Hendrix Boys,' said the hippy, avoiding my quizzical and bemused glance. 'Or GHB for short – we're NBG, that's Next Big Thing.'

'GHB, what a marvellous name!' exclaimed our host. 'I think I may have seen you on some appalling rubbish they put out on children's television,' he replied, putting a cotton-cream handkerchief up to mop his sweaty brow. 'Not you boys of course, but the show. Just wait until I tell them down the local. It does a late lock-in you know, would you *care* to join me?'

'Oh no,' startled the hippy, taking a step forward to stand head to head with the man. 'We couldn't and we'd rather you didn't tell anyone as it attracts fans. It's why we've had to stay out here before Nottingham concert tomorrow. We've got some *News of World* reporters onto us as well, so we'd appreciate it if you'd not say anything to anyone, especially if some big blokes in suits come asking questions. Right bastards they are.'

'Oh, right you are,' flustered the reddening landlord. 'Right you are. Well, let me just call my friend, delightful young boy called Simon, to see if he's heard of you. He won't say a word. You see, though, he knows all the latest fads. Comes and stays here once a month for a...' – and he stretched the words out – '...long, lux-urrr-ious weekend.'

He coaxed us into the small hallway and asked us to stay there while he telephoned young Simon. I shot the hippy an all-questioning look that said, 'What the hell?' and he responded with a gloopy grin and a shoulders' shrug. In the kitchen, the landlord dialled on an old-fashioned dial and pomm-pommed a big band tune as he waited for a reply. As he dialled the three of us leaned into the kitchen doorway as much as we could to listen to his telephone conversation. Keeping my ear to the kitchen I looked round to check that no-one else appeared in the hallway to catch us listening in.

I glanced at the mismatched entrance area: this slim hall had a white bedroom lamp on with damp marks around the shade, the light it cast highlighting brown and pink paisley wallpaper running down to a disgusting lime-green psychedelic shagpile carpet, almost, thankfully, worn bare; faded photographs of such holiday hotspots as Blackpool and Brighton were hung on the walls, tastefully framed in plastic fake wood; a low brown-painted coffee table stood by one wall with some faded pink fake flowers and a few leaflets scattered on: Rochdale Canal days out, the London Dungeon, Edinburgh park walks, a Bethnal Green leisure centre and a couple of cheap Earl's Court hostels. It had been a very long while since a woman had even slightly graced his life.

After the usual telephone greetings, we heard his voice go into an even more exaggerated theatrical manner. We three listened intently. 'You'll never guess what. A boy band has just arrived in town. Yes, apparently they're playing a pop concert in Nottingham tomorrow night and need to be away from their fans tonight. They're called the, erm, the, erm, Disgraceful Andrex Boys. No, that can't be it, their initials form GHB... yes, I know! Trouble is there's been a cock-up with their booking and I can't call their bosses until the morning.' Silence. 'Oh, you've not heard of them... Oh you may have... It does, does it... They do, how exciting! I'll go and ask them. It's such a shame you won't come ... Anyway, I'll let them stay, I'm sure I recognise one of them... Yes, absolutely. I must go then Simon and show them their beds... That's right, nothing to lose but my virginity! See you in a fortnight then. Bye Si. Bye.'

As he replaced the receiver, he pomm-pommed to himself again, finishing off his big band tune with a crescendo of pomm-pomms and an abruptly loud climax that suddenly halted. We stepped back sharpish as he opened the hall door and came back in. He stood and nodding with a satisfied, almost proud look surveyed the three of us.

'Well, Simon said you might be the ones he's seen who do a fabulous dance routine and he told me how it goes. And the deal is, you dance the routine, you stay the night.'

We looked at each other, thinking of what to do now, our adventure taking a surreal turn, but the hippy took the lead and started to shake his hair from side to side à la Quo with his thumbs tucked in his front belt loops. He threw myself and the carjacker a look that said: 'Do this or else you're out there again at mercy of gang with their guns' and he was right, so I shuffled about next to him in the small hallway like something from *The Full Monty* meets Boyzone and me and the hippy were away. I solely concentrated on shaking my butt while doing a Travolta *Saturday Night Fever* special with my arms, but the carjacker just stood there with folded arms.

The landlord looked at him wondering when he was going to join in and when it became apparent that he wasn't – and by not doing so he was risking our shelter for the night, and consequently our lives – the hippy paused his headbanging for a second and pointed at the carjacker. 'He's hurt his leg, so he can't do the routine. In any case, it must be hard to dance,' he said, casting a stern eye at the 'jacker, 'with devil on your back.'

The landlord looked on, too excitedly delighted to take in what the hippy had just said. We lasted a full thirty seconds more and as they ticked by the hippy got more and more into his headbanging. It was like the fever had grabbed him and I, and we were at that moment the two most ridiculous people on the planet. But it worked. The landlord loved us and ran his tongue round his gums with zeal.

'Oh fantastic, fantastic. It is you!' he exclaimed, although I'm not sure if he cared. 'That's enough excitement for the present. I need a drink or seven, but first let's get you boys to bed, up to those waiting bedrooms. You've got a busy day tomorrow.'

How right he was. And how thankful we were to our saviour that he hadn't turfed us out into the tightening knot of the Nottinghamshire night.

PUNCH-DRUNK

NICK CLARK FELT his throbbing eye. It had swollen so quickly he could hardly see through it. It had been a total mismatch. Both punches. The big bloke in the pub had managed to land him one at the same time the young Irish lad had knocked the big bloke flat on his back.

'Fecking amazing eh?' said the Irish lad. 'We could get banned from a shithole like the Dog and Toilet. And at last orders. Tanks for the drink anyway.' They shared a smile together and Clark pressed an ice cube to his face.

He looked around the late bar they were in with his one blurred eye. 'This place is not much better.'

'Right anall. They've got a jukebox and pool though. Do ye play?'

Clark shook his head and then hung it as he recalled the conversation with Jill.

'So what's with the missus?' asked the Irish lad as though reading his very thoughts.

'Just found out she's...' Clark couldn't finish his sentence. He had no need.

'Oh well, plenty more in the sea.'

'That's all right for you to say. You're young. I'm getting on a bit. Starting to sag and go grey and bald. Where I used to have a six pack I've got a party pack with twenty per cent extra. As it goes, I've always been a bit out of shape. Job gets in the way of any keep-fit ideas I have. And I've got a kid with her.'

The Irish lad looked at Clark and took a sip on his Guinness. Clark noticed that he was speaking with more of a London accent than his usual speech – it was a 'skill' he'd acquired over the years so he could get on with people from all walks of life. If he could walk the walk and talk the talk it helped him get the best out of anyone he was interviewing. He prided himself on being able to get on with a Tory councillor and get on just as well with the cabbie on the way there. It was a trick all good journalists used. Not that it had helped him much. Not that he was a good journalist.

'That's a tough one all right,' agreed the Irish lad.

'What is?'

'The kid. I've got three that I'm keeping back home.'

'Have you?' Clark couldn't hide the surprise in his voice.

'Have anall. Why I'm over here in a city I don't like.'

The lad's confession sobered Clark up a little bit. 'Split up?' Clark asked.

'No. Not like that. Only because there's no work where I'm from.'

Clark put the ice cube down and offered his hand. 'Nick.'

The lad looked a little taken aback, as though shaking hands wasn't something he did very often. 'Liam. Grand meeting you.'

They both took a couple of mouthfuls of their preferred poison.

'What's that job you do then?'

'I'm a reporter.'

'Oh right. Interesting job. Big paper?'

'No. Shitty little one.' They laughed together.

'That's okay,' said the Irish lad, indicating to his dusty clothes. 'I'm working on site in case ye hadn't noticed. Shite big one.'

They laughed again and drank some more. An old Irish man stood behind Liam and ordered a couple of whiskeys in a voice with a throat that sounded as though it had just been whisked. Liam raised his eyebrows at Clark to show that he'd heard it too.

'I used to work on a site,' said Clark. 'Labouring. Hard work.'

'No offence, but I bet ye it was while ye where a student.'

'Yeah. How'd you know?'

'Lots of lads do it while they're students. Bit different when ye know it's your living forever.'

'Yeah, you're right. Still it was more fun than working with the wankers that I work with now.'

'Ye go on any interesting jobs then? Chase ambulances and that?'

Clark indicated to the young girl behind the bar that he wanted another couple of pints of the same. 'No, just crap jobs. Been after a carjacker who's been active in the Tottenham area. Got nowhere with that story. Even so I'd probably be out of a job if it hadn't been for him. Before that this boring court case, that boring court case, the odd flasher, the odd row at the football. Support a team?'

'Arsenal.'

'Me too. Here, have another pint.'

Clark handed the girl his change and took a delicious neckful of the Red Stripe. 'And all the football news my rag covers is bloody Spurs.'

They had a drink together, chuckling.

'Ever been on one of those jobs where the journos wait outside a star's house.'

'No. Once I had to wait around for a pervert though.'

'How's that?'

'Oh, this was a fucking farce I can tell you.' Clark drank some more, not letting go of the pint glass now and keeping it close to his lips as he spoke. 'I had to hang around the shoe department of this department store. Fenhards in Wood Green.'

'So what's this bollix doing?'

'He was pretending to look at shoes, all day, but he used to secretly film women slipping shoes on and off. Had a camera in this holdall with a hole cut in it. Sometimes he'd pretend to be an assistant so he could touch their feet as he helped them on with shoes. He used to wear disguises, so they couldn't get him.'

'Did ye get him?'

'No,' replied Clark. 'After three days the fucking cops arrested me! Worst of all I was living in Feltham at the time and I got a call on my mobile from my news editor when I'm in the nick. He said: "Get off that job now you useless twat. They've got him and this is the headline: 'He felt 'em from Feltham!' Bloody genius! But no thanks to you." I never lived that one down. At least they couldn't use that crap headline.'

'Good job ye weren't living in Cumloden then,' laughed Liam. 'Did they ever get yer man?'

'Yeah he was from Cockfosters funnily enough.'

'Will ye have another drink? And stop feckin' winking at me will ye!'

Clark laughed out loud for the first time in weeks as he pushed his empty pint glass towards the bar girl, the numbness of his head turning the pain off from his swelling eye. But through his hazy state he knew what he had to do. He had to get out there and turn it on.

LOST IN LUST

THE GIRL wrapped her lips around Ged's throbbing helmet, bobbing up and down, going almost the whole length of it at times and then grabbing the base of his penis and wanking him in the same rhythmic motions as her bobbing head. Fair's fair he thought. He'd just taken his time kissing every part of her body, from top to toe, eventually centring on gently licking her clitoris which he'd taken as much pleasure in doing as she appeared to be from receiving. Loads of other black guys he knew had told him they didn't care for the craft of cunnilingus. In that case, Ged was happy to be the exception to the rule.

The teasing flicks of his moist tongue had sped up as the cocaine he'd placed on her pink clitoris had taken effect in his mouth and the numbness on her had worn off to leave her feeling warm between her legs. From the noise she'd made, it seemed to have given her the best orgasm of the evening, or morning as it was now. They'd been lost in lust for hours.

He'd heard people knocking on the office door for ten minutes now, but here as he closed in on his climax of an hour of intense sexual pleasures, he was virtually oblivious to what was going on outside his physical feelings, centred on his... oh yes, there it was, what he had been waiting for. He cried something to her, something that in normal conversational life would be mortifyingly moronic, but at this moment, it only heightened the excitement and increased his heart's thumpings and throbbings. 'That's it, I'm here, I'm here, yes, yes, bob baby, bob, bob, bob, bob. BOB, BOB, bob and suck, bob and suck, suck me, suck, suck, suck as hard as... yes, come on! Baby, you've got me. Bring it on... yes, oh YEEEEEERRRRSSSS!!! YEEEEEEEEERRRRRRRRS! YES! YES! YES!'

She stayed with her face resting near his penis as it slowly deflated and Ged lay feeling the empty wooziness in his head after that perfect physical release. He was in total contentment, as total as it could be and he could feel himself, hear his heaving breath and the thump of his heart slowly subsiding. Thump-thump, thump-thump. It sounded so loud it was as though it was from outside his body. It was.

'I think they really want to come in,' said the girl pulling her face into sight as Ged opened his eyes. He scanned around her lips. 'They really want to come in,' she repeated, 'whoever it is.' Ged listened, outside the pleasures of his head for the first time in a while. Thump-thump, thump-thump. He heard the knocking as it was this time and the strangled cry of his name following it. In fact the person outside was hollering, but the door to his office was purposely thick to keep the club noise out – and, fortunately, any noise from within, in.

'Come on,' said Ged, gazing admirably at the girl, 'let's go and join the party for a while.' They both got up and threw some clothes on again. Ged unlocked the door and flung it open to a wall of noise and the beaming skull-like face of his mate Tomb. He looked at Tomb and let out a laugh, grabbing hold tightly of the girl who had joined him by his side. He looked at her and she was laughing too.

'What's up?' asked Tomb in a Surrey accent. Ged stepped aside and indicated for him to go in the room.

'Have a look at the state of your face,' laughed Ged.

Tomb rushed to the mirror in the office, looked at himself and started cracking up. 'Fucking hell, it looks like I've dipped my face in a mountain of flour!' he laughed, before wetting his hand, wiping it round his face and virtually chewing the powder from his hand. He turned to Ged. 'Just thought you'd want to join the after-show. It's fucking mental, you understand what I'm saying.'

'I *over*stand what you're saying. Yeah, we'll have a look,' said Ged, looking at the girl. 'Sophie, meet Tomb.'

'Hi Tomb,' she said giving him a peck on the cheek as he joined them back at the door.

'Why do you call him Tomb?' she asked as Ged locked the door and Tomb bounded off back into the club.

'His real name's Tom Brown. That's Tom B and he's such a party animal he lives life like every day is his last, so most of the time he looks closer to a tomb than a Tom B. Look, he's back.'

They both looked as the double doors that led from the small corridor to the club dancefloor and bars swung open and Tomb appeared through them carrying a magnum of champagne in one hand and three glasses in the other.

'Here you are,' he smiled, handing them a glass each, 'And here you are,' he added handing them a small pure white pill each. 'And,' he said, popping open the champagne bottle and pouring the bubbling liquid, 'here we are, we three fine people, here surrounded by lovely, happy, caring friends in a club in London in the middle of a world out there that's full of hatred and horrors, backstabbing and bile, paranoia and protests, war and waste. What else can we do, but celebrate our good fortune in finding a place away from all that and people who we can love without fearing of them hurting us? Cheers!' The three of them flicked the pills into their mouths and took great mouthfuls of champagne.

'How's the acting going Tomb?' asked Ged.

'Wonderful, wonderful, bloody marvellous. Just got a part in a new British road movie. Now come in here and act up with me.'

'Okay, but it's film.'

'What is?' asked Tomb, finishing off the champagne in his glass with his head as far back as it would go.

'Movie's an American word,' replied Ged putting on an upper-class accent. 'We call them films over here old boy. Little point, but I think we should keep the English language as it is.'

Tomb topped up Ged and Sophie's glasses. 'You're quite right. British road film.'

He opened the doors and the three of them went into the club. The music was still pumping but turned down slightly and Ged saw there were about fifty people in there, the ultimate hedonists, those who knew no other way and if they did the boredom of it would be killing them more than the drugged-up lives they were living now. Ged recognised most of them by sight and about twenty to chat to, including a couple of Dead's men and three or four of the large group of girls who were still dancing as though it were the first dance of the night, not the heady climax of forty-eight hours of partying.

He looked around and felt pleased, not only for himself but for everyone involved in what he termed the 'Beautiful Scene'. In there he could see club faces he knew from Nottingham, Manchester, Cardiff, Brighton, Leeds, Sheffield, even Glasgow. Before the Beautiful Scene, he thought, half of the guys in here would have been fighting each other at football matches, not dancing together in the same club. The drug, the scene, the music, all together it had improved Britain, providing the country with the social mixing it needed and allowing everyone to realise that whether from north, south, east, west, England, Scotland, Wales, Ireland or wherever, everyone was basically the same.

'What part have you got in the film?' Ged heard Sophie shout in Tomb's ear.

'A brilliant part!' Tomb exclaimed, slumping by a wall as

the combination therapy of champers and pills momentarily grabbed him by the scruff of his frayed collar. Pulling himself quickly together, he continued. 'I play a complete party animal who's falling apart in a club, ha ha! So that's easy. See you two later. Here, have this.' He handed Sophie the magnum and with that went to dance with the girls, his arms up in the air and whooping with delirious delight at the new tune that was just being mixed in.

Ged felt himself already starting to sway to the beat and his shaven scalp starting to tingle. With a smile and his arm round Sophie, he watched Tomb leading the party as usual. 'Music!' shouted Tomb, both arms flailing around like a monkey swinging from bar to bar and his knees bending outwards as he got lost in the pounding beat. He was lost, escaping in ecstasy and writhing in the rest. 'DJ, you've got me. Bring it on… yes, yes, oh, oh, oh… OH YEEEEEERRRRSSSS!!! YEEEEEEEEERRRRRRRRS! YES! YES! YES!'

Ged couldn't remember from exactly where, but he was sure he'd heard Tomb or someone shouting out the very same earlier in the evening.

KILLER KNIFEMAN GOES ON THE RUN

WE LEFT EARLY the next morning for two reasons and both were for purposes of avoidance. The hippy, myself and the carjacker were all given separate rooms in the b'n'b, but the hippy and I decided it would be safer to stay in one room at the front of the building, taking turns to sleep on the floor with the bed hoisted against the door, and we took turns watching out through a crack in the curtain.

I realised this allowed the carjacker to have a better rest, but I couldn't trust him not to run off and mess everything up. He'd complained about sleeping on the floor and I told him he'd made his bed and he had to lie in it, but he didn't quite get what I meant. I really feel it was from a lack of wanting to understand rather than plain stupidity. Or maybe he did understand, but he just wanted to wind me up.

During the night, I didn't sleep at all. I'd heard our larruped landlord turn back in after what must have a considerable lock-in at the local. He'd arrived back mumbling to himself and once loudly cursing when he'd tripped at the top of the creaking stairs, before unsuccessfully attempting to be quiet as he tried each of our polished brass door knobs in turn. He was out of luck: with Dead and his men out to kill us we were all locked up. We were actually in the bedroom assigned to the carjacker, but myself and our hippy friend had locked our doors from the outside and pocketed the keys. So after three huffy sighs the landlord had crept back down to his lonely bed.

We sneaked out to avoid the 'breakfast in bed to fill any young belly' that he'd promised us, leaving a note of thanks and promising that we'd wave to him when we were on *Top Of The Pops* next week. By the look of GHB's darkened eyes, I don't think any of us had slept.

As the sun rose we formed our plans for the day as quickly as the bulging clouds built up over the hills again, like massive sky mountains with their summits in the heavens. Away from them the sky was pastel-blue at the horizon, slowly merging upwards to a deep electric blue. For an inner-city chap like myself the silence was stunning: an occasional snapped twig as we stepped or chirping early-morning bird and that was it – no tooting traffic, no wailing sirens in distress, no shouting dustbin collectors, no clattering bins, no slamming doors, no car stereos blaring, no trains or planes, no shots fired, no drunkards cursing the world out loud, no rumble in the jungle. It was deadly quiet – ominous in our circumstances.

We were like foxes being chased by the hunt in red and they could smell us, so we hatched our tracks to avoid the gang and get to where the hitchhiker wanted to go to join hearts and where I wanted to bury the burdening weight on my mind. I imagined the hunt in red would now be joined by the local hounds in blue for as soon as the disappointed landlord realised through his hangover that we'd duped him, he'd be onto the police. For these rural rozzers it would be a great big deal. We had to keep moving or we'd be torn to pieces.

Of course, first of all we were going to Gran's – so long as the BMW bandits didn't show up again.

About one hundred and fifty miles to Gran's

I'd been promising Gran the treat of a journey outside her Pennine village for far too long and there was no way I was going to let her down. Gran is one of those old ladies who you can really see the child in and a quite mischievous one at that. She's small, about five foot, frail yet active, with rounded shoulders and see-through white hair in the perm style that most old ladies adopt. Her face is as lined as unironed linen on a skin that has become as delicate as a new-born baby's, and her watery pale blue eyes are full of wisdom, sadness, happiness, life and love. She has been told she'll be blind within ten months. That's what the doctor says but she refuses to believe him, won't let Doc play God.

She loves life, is deaf when it suits her and more liberal than Brighton. I used to visit her just several times a year, always at her small house, but we have never been further than the village shops at the end of her road and conveniently close to the Rose and Crown. Gran relishes half a lager, which by the end of drinking always leads her into telling a tipsy tale about the old days, great tales like how she'd always go to the pub during wartime air raids – 'If you're going to go, you may as well go happy' – or one of her scrapes with authority, or one of her early lovers and she wished there'd been more before she met Albie, my grandad, but how she missed him – 'Just as well for you that the Pill wasn't invented when it was my dating days or you may never have been born,' she laughed. 'Mind you, your grandad was a most skilful lover, he'd –' 'Another half? Gran, I'll just get it.'

We reached the car where and as it had been left. I unlocked the doors. 'Can I go in front?' asked the hippy, stretching his arms as he grew into the new day. 'Because of me long legs, like.'

I pushed my lips out as I thought and eyed the 'jacker. He was stood across the car from me next to the hippy, looking expectantly like a doggy waiting to see if he was going on walkies. He really was a loathsome piece of filth and we couldn't trust him in the back alone.

'As we were really,' I spoke across the black pull-back roof of the car to the hippy who stood towering above the 'jacker's skinny head. 'He knows his way round here,' I added as way of explanation. 'You can put your feet up on the back seat and keep an eye out for our friends.'

The next thing happened in slow motion and he was several outstretched paces away before I reacted. I'd watched him turn and start to run, but through a mixture of tiredness and disbelief it had taken me a few seconds to react and get off after the carjacker.

He was making a run for it.

'He's doing a runner!' I exclaim as I take off in pursuit and speed past the hippy. As I brush by, the mighty giant hippy sleepily peers round at the happening. I pump my arms into the air quickly and my legs move with them, but although I'm making some ground on the carjacker who's waist-high in wheat, the mud from the field is sticking on the leather soles of my loafers. I'm slipping all over the place and my hands are getting whipped by the wheat stalks.

We're halfway across the field now and I can see a metre-tall hedge up ahead that he has to somehow get through, so if I can just catch close to him I'll have him at the hedge. He has to stay on this car journey now, it's too early for him to go yet, back out into the wide world just as he was when he jumped in on my life. He's not ready.

The field slopes upwards slightly making it even harder to get across, and neither of us are running, more like taking wide paces and we have to lift our feet up high to pull them from the suction of the ever-collecting heavy mud. He is tiring, and finding it difficult to get the strength in his weedy muscles to lift his loosening desert boots from the ground. In fact, we're both struggling, like flies in a sticky web getting more tangled in our bids to escape. Suddenly, as I continue to close in he stumbles slightly and looks round as he regains his way. I'm just a couple of paces behind him now and catching, when my foot sticks solidly in a plough-line. As I fall forwards I lunge for him. It's all I can do. I stretch like a cat and my hands grasp out at his tracksuit top, but my fingertips brush agonisingly past the velvet material and I fall in a crumple, crushing the spiky stalks and laying motionless in the mud, seeing the wheat from mouse height. I loosen my ankle from the rut that caused me to fall; it feels fine, but my chance has gone and he's away. I'm exhausted, panting as I lay there, and he will... then I hear a swift rustle and feel the air rush past me.

I look up. It's the mighty giant hippy moving in a blur. I abruptly kneel up, looking from the wheat like a meerkat and see him flying towards the carjacker who is now perched on the side of the hedge, about to clamber onto the top when the hippy highjumps into the air. His legs are moving back and forwards as he launches towards the carjacker, as though he has leapt to bound up some steps that actually go down. As he descends, his heaving figure pounces on the 'jacker like a rock falling from a huge height, causing the hedge to quake, shake and then give. There's a cry of pain followed by breathless gasping as the carjacker is crushed.

I brush some of the mud from my jacket, straighten myself up and walk to the two who are heaped where the hippy's considerable frame has clobbered the carjacker who is now held in a twisted headlock as he hopelessly tries to struggle free and curse the hippy at the same time.

As I get up to them, the hippy's teeth in his alluring grin glistens from within the base of the hedge. 'No shoes see,' he says, holding out his bare feet. 'Took me while to get off boots, but when they were gone I flew like lightnin'. Did you see?'

In tired silence we walked back to the car with the carjacker between the hippy and myself. We got in and set off on the morning's journey, all deeply in reflective mood. Occasionally the carjacker muttered a word in monotone to tell me a turning to take. I couldn't be bothered to ask him what he thought he was playing at. He'd obviously decided the money wasn't worth the risk of getting caught by Dead. He'd run, leaving us to them, not that he'd be any use if they caught up with us. Still, I had plans for him and for now he was steering us towards all of our destinies.

SEX AND THE LUSH ENGLISH COUNTRYSIDE

WE WERE PASSING through lush English scenery and the day was beaming brightly, the scenery as still as only nature can be. The sun beat down on my chest through the windscreen and on my forehead. It was baking, but even so I kept my mud-caked jacket on. Despite the stillness of the day, as we sped along with the sunroof down a slight cooling breeze gloriously rippled our hot skins.

The Saab I'd borrowed from Ged was purring lovely. We'd been going along the spine of England, running on its nerves, sending tingles through this sensitive land. With the roof down, the sky and sunshine filled the car, the rapidly shwooshing air blowing the hippy's long sun-streaked hair in a dance of zagged bright yellow fanned flames. All in all it was a beautiful day and I was really enjoying myself.

We were passing through typical hedged-in England now, keeping the countryside divided, running up and down the tilted landscape, criss-crossing each other or angling away. Chestnut-brown horses were in fields on either side, and black and white cows were next to them, eating. Rows of grand, proud oak trees overhung the road in a spot they had looked down upon before the roads passed them by; or occasionally an oak stood alone, in the distance, its branches politely nodding in the friendly breeze.

I put the radio on: Korn was just finishing off and it went

straight into another song. '*There's only one way of life, and that's your own, your own.*' I smiled to myself and toed down as we came out of a bend while The Levellers' Mark Chadwick sang to us. I cranked the volume up and started to sing along, such was my mood enthused by optimistic happiness. I should have been hungry, but wasn't. I asked if anyone else was and received two shaking heads. Fear and anxiety are not appetisers. In any case, the hippy was preparing his first J of the day, saying high to the new morning.

When he'd finished rolling it I watched him light a match and covering the joint from the breeze he sparked up. As he took a few long drags on it, he leaned forward, held some smoke in his mouth for a few seconds and then let it out.

'Miraculous man. Check out the road surface,' said the hippy.

I did, but couldn't see anything miraculous about it. 'What about it?' I asked.

'Look at the white lines being devoured,' he replied. 'We are devouring white line after white line, continuously with an unrelenting appetite.'

'You mean lines of coke?' I enquired

'Exactly!' he exclaimed. 'Coke and roads. Charlatans of genius that are elected make certain laws, but we ignore them. I'll tell you why.' He paused for effect. 'It's so we can get white lines to disappear as quickly as we can in our pursuit of somewhere else, that awaiting nirvana at other end of lines and all time we're going faster, so much now that we don't even notice where we are. We are spinning, keeping up, spiralling, competing, running scared, revolving ever more rapidly.' He leaned back in his seat.

'What the fuck are you getting at hippy?' asked the carjacker, feeling safe enough to be scornful again.

'What I'm getting at is that because we're in it, change is so tiny each moment that we don't even notice it, and yet one day

– puff! – we'll all burn out and disintegrate to dust in an angry ball of seething heat and as flames lick at our future, only then will we realise that we were to blame, that it was us who created hell on earth.'

It shut the carjacker up and as the hippy puffed on his joint I looked at the earth that he said we were creating hell on. Simultaneously, I slowed and turned the music down as we entered a village with a tiny flint-spired church to welcome us as it had welcomed travellers for centuries, first on foot and horse, then on stage coach and bicycles and now in motor vehicles. Maybe in the next century it will be welcoming people who have beamed there *Star Trek*-style. Its tall, proud spire stood majestically sure of itself against that never-ending azure sky. Nothing much was happening in the thatched white cottages of the village or along its winding and narrow roads. Nothing much had ever happened there.

Outside a red-brick and black-beamed Tudor pub, a stocky bald man watering red and yellow climbing roses briefly glanced up to see who was passing through. A small tubby boy in baggy blue shorts and a white vest with a dangly fringe huffed while he pedalled furiously, precariously balanced on a bicycle too big for him with a basket at the front that contained a loaf of crusty bread wrapped in white paper. Each time he puffed he blew his floppy fringe from his eyes and then stood up to tackle a slight slope. At a junction as we left the tiny community we pulled up alongside a phone box – an old bright red one, the ones everyone likes – and I listened for the sound of a red BMW. It sounded *too* quiet out in the English country. As we sped up, off into the winding rural scenery I put the volume up again to hear another Levellers' song playing: '*What a beautiful day*,' sang Mark. '*And nothing is impossible in my all-powerful mind...*'

As we approached bends I eased the vehicle to perform to perfection; down a gear, eerroom, a touch on the brake pedal, accelerate, gear up, and off we sped, verrummmmmmm, out of the turns, faster, faster. I checked the carjacker – he was staring out cursing the countryside scenery that had been swapped for his city scenes. In the back, the hippy, head down, studied the simple map he'd drawn of the stones. In fact, he'd been studying it so hard, and was possibly so very stoned, that he'd nodded off in that position. Tiredness entered my head, as though floaty dreams were gently pulling forward my eyelids and my heavy head was following. But I had to fight it. I took a deep gulp of the fresh air. I had to keep my senses as those four slavering dogs were still with us, somewhere not far.

About one hundred miles to Gran's

I gazed in my rear-view mirror at the hippy, looking so serene after finishing his joint. He was a decent guy who without provocation would go through life giving out only love and happiness. Pushed too much, I reckoned, he could be a killer. He started to lean to one side in his slumber and the map slowly slipped from his loosening grasp until he sat up with a start, grabbing it back and holding it tightly. He blinked a couple of times, pushed his lanky hair from his face and curled it behind his ears, then slowly glanced around to figure out where he was. After quickly checking to see he still had the map firmly in his hand, he raised his backside and slid it safely into his back pocket. He looked at me in the rear-view mirror in which I realised he could only see my green eyes and dark-black eyebrows.

'Errr, where are we now man?' he asked, sleepily.

I could see the whole of his upper body filling more than half of the back seat, and noticed a new small tear along the left on his scarlet T-shirt, exposing his deeply tanned muscular shoulder.

'We're here,' I replied. He looked at my eyes in the rear-view mirror and nodded.

'Okay,' he said still looking at my eyes, 'that's okay, so long as we're not there yet.' We passed a cyclist pedalling furiously in bright, tight Lycra gear. 'When you're on road, professional cyclists, they're always good for a laugh,' cracked the hippy and he broke into a grin.

I checked what he could see of me in my mirror: he would see that I was smiling back as a few crow's feet creases appeared around the eye sparkle that laughter causes. That was it really though; he was talking with my eyes. I looked tired too, I was tired too.

We were all right, me and the hippy, on a similar level and quite happy in each other's company. There was no need for either to wear any sort of mask and I felt that I could see him and he me, for who else could I be and who else could he be? Now, I looked over to the carjacker. It was his turn to take a quick kip, slumped as he was against the passenger side with the wind whooshing past his wingnuts.

'According to a sign a few miles back we're heading for Stoke-on-Trent,' I told him as Toploader came on the radio, 'which is not where we want to be heading. So I'm going for the A515 which will take us near enough into the Pennines. Gran lives near, don't know the road. I don't even know if it's got a name, but I know the way and then after we've picked her up we can go for your date near Hollingworth Lake.'

'Brilliant. We should be in time to get there. It's tomorrow.'

'I know.' He gazed at me earnestly, then raised his eyes skywards for a moment's thought. My eyes flicked between the road and him.

'I can't wait to see if she's same,' the hippy said. 'See if she still shines from heart. You know what I mean?'

I thought of my mum, wondering where she was and I remembered her telling me not to pull flowers from gardens, not because I wanted to destroy the flowers, but because I liked them so much. I recalled walking on long summer days and the warmth of her love.

'My mum was like that,' I said sadly.

'How do you mean "was"?'

'She died a few years back.'

'I'm sorry man,' he said softly to me. 'She's still here though, within you and within me and in air we breathe.' He nodded at me reassuringly. 'I've never had such a loss, but then I never knew my parents or any family. I don't even know my birthday.'

'How's that?'

'I was orphaned, just like boy in story that Basque bloke told us. I was fucked up about it once, but I'm okay now.'

Then he leaned forward to show me his upturned forearms. On the underside were several long, wide pink, shiny-smooth bits. He quickly pulled his arms back out of sight, but remained leaning forward.

'I cut myself to ribbons one day,' he explained. 'I wanted to let all badness out. I'd been dumped. My own mother couldn't stand sight of me, so much that she left me. I didn't want to kill myself, just to let bad blood out.'

'So you cut yourself like that?' I asked.

'Yeah, blood everywhere. Then, next day I started to think about doing myself in. Only time I ever have. But I remembered Kar from school. See, he thought that by killing himself it would do world and his friends a favour because he was so down he felt such a burden on everyone. But really he left a trail of sadness and I still think of him loads.'

I didn't really know what to say to him, so I just looked ahead and then glanced at the sleeping carjacker.

'He's a tosser, isn't he,' stated the hippy, pointing at the 'jacker. I nodded. 'Was it definitely him at that school?'

'Definitely man. He's a rich kid acting up.'

'That's what I figured. But why?'

'Don't know man. Do we need to know?'

'I think we should. There may be a way to take him back to how he once was.'

'What if he's always been like this, always been a bad person?'

'Do you reckon he has?'

'I reckon he was. Little tosser.'

'What can we do?'

'Open door and shove him out.' He was only half joking.

'I couldn't do it,' I said to him, 'kill a stranger.'

'Couldn't you?'

'No, I don't think so.'

'What if a stranger threatened your life? You or him?'

'I suppose I would then.'

'See man, so you would kill someone. What about someone you knew?'

'No, that would be harder.'

'Even if you knew they were really evil piece of work? Surely that would be easier.'

'I don't think I could.'

'Shouldn't we leave the world a better place?'

'Yes, I suppose –'

'Well then.'

'What are you getting at?' I looked at the hippy in the mirror. He leaned over to one side, so that his face was out of sight of the mirror.'

'Kill him,' he commanded in a whisper that seemed to hover.

'Kill who?' I asked, searching for the hippy's eyes to communicate with, but in vain.

'He should be a victim so he can see what it's like,' said his voice from the back.

I looked round to get a quick view of his face. It looked dark and the most serious I'd seen him, almost as though he was a different person.

'Make him a victim,' said the hippy, staring at the carjacker. I quickly turned back to look out over the road, feeling a chill running through me.

The hippy moved his face back into sight of the rear-view mirror.

'I could kill someone like him,' he said to my eyes. 'I'm sure you could too. Imagine, if he were dead, world would be better off.'

I imagined.

'Like if someone had killed Hitler,' continued the hippy, still staring at my eyes. 'If I'd been alive and they'd thrown me and him together in same cell in 1925 when he was writing *Mein Kampf* and I'd have had that blade that him in front held to your neck… I'd have killed Hitler. I'd have taken delight in running that blade around his bad body while he watched. Then I'd have sliced his stomach to bits until all his evil guts spilled out.'

He made a slashing motion with his right hand and the noise of a blade cutting.

'But wouldn't you have been as bad then?'

'No, good would have beaten bad by being evil.'

'So then surely evil would have won?' I asked

'No, if I'd done that,' the hippy said, smiling now, 'I'd have left the world a better place. What I'm saying is that to reach heaven on earth, we may have to go through hell. If I'd have killed Hitler, I'd have saved millions of lives – by taking just one life. And all Jewish people alive today like me would have had families twice as big.'

'Are you Jewish?' I asked, slightly surprised as I suppose I imagined all Jewish people to be orthodox, certainly not some smiling stoned hippy

'Yeah. Scottish too. I'm a Jock Jew if you want!' he laughed. 'But that's all I know about my family, from note that was with me when I was left outside synagogue. It was written in Hebrew by my mum. I'd give anything to meet her.'

'Would you be angry with her?'

'No, I wouldn't be angry,' he said thoughtfully. 'I need to see who she is and why she dumped me. And see who I've got Jewish characteristics from. Not that I look like a typical Jew. But then, what's a typical Jew look like?'

I shrugged.

'And I grew up round Pennines before heading off round world, so I'm not especially Scottish either,' added the hippy. 'But if people need to know, then I'm a Scottish Jew.'

'Did you enjoy growing up in Pennines?'

'Yeah, until I was about eleven and I wanted to get girls,' replied the hippy. 'Then I started getting off my head. I think Chaucer was wrong. It's not money, it's sex that's root of all evil.'

'You mentioned that when you first got in the car and in the Spanish story.'

'Yeah, man has drive to have sex,' said the hippy with enthusiasm. 'No matter how many planets we visit or how many computers we invent, man wants to make love. Essentially it feels great, and we know deep-down we have to keep forming. We don't know why, but we know we have to for one day. When man reaches a certain age, when first grey hair appears – our white threads to heaven – he knows he's going to die and most men, and women too, want to leave an image of themselves behind.'

I switched the radio off to listen more intently.

'Take away man's sex drive and you'd see wars subside,' continued the hippy.

'You don't think it's all to do with capitalism then.'

'Yes, all to do with capitalism,' he said, opening his arms in agreement. 'But what I'm saying is that man's sex drive is reason for capitalism. Squabbles over land are related to power which is related to sex – for oil gushing in Gulf think sperm gushing from man. A fiercely ambitious man, who wants material richness, does so only so that he can increase his sex appeal. He does it unknowingly, thinking it is for purely material gain. But it's not. It's for fear that he'll be old and have nothing with which to replace his youthful sex appeal.'

'And what about hunger? If someone has more land they have more places to get food from.'

'Part of reason, I agree. But what would you choose – free food and no sex, or foraging for food and sex?'

'I'd forage,' I answered with a smile.

'So you see which drive is biggest,' he grinned back at me. I'd never heard him get so excited about a topic. I felt that I was starting to know this hippy. I wanted to know more.

'What about religion?' I asked him. 'That causes more wars than anything.'

'Religions have often come about to keep women in check for the men,' he replied. 'So that's sex, not religion. Of course, love comes into it as well.'

'What about you and Sarah then?' I asked the hippy. 'It's been a long time.'

'I know,' he sighed, running a hand through the centre of his fine blond hair, before flopping his arm back down in his lap where it came to rest on his other hand. 'There was something amazing happened up there.' He stared down at his hands, then looked back to me. 'Weakest person in love becomes strongest, smallest becomes tallest and worst can become best. With love we have found everything we need. All and everything.'

Only about fifty miles to Gran's

'Do you think he'd change with love?' I asked the hippy, nodding at the carjacker.

'No, no chance,' said the hippy, emphatically shaking his head. 'No chance,' he repeated without taking his look from me. 'There's only one thing that will change him.'

Thoughts of Julia flitted across my mind and how I'd lost her when I'd put too much time into starting up my old flower stall by the station. I don't know how I ever lost her.

'Without love I'm lost,' lamented the hippy, sounding like an ocean echo to my mind. 'But I'd never end up with such hate as he's got.'

'Have you kept in touch with her?' I asked, forcing my thoughts of Julia away.

'Now and then. No, sometimes.' He seemed disturbed and looked away from me. 'And I'm not even certain that stones place is there.'

'You said you'd met Sarah there. I've heard of them.'

'Everyone's heard of them round these parts. But how many do you know who's actually seen them?'

'Well, you've seen them.'

'But I'm not right certain. It all just seemed too special…'

'You sure you weren't too stoned?'

'Like tripping?'

'Whatever. I'm not sure about drugs. I don't touch them.'

The hippy's jaw dropped at the same time as his eyebrows raised.

'You mean you've got half of Columbia in boot back here,' he said, grinning widely, 'and you've never taken any.'

I nodded. 'That's right. Never even had a joint.'

'Bloody hell fire!' he exclaimed, sitting upright. 'Pleased to meet you. Apart from President Bill Clinton, you must be first person under fifty who hasn't taken drugs! And of course even Clinton took them, didn't he. His excuse that he didn't inhale is as bad as a girl who says she's never given a blow-job because she never swallowed – and he knows a few things about that as well!'

We laughed together, and he looked to me expectantly as though I was suddenly going to tell him that I was only joking. He realised that I was telling the truth.

'You really haven't have you?' he said. 'Do you realise how many big nights out you're carrying back here?'

I shrugged.

'I don't believe it. Why have you never taken any?'

I thought for a second and checked the fuel. Nudging red.

'I like to have control,' I told him. 'And I don't want to die young because of drugs.'

'What about if you get shot for drugs?'

'That'd be ironic.'

'No, anyway, I weren't tripping that time I saw stones. Or thought I saw stones. I don't think so. I'm not sure. It was around time when I took too many mushies. I used to think I were main character of books I were reading.'

'How do you mean man?' I asked, noticing the carjacker slightly stir.

'I couldn't help it. I'd become a character in a book. Everyone around me would be other characters in book.'

'You lost the plot then.'

'More like I was in plot! It was okay when I read something by Nick Hornby or Roddy Doyle. Charles Bukowski and John Kennedy Toole were a lot of fun, but Stephen King caused a few problems. Worse were when I took to reading Enid Blyton though. That were mad. Still, in madness lies freedom I reckon.'

'What do you mean?'

He leaned further forward and put his huge hand on my shoulder. 'When I was mad I could do anything and no-one bothered me,' he said, his northern dialect becoming stronger in his excitement. 'You can do bad and you can do good or you can do nothing at all. Like if you were to do something that you know is good and you're a good person like you are, but laws of a rotten world say it's bad, who's wrong?'

'What are you getting at?' I asked.

He took his hand from my shoulder, before he spoke again, raising his voice as he did so. 'If you did something that you knew was good, lawmakers and those that don't question anything might call you mad. But who's really mad?'

He paused and then continued, his volume still rising. 'Forgive them for they know not what they do. But should there be forgiveness for those who know full well what they're doing and how bad it is, but refuse to stop? Sometimes you have to get mad to get even with people like that. So I say, in madness lies freedom.'

I shifted my grip on the steering wheel from ten to two to something more like twenty to four. It was microwave weather and the sun still shone like a golden glowing egg, although I think the hottest part of the day had passed. We drove on for a little while, the carjacker still sleepy-sound, only stirring momentarily when the hippy had raised his voice.

In the quietness I thought more about drugs and then sex and oil and wars and Gran and the four gangsters, the knife that had been at my neck and what the hippy had just said about getting mad, and good and evil. I glanced back down at the snoozing passenger to my left. Another sweat droplet trickled from his temple, shifting the grime on his face in its trail. Even in his slumber he was snarling nasty, his skinny face made ugly by his contorted features. I smelled submission in him and I guessed he would let me take his throat by my teeth.

We were on a minor road now, with unkempt grass verges and hedges, a few signs indicating local places and speed limits, while the occasional house or pub or phone box or pillar box flashed by us as we ignored those speed limits. Towering straight factory chimneys stood in the distance, landmarks of the north. The hippy was staring at them too. 'Look at those,' he said pointing glumly. 'Monoliths to money, birthplace of the bourgeoisie, the diseased cunt that delivered capitalism.'

He was right. Around the soot-stained factories, land appeared to creep up and growl as though it knew what these forbidding buildings were there for, and how they had ravaged. Wild grass grew tall around the darkened dry-stone walls with patches of green moss growing on them as they snaked the landscape, crawling to the distance, to the range that is the Pennines, that is Gran's place.

My body ached from driving and I wanted to have a pee now. 'I need to stop for a pee,' I said.

'Me too. We'd better wake him so we don't have to stop again.'

I pulled over on a turning that was a tractor track through a field of luminous yellow mustard-seed crop and poked the carjacker. He woke with a jump. 'Urrrgh! What? What's up? Where the fuck are we?' He blinked his pinky eyes at me.

'Pee break.'

'Uh, okay,' he mumbled, wiping the dribble from his chin with his grubby sleeve. 'Where's the gang?'

'Away,' I said. 'For now.'

I opened my door, leaving the engine running and we all left our doors open as we lined up, carjacker in the middle, and wet a dry-stone wall.

'You two looked like wankers dancing in front of that fucking battyman,' said the carjacker, his nazty person fully awake again.

'What?' asked the hippy to the carjacker in our mid.

'You looked like wankers,' he repeated.

'When?' asked the hippy.

'In front of that fuckin' gay landlord at the b'n'b.'

'That was ridiculous,' I said, my spray in full force, 'but at least it got us a room for the night. You're the wanker for nearly getting us turfed out.'

'Yeah,' said the carjacker. 'Well, I wouldn't have even stepped foot in there if I'd known the cunt was a bum bandit.'

The hippy and I both shook our heads as we all shook our knobs, making sure our eyesight didn't fall in the direction of another's penis, as heterosexual men do.

'As it goes, there's no reason why we couldn't be boy band,' declared the hippy emphatically. 'I mean there's so many crap celebrities at least we'd be able to say something interesting. You know, word "celebrity" means to be celebrated and there's so many of today's celebrities that we shouldn't celebrate. But media makes stars and we've become obsessed by cult of celebrity.'

'It's a career choice to be a star now,' I said, stepping away from the wall and buttoning up my trousers.

'Exactly,' said the hippy, giving his dick a final vigorous shake. 'We should all be allowed to fulfil our potential, then no matter what we do, we'll be glowing. If you shine with the stars you don't have to look up at them.'

I nodded. The carjacker finished pissing.

'I were main singer in GHB anyway,' laughed the hippy.

'Who says?' I asked.

'Record company would insist as I'm best looking, man,' he chuckled. 'I've been told I'm spitting image of Robbie Williams! I'm hungry. Can we buy a veggie burger round here?'

'We should be at my Gran's soon. We can eat there. She's bound to have got a bit of grub in. A cow or something.'

'But I'm a veggie,' protested the hippy, still smiling.

'Might have fuckin' guessed. Does she know I'm coming?' the carjacker nonchalantly enquired as he buttoned his army trousers up.

'She's only expecting me,' I answered, turning back to the car. I couldn't help but notice that the hippy had flapped away a massive penis. No wonder the big fella was always grinning.

We clambered back into the car and slammed shut the doors. I pulled out, moving through the gears like a skilful football star slipping through an up-for-it defence, and indicated, even though there were probably no cars for absolutely miles around. Except, I suspected, a red BMW. We were soon up to speed, cutting through a cool breeze on that hot August day.

'I'm knackered,' expressed the carjacker. 'Any chance of some of that Charlie to perk me up?'

'No chance,' I replied flatly.

'Oh go on, you don't seriously think I'm going to help you bury it without having a bit do you?' he said, laughing.

'No chance,' I repeated.

'You can have some of this when I've finished rolling it,' offered the hippy, opening his palm to show the nearly completed joint.

'Nah,' said the carjacker, curling his lip. 'It's hippy shit for shit hippies. I want a livener.' Suddenly the hippy's huge opened hand clouted the carjacker on the side of his head knocking his cap off. The carjacker turned round and flung a limp-armed punch back at the hippy who just caught his clenched fist with his hand. 'Shut it, will you,' he said, squeezing the carjacker's fist tightly. 'We're going to visit Gran and then Beloved Wood and you will keep it shut until we all have last sight of you. How was that for a livener you ungrateful little tosser?'

The hippy released his grip and pushed the carjacker's hand back.

'Fuck you!' snapped the carjacker. 'When we get out I'm going to deal with you.'

The carjacker stared at the hippy for as long as he could take the hippy's stares back, then collected his cap from the floor and placed it back on his head before sliding his upturned palms under his thighs, sitting on them and staring ahead.

'In any case,' I said to the carjacker, 'it's not been paid for yet.'

'Exactly, so…'

'I warned you,' menaced the hippy.

The carjacker pulled a face at the hippy that only I saw. 'But you're still giving me a load of Charlie for helping you,' the carjacker directed at me. 'That's the deal isn't it? That still the deal?'

I said not a word.

MINDLESS VIOLENCE CONTINUES TO RISE

THERE WAS PANIC in his voice. 'Can you at least tell me where we're going? Where are we going?' asked the carjacker. I thought about that moment I'd met him, when you first heard of him, and who we were back then and how we are all constantly evolving and who we were becoming and how meeting him has changed me, changes everyone who hears about something like this happening, and I kept my eyes firmly frontwards.

'Where are we going?' he repeated, looking desperately between the hippy and myself to discover the answer.

I'd discovered a lot about these two on this journey, and I'm discovering a lot about you: just from the fact that you're still here I know you have it in you too. You have compassion, you have empathy, you have a heart, you have understanding. And you may even have the will to kill. I mean, just how far would you go to do what you know is right? All the way? It's what I had to think about then as we sped along.

'We're going to Gran's,' I finally replied to the carjacker. 'Not far to go now.'

What do *you* reckon? Are you someone with good will? Could you do it?

Then the hippy, who had sparked up, chipped in: 'We're going to the future,' he said. 'Each millimetre forwards is toward future and away from past. There's future, ooh now we're in it, no, now it's past, no now it's present, ooh there's future, no it's present, and now past. Shit, we'll never be in future. You'll have to drive faster.' He chuckled and took, what appeared from his satisfied eyes-shut expression, a delicious drag on his joint. Do you remember those T-shirts that read 'Stoned Again'? Well, the hippy didn't need the 'Again' part on his one.

'I don't suppose any of you want any of this hippy shit?' he asked, holding the joint out. 'Nope?' He was on form, having fun. I should have been too, but in my anxiety caused by the gang and my deep thoughts about the carjacker, I'd lost some of myself. I'd also gained some new self. It was scaring me.

'Yeah, I'll take some,' said the 'jacker putting his hand back to take the burning baton. He snatched it and took a couple of swift tugs on it before passing it back.

'Can we put the radio back on?' asked the hippy. 'I love those local radio stations – they play loads of Seventies stuff.'

Seemed no harm, so I tuned in the radio, but it was some thumping dance stuff that crackled on.

'Underworld, we have here,' cocksured the carjacker.

'No underworld, we have after us,' replied the hippy, cracking up at his joke.

'No, the music's Underworld. I know that cos my wanker of a neighbour plays it top fuckin' volume through the night. Do you have to have it on? I fuckin' hate music.'

I wondered if the carjacker was so happy he'd got in now, yanking my door like he did when he could have been at home. Strange thoughts were gathering in my mind. It all felt unreal, as though I was outside of myself, as though I was elsewhere. I thought the show would only be a day, I didn't know the ride would turn out to be such a gurgle. He must surely be enjoying the ride all right. The Pennines are in sight and growing all around us. No cops had hassled which was good in these days and ages. Hippy man was a bonus. Liked him. He don't like carjacker Cool Cat though and nor do I. Four men still chase us, maybe more now if the Nottinghamshire cops had been put onto us and Dead may have called for reinforcements. If they see us again, they'll shoot, wherever it is. Losing life in the Pennines is not so bad. Me and the hippy dude would at least collect death where we'd collected life, to go full circle. The carjacker, he don't appreciate none of this gorgeousity or my generosity in bringing him here. We are on the edge of the Pennines now and I said to him, no promised the rascal, I'd show him their forever beauty. Wonder what he thinks now? There's towering hills as tall as the tower-block slums from which he crawled out.

He's had enough time now to rue his rude actions. But I don't think he's having any regrets, he knows only bad, he knows bad so well that he'll never meet any good. He needs to regress to have regrets. No way he can do it alone. Let him feel the noise, the heat, the retribution for his unkind ways.

'Do you like them then?'

'What?' he scornfully retorted, with the hippy looking on. 'Like what?'

'The Pennines. I told you I'd show you them.'

'Fuck 'em. They're only good for shitting on. I'd rather be at home.'

'Where's that?'

'Edmonton.'

'So why'd you jump me at Tottenham High Road?'

'More cars. Pigs are never around, they're chasing after those nigger murderers that live either side of the High Road. And that leaves me a clear route right down the middle.'

'You don't like a lot of the people you live with?'

'What d'ya mean?'

'You don't like black people?'

He snorted. 'Does anyone?' He spat his hatred out, turning to face me, spittle literally spraying from his mouth onto my face. 'Or the pakis, or the wops, or them fuckin' greasy bubbles in Turnpike Lane, and those yids down at Stamford Hill. They should all fuck off back to where they come from.'

'Why do you dig yourself up about it?'

'About what exactly?' he asked, turning to glare at me.

'Why are you so racist?'

'There's only one nigger I've met who was all right,' he replied addressing the remark to me but now looking ahead and speaking out through the windscreen, as though he were a murderer being interrogated through protective glass. 'He's my mate so you can't say I'm racist.'

'That old shit,' I remarked.

'What?'

'You're coming out with the old same old shit that racists always say. Why do you like Edmonton more than the Pennines? It's all honkies here, homeboy.'

'They're fuckin' northerners though. That don't count. In Edmonton, there's more chances. Edmonton's easy. What can I do with these fuckin' hills?'

'Look at them,' said the hippy to him.

'And?' demanded the carjacker.

'Look at them and feel their wisdom,' said the hippy. 'You could stretch and grow in their space. Look at them and realise that they were here long before any of us and they will be here long after we've gone. Maybe our children's children's children will be looking at this same spot.'

'More hippy shit!' declared the 'jacker. 'I don't believe this. They're only fuckin' hills. It's not like they're worth anything. They should fuckin' flatten them. Flatten them and build a city on top of them. Then I might live here. Then I might have a chance to survive on those bleak fuckin' mountain lumps. How I ever... what the hell am I doing here?'

'You made your decision,' I said, staring at him. 'And here you are. But we should have let you run off back in that field. Leave Dead Cloutner to kill you.'

'Piss off,' he scowled. 'I'd get on with him all right.' I

148

raised my eyebrows at him. He carried on. 'Course I would. He'd know where I was coming from. It's not usually, shit… In my manor it's usually so easy. You know…' He was on a roll '…in some American states people can legally shoot carjackers on the spot and in South Africa – where most carjackings end in murder – loads of cars have a device fitted that can blast a ten-foot flame out of the sides of the car if the driver doesn't like the look of someone approaching. I've read about it, see.'

'And what if the driver doesn't see the person approaching?' I asked. 'Say he's in a busy city street for example.'

The silent movement of his shoulders and the smallest suggestion of a smile which played about his lips indicated the equivalent in other human beings of a large laugh. 'Listen mate,' he said, turning to face me. 'It's the car manufacturer's fault. They've made car security so good there's no chance of nicking a decent car from the street like there used to be. So I've been forced to go for the next weakest point – and that's you in the car with your keys. It's not just me, it's most car thieves.'

'You're a tosser,' stated the hippy. 'We're all losing patience with you and your sorts.'

'You don't get it mate,' said the carjacker, getting agitated and spinning round to look at the hippy. 'You just don't get it do you? It's about bottle, doing what I do. And some skill. You know I can spin this knife round my fingers like a Harlem Globetrotter.'

He leaned down to pick up the knife and I stared right at him. The hippy behind blew a fog of smoke at him to let him know he was there, watchy-watchy. Cool Cat blinked his dry eyes in the smoke, wafted it with one hand and then with some considerable dexterity span the knife around his fingers, flipping and twisting, lapping and levering like some sort of heavy-metal drummer twizzling his skin sticks in front of an audience of adoring metal muthafukkas. With a final flippety-flip and up into the air, the carjacker caught the knife's handle and pointed the shiny blade right at me. I looked away from him, eyes on the mission ahead, more focussed now than ever.

'Drop it now,' said the hippy, no messing in his tone.

The carjacker ever so slightly turned the knife towards the hippy, then slowly placed it down by his side of the gear box, all the while creepily looking at me.

'When I jump in,' he said, 'if there's any hesitation when the blade's at their throat and I start doing that, it's usually got me the keys, cards and cash of anyone before you can say pooper!' He turned his face directly to me and spoke with a smile. 'I love the look on middle-aged women's faces the best.'

'So why did you not do me?' I queried.

He pondered for a moment, his eye-pinnies flickering up and down my face. 'You looked different. You showed no fear. And you told me about Dead Cloutner following.'

'Not straightaway, I didn't.'

He didn't say anything. 'So, you cut people before?' I asked, studying him for the truth.

He looked away and lowered his face, rubbing his nose as he spoke. 'Yeah, mate. Bit of jibbing never goes amiss.'

He looked back at me before staring out again through the front of the windscreen with a cocky smirk. There was something about his endless evilness that made me feel frightened. For the first time, after all these hours in his company, I was fearful for us. All of us. There seemed no getting through to him. He was as naturally bad as a decomposing corpse. His racism, his manner, I didn't know why. Something that I couldn't comprehend had made him as he was and perhaps I had better see him right, you know what I mean? He disgusted me. There was as much hope for bringing goodness out of him as there was the chance of smelling glass.

I sensed the hippy shaking his head and so did the 'jacker.

'What's up with you?' scorned the 'jacker. 'Twat.'

Suddenly the carjacker shoved the hippy in the face with his opened hand. 'You're getting on my fuckin' nerves,' snapped the carjacker, 'all your righteous shit!'

I watch, frozen to the spot, as the carjacker reaches down to grab his knife again, but just as he curls his fingers round the handle a mighty fist cracks against the bony right cheekbone of the carjacker's face. Followed by another and another. Then some more digs as the hippy rises from his seat standing at full height to get at the carjacker who's punching back. A couple of the carjacker's punches land on the hippy, but all they do is fuel him with fury.

Realising he's coming off worse, the carjacker defensively puts his hands up, but the hippy's powerful punches go right through his weedy arms.

'*Fuck off hippy!*' screams the carjacker, trying to get his hands down to reach the knife again. 'Fuck off! Or I'll kill you!'

The hippy replies with a real bone cruncher in the side of the carjacker's nose, immediately afterwards indicating with a nod to the dashboard. 'I like that magnetic Saint Christopher compass,' he says before aiming another whack. His vast knuckles connect at the edge of the carjacker's right bony eye socket. I knew he'd been close to losing it with the nazty one and now he had. Blood starts to drip from the end of the carjacker's nose who's whimpering now like a lost baby chimp. He takes the punches quite well. He has to. There's loads of them.

As the hippy punches I notice a loosely tied woven brown leather friendship band on his thick wrist. The force of his connections causes the band to slip back along on his arm until the muscular width of his forearm stops it sliding further. Immediately after a punch he loosens his fist so that his fingers dangle and he shakes the band back down onto his wrist before forming another tight clench, knuckles at right angles and fingers and thumbs tucked tightly underneath.

There's a certain anticipation of the next punch to come. I stick my foot down as we roar through the dales, the hippy's hair flowing wildly as he stands up in the whooshing speed breeze. I'm ready to grab the knife if the carjacker is foolish enough to make another snatch for it.

'I always get my mates fridge magnets if I go away somewhere for a holiday, rather than travelling that is,' continues the hippy. Thwack, thwack! 'Last time I went to Isle of Wight, a few years, fuckin' shut it you wazzock, ago –' Bup! Bup bup bup – 'I bought my mate Simon a pint of beer fridge magnet as he drinks a lot; then Danny I got a – look shut it –' Knunch – 'smiley face as he's into clubbing. What' – Ud! – 'else? Oh yeah, I got Josh a skull with a snake crawling through eye as he's into macabre.'

For the time satisfied, he sits down and leans back in his seat, slightly breathless while the carjacker mops blood with his sleeve, his cap hanging loosely over most of his face and not daring to look around in case he gets another slap. 'And I got Clifford this black bloke with dreads playing bongos, because Clifford's a black bloke with dreads. And I got Tree a tea towel.'

I didn't like the violence, but the 'jacker had something coming to him from the hippy from schooldays and from this journey with his perpetual boasting and filthy lies. Some blood's already starting to darken to a dark scarlet as it solidifies on the end of his nose and the 'jacker glances a hateful look at me before pulling down the sun visor and checking his bloody damages in the vanity mirror. I tilt my head back a bit to see the hippy in the mirror scooping up his unfinished spliff from the floor mat.

'Why didn't you get Tree a fridge magnet?' I ask him.

He looks at me as though it's obvious. 'He doesn't have a fridge.'

BULLY BOY

THE AIR WAS CLEANER after that incident, like after a storm on a humid day. I wondered if I was turning as bad as the carjacker, as though his evil was seeping through my pores, for I didn't feel any of his pain from the beating he'd just received.

The hippy turned back to me and spoke out of one corner of his mouth with the spliff balancing precariously in the other. 'Sorry about aggro, man,' he said. 'Once every so often I lose my rag, and I've had enough of him, understand?'

I understood.

'What the fuck was that for hippy?' spat the carjacker, who was wiping some more blood from his nose and patting his reddened face.

'You must be used to it anyway,' said the hippy as way of explanation. 'Man, I'm talking to you.'

'What?'

'I said you must be used to getting punched, little tosser like you.'

'Nah.' The carjacker was cocky enough to smile to himself.

'I really wanted to punch you and your arrogant mates at that school when I was gardening.'

'What school?' asked the carjacker, still trying to cover his true identity.

'Well, it was worth the wait,' said the hippy. 'You deserved that a long time ago. You're just lucky I was only playing.'

The carjacker stared at him with an ugly look. Silence resumed and I gazed at the Pennines, a great green expanse running to the edge of the world. Nothing was getting through to the carjacker. Nothing. He was as he was, but we couldn't leave him like that.

We passed a massive old lone tree on my side and high up in it away from harm's reach I spotted two black and white magpies – joy. Both were stood on a long branch, just stood there. It was cooling down around us. Outside I could see from the stillness of the branches that there was not so much as a breeze.

I watched in my wing mirror the two magpies remain there and then they were joined by another magpie that swooped and hopped across the greenish branch, squawking. I saw the other two hop and shuffle to make room for the newcomer, but the new magpie crowded them, crowded them some more and they shuffled along until the branch became a twig and the twig became the sky into which the two magpies flew.

As we shifted round a sloping swerve, I recognised a rocky crag to the right from previous trips to Gran's and watched it in my side mirror as we sped away. We were close to her little place now. I looked again in my wing mirror and saw the tree in the distance with a magpie on, squawking loudly, its beak in the air and its little head swinging from side to side. Then I felt the carjacker's beady eyes upon me, making me uneasy. I pressed the radio off and turned to him.

'What's up?'

'Nothing. Just looking.'

'Are you still in touch with your family?' I asked.

'Never hardly knew 'em.'

'Where'd you get your desert boots?'

'Look, you don't have to try to make friends with me.'

'I'm not. You can't *make* friends.'

'As soon as I've buried the nosebag I'm getting my cut and I'm off. I'll even walk to the nearest town, get some money from someone and get home.'

'Then what?'

'Sell it. Then buy myself some things, clothes and that. Anyway it's up to me what I do with it.'

'Course it is.'

'What you going to do with yours?'

'Take my Gran on holiday.'

'Is that why we're picking the old bag up?'

I didn't answer, the hippy did though as he stubbed the butt of his joint into an ashtray, knocking the seat in front of him with his knees and its occupant in the process.

'You shouldn't talk about old people like that,' said the hippy, staring at the carjacker.

Quickly the carjacker looked away somewhere out of the front of the car. I looked at him, at his skinny face and at his sky-blue and cream velvety Fila BJ jacket and his too short brown army trousers and his pale smooth skinny ankles and his smart desert boots and his blue Motörhead cap crookedly placed on top of his wide brown Mohican cut. He sneaked a look at the state of his face in the vanity mirror. Flakes of crisped black blood were peeling from his nose and lower lip now. He tugged at them and flicked them into the wind with his arm hanging out the side of the Saab. I asked him a question.

'Have you got a grandmother?' I asked him.

'No, got no family,' he answered, still staring ahead, still picking and flicking his dried blood.

'What about your rich parents who paid for you to go to that school?' asked the hippy.

'Didn't go there. Got no family.'

'Are they dead?' I queried.

'Don't know.'

'Where are they then?'

'I don't know. Australia.'

'All of them?' I continued, still looking at his reddened face. Behind him, the hippy sat forward too, his knees pressing into the back of the seat, breathing down the neck of the carjacker who hunched while shifting uncomfortably forward, expecting a repeat cuff at any moment.

'All of them are in Australia?' I asked again.

He shrugged.

'Do they know you?'

He shrugged again. 'No. Not now.'

'Do they like you?'

'No.'

'But they don't know you.'

'They probably still hate me.'

'Why?'

'Cos I am who I am. Look, give me a break.'

'Do they know you're a mugger?'

'I'm not, I'm a hijacker. A professional carjacker. A Twenty-first Century highwayman.'

'Do you get job satisfaction from this "career" of yours then?'

'Yeah. I do as it goes.'

'What do you tell your family you do?'

'They never ask anymore.'

'Do you love your mother?'

'Don't want to know her.'

'What about your grandmother?'

'Don't want to know her either.'

'But they're all still alive?'

He quickly looked out of his side window. 'I don't care.'

'You should have more respect for other people,' the hippy breathed into the carjacker's ear. 'Just because you don't know your relations doesn't mean you can have dig at others.'

The carjacker leaned forward to create some space between himself and the hippy. 'Bollocks!' he threw back at us.

'This old lady we're going to visit has a lot to offer,' said the hippy leaning further forward, ignoring the carjacker's goading.

'Like what?' answered the carjacker indignantly, leaning as far forward as he could without looking too cowardly.

'Like she's been through a lot,' replied the hippy. 'You should be decent to her.'

'Give me one reason why.'

I answered this time. 'Because she's lost the person who was closest to her, a person who she shared so much with over a time we can't yet imagine. She's not even got a chance to visit his grave. Can you imagine that? I can.'

'Not my fault mate.' The carjacker hunched his shoulders some more, realising he was on a dangerous course.

'Can you imagine that?' I repeated through gritted teeth while looking at him.

'Fuck this! No I can't.'

'Can you imagine that?'

'No!'

The hippy leaned towards him. 'Do you know why I remember you?' he asked.

'No.'

'You were school bully,' said the hippy accusingly.

The carjacker smirked to himself.

I looked back to the road, settling back as I started to feel that we were getting somewhere. The hippy leaned back too.

'Are you sure?' I asked. 'Why not let it out now, whatever it is.'

'I've had enough of this,' spat the carjacker, his twisted mind contorting his skinny face. 'Let's just get this nosebag business done with, so I can get the fuck out of here. I didn't even go to any public school. You two are just wankers.'

'I think he did,' I said to the hippy who was looking at me in the rear-view mirror, his look penetrating my thoughts, nudging them and getting underneath. He understood that we'd just found out something about our little aggressor. That what we had was a dirty liar on our hands here. School bully was lying. The filthy, rotten scoundrel. What option did I have then? You'd have done the same, wouldn't you? Come on, wouldn't you?

'It was him,' said the hippy, nodding at me as he kept his eyes firmly on mine in the mirror. 'It was him all right. Even then he went around bashing kids, kids who were smaller than him, kids younger than him, nicking dinner money. Even then he was a little bastard. I used to watch it every time they had a break. He had a couple of bigger lads that he got in with. They had muscle, he had devious mind. He was a skinny little tosser then too.'

'You know nothin',' snarled the carjacker. 'And if you did, you'd know that I get my way. Pair of wankers like you won't stand a chance. Any case, I went to school in, er, Hackney. If either of you two had been there, you'd have got battered. Especially you, you fuckin' hippy wanker.'

'Like you did that time.'

'What you on about now 'ippy?'

'Twenty of those lads had enough of you. Rugby boys. You remember. It was me that saved you when they threw school rules out and took law into their own hands. You'd still have bruises today if you hadn't grabbed hold of my spade that I'd left in ground. And if I hadn't waded in to save you and my spade. You really know how to dig more trouble for yourself.'

'Bullshit.'

'Okay man. But I won't be stepping in again for you.'

'Big deal,' gobbed the carjacker as he shrugged.

The hippy said nothing more, instead he turned his attention to the scenery, but there was an unspoken knowledge that had passed between us.

Sneaking through the northern landscape, I'd been involved with the conversation so much that I hadn't realised we were virtually at Gran's, at that old lady's who had loved and lived, and who had lost one and who was close to losing the other. I was excited to see her again, to be able to take us all on a little adventure. Maybe there was danger in the car, but time's running out for Gran and I'm sure she preferred to be with us than to be left at home on her own. I still think that. As with all of us, time always get the better, always beats us. Everybody here and now, and that's everybody, will be dead in at the most eighty, ninety - at a push one hundred years - so how long do we have left? How long do you think you've got left? How do you think you're going to die? Will you wish you'd done things differently? What day of the week do you think you will pass away on? Will it be summer, will it be pissing it down with rain? What will be your final thought?

So Gran wants adventure and I want her to have adventure, to have no regrets when she lays on her deathbed which isn't so many steps away from her. I haven't given her any great-grandchildren, and I'm alone so we may as well be keeping each other company, giving each other life and love. She knows me better than anyone, better than Julia, better than I know myself. She's seen me from the day I was born, from baby to child, from teenager to young man. She might not be able to see for much longer, so let her see life now, let her see it all.

We took another couple of twisty turns and winding bends until there was Gran's tiny house peering at us from the middle of a small row of terraced houses. Behind the gathering of houses the field flowed away with dry-stone walls running across them like the veins in a man's hand. All shades of green, from lime to olive to a green so dark it was almost black, randomly picked their patches on the land, broken up by the walls and a small lake, bluish and silver-white in the distance. A lone grey house, probably a farmer's, stood far away in the hills that rolled forever and ever like the mammoth green waves of a vast ocean.

We've made it this far. Well done you and me, the hippy and even the mugger nazty.

We're at Gran's

PRINCE CHARLES IS 'SAFE AND WELL'

OUR WORLD WAS TURNING away from the sun and long shadows of the early evening stretched out before us. We passed an old wooden bus stop shelter where the young crowd who lived in this village probably hung out thinking of something to do, some way to escape. Beyond the shelter, grassy fields ran away and dipped before popping back up for the horizon and an overgrown verge ran immediately beside the road.

Between the bus shelter and Gran's row of sootied red-brick terraced houses was a small darkened red-brick grocery shop and post office standing on its own with a couple of net-curtained living rooms above it. Even this far out, everything had been covered by the dark shadow of soot cast by the pollution of the industrial revolution.

Outside the shop on the verge, slightly tangled with long loose weeds, was a billboard with a poster headed *Pennine Weekly Post*. 'BURGLARS ROUNDED UP IN DAWN RAIDS' was daubed in black felt pen. In the cluttered shop window, alongside a poster for Wall's ice cream and some local For Sale cards, another poster for the local paper screamed 'PRINCE CHARLES IS "SAFE AND WELL"' – Read All About It!'.

'Heed all about it would have been more appropriate,' said

the hippy while pointing at the headline. 'That's made-up media, at both its greatest and most horrific. It's non-news. Old Chas hasn't been in an accident or anything in last week. He is as he is most days, but even bosses of a local newspaper know that a royal story sells and that royals rarely sue. That report will most probably say that a spokesperson has heard this and seen that, but nothing was wrong with him in first place. It's bullshit.' He was shaking his head in disgust.

'And if you start silly rumours,' I said in response, glaring at the carjacker, 'you cause all sorts of trouble, trouble that wasn't there in the first place, you know what I mean?'

'Yeah, that's it,' agreed the hippy. 'That's whole point.'

We parked round the side of Gran's on a bumpy mud patch with no sign of other cars in the village. I asked the other two to wait while I fetched Gran. The hippy gave me a knowing nod while the carjacker just slumped further down in his seat and pulled his cap's peak over his eyes as though he was going to kip. But he wasn't going to sleep. No, he was going to sit there thinking his malignant thoughts, thinking what he could take from life. Greed ruins everything and it had certainly ruined him. I pulled out the car keys and put them in my trouser pocket.

'No messing about, right,' I directed at the carjacker. He nodded slightly, then yawned.

It was cooling by the minute now and I shut my door softly for the quiet filled me up here. It was the sound of silence. It felt great to stretch my legs, arch my spine and I clicked my neck from side to side, then took some purposeful strides towards Gran's.

Fairly soon it would be pitch-dark, in a countryside darkness the carjacker and I had rarely known. Smells of nature and brick and trees wafted as the heating effect of the sun lessened. There was no sign, or noise, of the gang. Maybe we'd lost them. I looked back at the two faces in the car and decided that perhaps they were still around: the hippy wasn't quite so happy sat there and I could see in the carjacker marks of weakness.

There's no gate or no border as such marking Gran's decaying two-bedroom rented property, just a front garden and the only boundary of sorts here is a hydrangea that spreads itself out in a bushy pink display during the summer. Gran's a socialist going on communist in many of her views and doesn't believe that we have the right to own any of the land, that it belongs to everyone. Her home is on the end of a terrace of four, typical of homes built quickly a century or so ago to house the desperately eager new workers needed for the cotton and wool factories of Lancashire and Yorkshire. Of course, those factories have long gone these days and these sort of towns are almost extinct now, as old in town terms as the people who live in them are in life terms.

I peered through Gran's nets as I rapped lightly on the door. She'd had newspaper sheets stuck up at her windows once, to keep her privacy and to stop inquisitive eyes from glaring in at her bare poverty. Now she was past caring. I knocked again and waited glancing back at the car. The hippy waved at me and gave me a brave smile and an encouraging nod; he knew what it meant to meet your Gran while the other one just grimaced under his peak, arms folded, probably dreaming of the money he was going to make from this little job gone wrong and now to his mind, financially at least, wonderfully right. Although I was going to sort him out, I really would have felt better about things if he did some listening.

There was still no reply from Gran's, so I walked to the side door and cautiously let myself in. I didn't want to frighten her. I knew she'd be in at this time; she's in most of the time. I left the door open and took a couple of small, quiet steps into the tiny kitchen.

'Hullo, Gran? Hullo? It's Patrick.' I listened, the house was totally silent, nothing stirred. I glanced around the kitchen: those old orange and black pans on the cooker to my right, the pale yellow faded flowery wallpaper still slightly peeling behind from years of cooking condensation, a couple of old thin wooden cupboards – modern when they were put in during the Thirties – to the left above the fridge and next to them the net-curtained window which, in the summer, lets in some pale Pennine light onto a spindly spider plant in a red pot and then onto the red tiled floor. There wouldn't be much in her cupboards, just some tins, sugar, and definitely semolina. Gran loves the stuff, which is why I like it so much too I suppose.

Inside the slightly open cupboard door, hidden away as though it's naughty – and perhaps it is in Gran's mind after her long marriage to my grandfather – is a picture of David Soul. She's always loved him, for as long as I can remember, even when my grandad was alive. We'd often ended up chatting about Starsky and Hutch, mostly Hutch. She knew every episode really well. She quite liked Huggy Bear too, but not in the same way that she felt for Hutch.

On the small chopping surface beside the cooker there's a white tin bread bin, a really old one like they sell in antique shops or try to recreate in IKEA or some furniture place like that. A lemon-yellow Jiffi cloth which Gran uses to keep the place spotless is always neatly folded on the back edge of the heavy old free-standing sink under the window and hanging as ever just to the further side is the grey milk saucepan, bashed out of shape from being dropped several times over the years, but used regularly for that semolina and to boil water for cuppas. I nudged the door that led from the kitchen into the living room. Suddenly a cold shiver ran up my spine to my scalp and once more I felt out of myself. I sensed someone watching me here. Or watching this house more like, someone not in the car, some strange old lady, someone small anyhow, and someone ever so beady bad. Not too comfy with that really; I felt itchy and paced one way then the other. Something seemed amiss.

'Hullo,' I called out. 'Gran?'

I scanned the sparse living room. Tidy two-seater velvety worn brown sofa with tassles, thin beige carpet with Granny's fluffy yellow nylon rug laid on it in front of a gas fire that she had not had on for a while judging by the slight chill; above it a chipboard wood mantelpiece is covered in little junkets: a frog made from seashells, a golden metal replica of Blackpool Tower, an old white-faced clock with Roman numerals, a glass paperweight with dried flowers inside and other things I remember seeing and playing with since my memory began. In the far corner there's a big wireless and a small dark wooden table to its side pushed against the wall under another net-curtained window with a bulging rack of women's magazines. All of them would be there, some going back years, but not *Woman's Own*: Gran hated that one.

On both the mantelpiece and the small table there's photographs and also on the wall in an assortment of wooden frames: some bright colour ones of me when I was six, seven and eight dressed in the fashions of the time with blond hair and a chubby cherub's face; there's some of my mum in colour, looking young and stunning; but mostly there's black and white ones, really small with white borders and most of them are of Gran and my grandad having fun at the seaside, sitting on a hill together having a picnic, at their wedding where Gran is younger than me now and Grandad about the same age. They look happy in those pictures, there with most of their lives ahead of them and to spend together. But whatever life gives us it also takes away. They were a happy couple, my Gran and Grandad, despite the struggle of poverty that life viciously threw at them. They were happy because they loved each other and that was priceless.

Anyway, to continue, a cheap dark brown wooden chair with Greek-style weave for the seat sits in the other corner of Gran's living room and that's all there is to see apart from the off-white walls. But there was still no sign of Gran. There was a smell, an old odour of Gran's flowery perfume, but also a slight stench like a bad egg, not pleasant, so I took a couple of steps over to release the window's lock and push it wide open, causing the nets to billow in the breeze.

I looked to the other door in the room. It leads past a tiny room where Gran has a few more paperweights and trinkets and Granny's junk to the narrow steps that lead upstairs to her bathroom, bedroom and small spare room with the springy bed that I used to stay in. Then, as I looked to the door it slowly swung ajar.

'Whether tha's yung, orld, single, married or widoor, you could win fifteh thousand,' said Gran coming through the door holding an envelope and talking in an old northern English that will be virtually extinct when her generation passes on. 'An' ah thought to mehself, ah've been all of thorse.'

She casually dropped the envelope on the floor and we met. I cuddled her frail bones and she squeezed back, then pulled away and looked at me, up and down.

'Gie owa tha mitheren. Ah always tell tha, that tha dorn't need to knock. Doors always orpen – int daretam aneh rords. Lookes lahk tha need sum food. Ah've sum int fridge. Come and looke.'

I followed her through to the kitchen, not yet finding my voice. She was Gran, but she looked more skinny than when I'd last seen her. She wore her brown nylon slacks, a lilac round neck thin wool cardigan with a pink floral trim, and a pair of worn blue cotton shoes. I followed her steps through to the kitchen where I went to close the back door I'd left ajar.

'Leave et orpen,' said Gran. 'Otherwise, kitchen steams upp when ah cooke.' She pulled the semolina from the fridge. 'Ah'll 'eat this upp, chuck. Blob of jam en and tha'll be raht as rairn.'

'So you all right Gran?'

She didn't answer me, not with words anyway, just gave me a quick look as she poured the thick semolina into the grey saucepan. The look said thousands of things and said them a thousand times: all her memories, all her feelings, moments of pain and excitement, and feelings of good and bad – the pleasure of life and the despair of death and the indescribable joy she got from loving me. And on top of it all the look said, 'Let's not ask questions like that, ah've not got long to enjoy tha, so let's bluddy well enjoy tha.' And she was right. She was always fucking right, this old tender, helpless, grey old sucked-in lady before me. My Gran.

She lighted the gas cooker and stirred the semolina, looking at the swirling pattern her wooden spoon made in it.

'Sor, that envelup came through mah door and says that if ah'm yung, orld, single, married or widoor ah could win fifteh thousand. What collops daft rubbish. Aneh rord, ahm beawnt throwen that en blummen estin. Tha look raht grand int suit. Bit muddy though int et?'

I told her that I'd slipped and Gran scooped the semolina and poured it into a dish before getting some jam out of the fridge and putting a dollop in it.

'Thanks Gran. Aren't you having some?'

'Ah've just eaten not long since. Ah've onleh watter to drink for tha or ah can brew cuppa. Were journeh throught dales all raht?'

I nodded and poured some 'watter' into a glass before going through to the living room where Gran picked some dead leaves from her busy lizzie, while I sat on the sofa to gobble up the semolina. I thought of those outside, but I'd tell Gran about them in a second. We weren't bursting into conversation simply for one reason, and that was that we knew each other so well. Just as I finished scooping up the pudding, Gran sat down opposite the two-seater I was on.

Under those fair brows that hung like old bridges, her eyes were pulverising in a caressing kind of way. Eminent and wise. And naughty old devil. Despite the whitening of her irises where she was going blind I could still see in her eyes the young girl at school, the daughter, the little sister, even the teenage flirt at the village dance.

'Gran, we've got to go. Are you ready?'

She looked away out of the window at the Pennine scenery, at her view, flowing away into the distance and ensuing darkness. The sunset was probably quite glorious, but we could just see from here some red tinges on the edges of a couple of bulbous clouds that were fading out of sight into the dark night that was soon to surround us, all of us on this green and pleasant land.

She hadn't heard me. 'Gran. Grandma!' I repeated louder.

'Sorry chuck. Did tha say sumthen'? Ah'm goen deaf as well as blarnd,' she said, turning away from the sunset to look sadly at me.

'*Isn't that what the doctor gave you that hearing aid for?*' I asked. She looked at me, just for long enough to let me know that she'd heard, before, without changing her expression, looking out of the window again.

'Isn't that what the doctor gave you...'

'Aye,' she snapped as she looked back quickly at me, cutting me mid-sentence. 'Butt folk can see et, dangleh bit, plat-stic anall. Dorn't care mutch for plat-stic. Ah think et causes cancer.'

I looked at her in puzzlement. 'How's that Gran?'

'Well, since we 'ad more plat-stic things there's been more folk wi' cancer, least round 'ere. Onleh last munth, Enid passed awere. Cancer of brairn, an' she always wore plat-stic 'elmut when she were riden push-bike to shops. Fit as thee everywhere else see, butt et were brairn where et got 'er. Ah dorn't want cancer getten int ear now. Ah'll go bluddy deaf fust. Aneh rords, et lookes daft.'

'Who lives around here who's going to be bothered about it?'

'Never tha mind, never tha mind. There's lahf en meh yet.'

I sighed and we smiled together, Gran displaying her

whitey-white neat row of dentures. She used to make me laugh when I was a child by pushing those dentures in and out with her tongue. I really love this old lady.

'I'm just going upstairs to splash my face, Gran. I'm shattered. Been driving for hours. And I've got an old friend and a work colleague out in the car with me.'

'Ah know. Ah wundered when tha were gorn introduce. Ah'll just get me bits uppstairs. 'Ave wash down int kitchun. There's sum butties made upp int fridge, if tha can fetch thorse. Sum special ones for tha wi'out butter. Lads must be raht 'ungreh anall.'

I watched the door swing closed behind the stooped, shuffling figure of Gran. She had a great presence about her and immediately the door shut I noticed the ticking silence again. I went into the kitchen closing the door behind me and pushing the back door shut, then carefully took my jacket off and hung it on the back door knob.

It was a dim light now, but I left the light off. Quickly I sat down on the hard, cold tiles and set about doing my sit-ups. I used to do two hundred a day. It's important to stay fit in this day and age. I rammed my way through them, hands at the side of my head but not touching, knees slightly bent, feet flat on the floor. I've been doing them for years and my stomach's solid. But I wasn't really doing them for a physical reason. Yes, I liked to be fit, but this was about keeping my mind in order too.

It took several minutes and I had a few deep breaths when I'd finished before standing upright without using my hands to push me up and peered through the kitchen window, brushing the straggly spider plant as I did so. I couldn't see much out of it except the faint outline of the white Saab and a couple of other houses. I went back on the floor, stomach down, and started to do my press-ups next. Two hundred also, sometimes more, never less, each day. It was a great exercise and I loved doing it, loved knowing that I was going to do it.

It was one thing I could count on in this unpredictable world. I looked at my splayed fingers as I moved up and down, sometimes reading across my knuckles as a way of counting: L-O-V-E-love, L-O-V-E-ten, L-O-V-E-love, L-O-V-E-twenty, twenty-one, twenty-two, twenty-three, twenty-four, twenty-five…

A few minutes later I kicked my legs up and sprang to full height. I felt great. I could hear Gran in the next room, and after putting my jacket back on and pulling the sandwiches from the fridge to put on the kitchen side I opened the door to –

When I saw him my first reaction wasn't to blare out: 'Who the fuck are you?' as I would have expected. Instead I was thinking: 'How did he get in?' I'd spent hours making Gran's place secure, but nowhere in Britain is safe from the burgling scum these days, not even a village such as this and I knew immediately that here was a burglar, one of the ones they'd missed in the dawn raids, if there had been any dawn raids, or perhaps one out on bail. I saw it as fate that here was another bad one to correct.

Okay, Gran left the door open during the day, but she lived in a past time and refused to believe that some thieving stranger would wander in while it was full daylight. I saw the window behind him that he'd just clambered through to get in. You can't even have fresh air coming in without some bad air coming with it.

Neither of us move.

I keep my eyes glued on him and my voice rises from within my calm anger and cascading adrenaline. 'Who the fuck are you?'

He just stands there, a squat little fucker with a greasy dark moptop and a sparse bumfluffy beard. He's a kid, early teens, standing in my Gran's house with a fucking carving knife that I'm sure belongs to Gran. I can smell the fear from him and take it in as I hear some church bells ringing in the distance. Pennine evening mass. I can hear my heart beating, thumping, and my rapid breath going in and out through flared nostrils. My face is tense, all on a downward tension. He is screwing up and breathing the same. I can hear his heart's beat thump-thumping. We are like two bulls waiting to charge at each other. He takes a couple of quick deeper breaths and gulps down a fearful swallow. He's making a move. Move first! Move now! I want to fucking kill him, kill him before they finished going in for evening mass. He lunges, his teeth clinking together as he does so and a small noise coming from deep in his throat. He raises the knife up above his head and as his upper torso leans towards me I bring my right leg up and catch him nicely in the chest. It is not even a full-force *mae-geri* front kick, more of a hard evenly weighted push so that he loses his balance and I help him down with my foot. I didn't want to disturb Gran by knocking him back through the window.

When I put the Browning at his temple, his face is a picture. Yeah, he quickly drops the carving knife then, the knife he'd have threatened my Gran with, the knife he'd have... I'm working hard to control myself here. She's the crème de la crème, he's just the scum de la scum. I could have broken every one of his bones with karate, but his lesson has to be learned quickly and quietly, and I do know how to handle a piece very well.

So this burglar can't take his eyes from the barrel of the gun I'm holding. He's shaking, then rigid with fear and I can't take my eyes off his petrified, unblinking eyes as I push his head with the gun so that one ear is tight to the beige carpet and the other stands out just below the barrel which I press and press and press. I could kill him this way, by pressing the barrel so hard in his temple that his skull caves in and his eyeballs pop right out. I wanted to, until that point. But then I thought of the mess, not just the blood in Gran's living room, but the whole mess of telling Gran why I'd had a gun in my jacket, blah blah and all that.

Oh yeah, then he starts trying to say something. 'D-d-do-

don't-d-don't k-k-k-k-k...' He's pleading, but this young cat is so petrified he can't get the words out. Yeah, he'd have been tough with an elderly lady, but he didn't bargain for a fit young man, with a gun. Go, go on. Go on you scum. I'm willing him to say it... 'k-k-k-ki...' Go on. *Go on! Say it!* Just say it.

The church bells stop ringing. I can almost hear the first hymn such is the silence in the Pennines. I could easily pop him swiftly and quietly: the Browning that Ged had left in the car for me is fitted with a silencer. I'd never wanted to have the gun, it's all too easy to take someone's life, like turning a switch on. It just takes a gentle squeeze and that small metal cylinder cuts through, and well, that's that. But Ged had put it in the glove compartment 'just in case' and I'd slipped it in my jacket pocket, ready to bury with the cocaine.

I think about shooting him, not killing him, just grazing this little cat. There'll be a reason for each shot though, nothing random. I want to shoot first his ears off so he can't hear if people are in on his robbing trips, then his nose for being so nosy about other people's homes, then his tippity toes so he can't creep about, then his kneecaps so he can't walk into other people's lives. I stare at his face, the magnitude of his horror showing in every part. Imagine dying and that being your last expression.

I notice the smell of Gran's busy lizzie and look at its pinky petals. There's not usually such a strong smell from lizzies, but it smells really pleasant and it reminds me of Gran. This cat's going to remember this day. Ha! He's made some situation that he don't like, and what is going through his criminal mind?

'You from Manchester?' I ask him.

I indicate with a slight nod for him to get up. He gulps and nods, staying where he is on the floor, his hands held out to show they are empty. Manchester: north England's cultural centre, a town of football and bands and rain and trams and kids like this one wearing sports gear. A friendly enough place with one of the most violent drugs scenes in Europe.

'Answer me. Where are you from?'

'C-c-can't t-t-tal-talk –'

'Where you from?' I demand again, feeling myself tense up. He's starting to play with my nerves.

'M-Mmm-Mmmmmm-Man-Man-chest-Manchester,' he stammers.

I feel a shudder run through me and my finger flinch on the trigger. Can't he just talk to me properly, he's doing my head in. 'Can't you talk properly or something?' I blurt, feeling dangerously agitated and losing more of my self-control than I have in years.

'N-nn-n, st-stammer,' he says pointing at his mouth. 'Stammer,' he repeats, getting the word out in one go and despite the circumstances looking pleased with himself for doing so.

I move the gun away from his temple, and drop it to my side. 'I'm not going to kill you,' I say, my voice sounding deep inside my head. 'I'm not a murdering man.' As I let out a relieved breath, he almost starts breathing again. Shit, he has a stammer.

I don't need to say any more to him. He's out of this game. Whatever his situation, burglary's not the solution. I check his navy blue tracksuit jacket and blood-red Man United shirt underneath it, his baggy jeans crumpled at his ankles running into a pair of black Adidas trainers. At least he's a Man United fan who's actually from Manchester.

'You going back to Manchester now?' I ask.

He nods, his eyes wide with terror. I indicate for him to get up with a backwards nod. He slowly stands, his eyes staying firmly fixed on the gun by my side. He steps back against the wall away from me, cowering, his hands up instinctively close to his face, as though they could stop a bullet.

'Go now then.'

I waved with the gun at the door and watched him walk past me, his eyes looking down, not at my face in case he gave me the wrong look. For what he'd done I should really have sent him to church I thought. To the graveyard. I looked at the knife on the carpet. I was fairly certain he wouldn't be back in anybody else's house. In any case, there is no discipline which will turn one person into another. Each man has a world within, greater than the external. His world within had just been changed by the external, but that's not a guarantee that he won't go back. I could have blasted him dead and that's a guarantee, but then what does that make me? I stuffed the gun back in inside my jacket pocket and buttoned it up. I heard the back door slam shut and some footsteps scurry off.

Now you may be wondering why I didn't use the gun on the carjacker back there in Tottenham, and I'm not going to keep any secrets from you, especially now we've come this far together. And the answer is, I don't really know. They're not really my thing, and I would never kill anyone, but I am pretty handy with them. My stepdad, Gran's son, was in the army and he took me with him to shoot rabbits and sometimes other animals, before he left my mum. We didn't eat the rabbits, or even sell them. He just liked killing them and the next greatest pleasure he got to killing them was seeing his son killing them.

On the other hand you may be thinking: why didn't he take the burglar with them? That would have been interesting, but the carjacker needed our full attention.

'I just heard the church bells pealing Gran,' I said to her as she came back through the door, smelling of peachy powder and with a bit of cover on her face pinking it up. Over her wispy white hair she wore a faded pink and purple headscarf reminding me of some old Thirties film star.

'Aye, getten late now. Church is en Mappelthripp orver dales. Wud tha mand shutten windor for meh, luv. Dorn't remember orpenen et, eeeh memory's goen anall. Then ah'll just mutter tara to my busy lizzie and we can be on ours ways.'

I don't want you thinking I'm an evil man either. I'm not, not at all, but sometimes love is not enough. It doesn't filter through to the others around. Our kid from Manchester needed some gentle persuasion to mend his ways. If I could have taken him for the ride, I'm sure he'd have come good, unlike that scummy carjacker. Perhaps what had happened was enough. I closed and locked the window.

'Let's get away Gran. We've got to find a place to stay.'

'Ooooh, ah'm raht chuffed to beh coming. Where weh goen?'

I shrugged. 'Just around until we find some place.'

'Well, thanks chuck, tha's made mah yure. Tha go on an' ah'll just lock upp.'

I went out through the kitchen and picked up the sandwiches before opening the back door and stepping into the cooling darkness. Gran followed, grabbing her pink cotton anorak from where it always was on a nail behind the door and locking the two locks I'd put on for her some time back. I was preparing for when she met the other two and hoped the carjacker would be polite. I had no doubts that the hippy and Gran would get on, but, well, we'd see. As we turned the corner I saw them sat how they'd been when I'd left, the hippy's bright eyes burning into the back of the carjacker who appeared asleep.

'One's a mate, the guy in the back, and the other I'm working with,' I said to Gran as I carried the sandwiches in their paper bag and came up to the car. I opened the back car door for Gran and she headed for it.

Then all of a sudden, she stopped in her tracks, her tiny little ankles not knowing which way to go for a moment.

'What's up Gran?'

'Narf. We need narf to cutt butties. Ah'm raht sure ah putt et in frunt rum to remarnd us.'

'Oh, it doesn't matter. The lads in the car have both got knives.'

You can imagine, I was getting fed up with blades, diggy-daggers and 'narfs' by now.

I apologised to Gran for not carrying her little brown overnight bag when I saw it and took hold to put it in the boot. I noticed that the carjacker really looked like he was sleeping. I was tired too, we hadn't slept much at all. I opened the boot quietly and put Gran's bag in.

'Oooooh, ah could do wi' sum weedkiller!'

I shut my eyes tightly as I quickly closed the boot. I'd virtually forgotten the cocaine was there, packed in those weedkiller bags, with a shovel laying on top that I'd brought for my original plans before the carjacker had invited himself in. Now this whole trip had become just one event, there was neither rhyme nor reason for it now – the coke may have started it. But now it just was. It was bound to be.

'I'll buy you some from a nursery,' I said turning to Gran. 'I haven't got much in there!' She chuckled, then tutted.

'What's et all for, luv?'

'I've got to go round with the lad in front. Get rid of the bad leaves, weeds and rotting parts. You know, before they spread and destroy everything with their disease.'

I really didn't like lying to Gran, but there was some truth in my explanation.

'Ah see, so all comes oop smelling rorses.'

'Exactly,' I nodded. Just as I had put one leg into the Saab, I heard the sound of another car. I watched the burgling kid go past in a Golf. He must have stolen that as well, but he had to get back somehow and we were a bit full up. I felt good about what had happened. I really felt like I'd done something worthwhile, that I'd done something for the benefit of society. While the means had not been ideal at all, the results would be felt by several people, several people who wouldn't get burgled now and who would spread their decent feelings and not be full of resentment, and their trust would rise over paranoia, and pass on to others around them, and that's how it all works.

That's how it all goes round. So while the means had not been ideal, the result had been. And this is how it's to be. Now theory and action are the same.

NAMING NAMES

STARTLED, HE WOKE with a jump when I whirred the roof back over to cover the four of us. Or at least the carjacker pretended to wake from his fake slumber and cursed at me under his breath for waking him. I don't think he'd really been sleeping at all, just scheming and drooling about what he could get out of us from this situation. It was chillier now we were dissolved in darkness, so I shut my door and switched the car's interior light on. Now we could see each other.

'Hello Gran!' said the beaming hippy leaning his huge frame over to give her a peck on the cheek. The other one turned and mumbled something.

'All raht,' said Gran. 'Sozz to wake tha – tha 'ad raht sock on.'

Even the half-asleep carjacker sat up a bit at this one and I was about to tell Gran to ease off on the sauciness so early when the hippy replied in their own Pennine language. 'Aye, raht sock on duck,' he said, 'butt now we're all slept upp an' that.'

'What's tha called then?'

The hippy looked at me and I realised I didn't even know his name. 'I'm Bruce and it's a great pleasure,' he said, going back to his New World northern accent.

'I thought it was Charlie in the back!' smirked the carjacker, straightening himself and his cap. 'Did anyone see that series on TV about that dealer who – '

'No that's Bruce,' I said, mostly so Gran wouldn't question it and give the carjacker a chance to press home his point. 'Introduce yourself to Gran then. And hello Bruce,' I added, checking him out in the mirror as I started the car up again.

'It's a pleasure,' Bruce replied.

The carjacker spoke to Gran with a sarcastic, robotic politeness. ''Ello, my name is Tom.'

'That's it!' exclaimed hippy Bruce leaning towards him and clacking his fingers Rasta-style. 'Thomas! Thomas Hungerford, if I remember rightly.'

The carjacker sneaked him an uncomfortable, defensive glance in the wing mirror.

'Well, all raht Thomas and Bruce,' said Gran, attempting to calm the commotion, before asking Bruce. 'Does tha know thee?'

'From school,' Bruce replied, staring at the carjacker. 'It's been a long time…'

'Aneh rords, et's raht grand to meet borth. Ah'm Gronnie. Granneh Gron to tha if tha pleases.'

She said it humbly, almost shyly. Gran hadn't been far from her village for many, many years and knew nothing much of strangers.

'I saw a lad running from house,' said Bruce, looking concerned at me. 'Everything all right?'

I replied that it was. 'Yeah, he was just asking if we wanted windows washed. Here's some sandwiches.'

'We dorn't usualleh get windor cleaner upp at naht. Oh well,' shrugged Gran before turning to Bruce on her left. 'Sor, 'ow long 'as tha knorn our Patrick?'

Now we all knew each other's names and it somehow made a difference. Thomas had tried to rob me back there in London and along the way we'd picked up big Bruce the hippy. Thomas! Not exactly the name I'd put to a carjacker.

Bruce seemed uncomfortable lying to Gran too, fidgeting a bit in his seat and covering his mouth as he spoke, to hide his false words and also his mouth that he crammed full with sandwiches, as we all had – we'd been famished. He made up some story about us living near each other in London and they got on well, chatting about the northern landscape and the Pennine people. We were back on the small dipping and winding road that we'd come along to Gran's. We could have stayed at her place, but we really had to be motoring towards the stones where hippy Bruce, had to meet his girlfriend. Also, Dead Cloutner would still be sniffing about somewhere close to our exhaust pipe, trying to locate the chemical smell of coke, and to keep moving as far away as we could from where we'd first met them was the instinctive thing to do.

I watched the pair in the back chatting away. The carjacker leaned round to look at Gran. 'Is that how everyone speaks round 'ere? I can't understand nothin'.'

I think he thought this would wind me up a bit, talking to Gran without any manners, but Gran was okay.

'Tha's not from these pats?' she asked.

'What?' he impatiently answered, just as he'd started to hum the theme to *Chicago*. He was doing his best to wind me up. But no need. I knew clearly what I had to do, what had to be done.

'Tha,' said Gran louder and pointing at him, 'is not from Lancashire?'

'Nah. I'm from Landun.' He was nonchalant and put on his counterfeit cockney even more to make the answer ring with some truth. Also I suppose he exaggerated his accent in the way that people with a different accent do quite often when talking to someone else who has a strong dialect. It's all a question of identity and projecting an image of who we want to be.

'Does tha lahk et oop 'ere?'

'What 'ere?' he scorned indignantly. 'Not really.' Gran

recoiled her head back with a puzzled look. I thought she was in shock at the carjacker's answer, but she was staring at his neck. She opened her eyes wide in mock horror, then she looked at Bruce.

'Where's tha's cutt?' she asked him bluntly.

Bruce looked back at Gran, his face slowly falling like a leaf from an autumn tree.

'Ah see these lads have borth got cutts ont necks. Is et all fashion these dares then?'

Bruce's face lifted and he chuckled. 'I thought you were talking about a cut of something, like a cut of... well, you know, something. Anyway, I've got this instead,' he said, facing Gran again and pulling aside the neck of his T-shirt to reveal the scar from where the pipe had been put into his throat after his car accident. 'Mine's from a car accident rather than from an accident in a car.'

'Raht, ah see said blarnd man,' spoke Gran hesitantly. 'Is that tatty shirt all tha's got to putt on?'

Bruce nodded. 'I don't feel cold ever,' he replied, 'and I like to travel light. If I need to wear something warmer I just get it wherever I am and then if I don't need it I give it to someone who needs it. Less you've got, less there is to worry about as I see it.'

Gran was nodding at Bruce, but I could see she wasn't really listening, her mind working and a frown appeared between her eyes. She was thinking about my accident and that now. There was a silence in the car as we whizzed up and down the little countryside road: I supposed the others were thinking about their car accidents too, if the carjacker had actually been in a crash. He lied so much that he probably didn't know. He lived a lie.

I switched off the inside light. Straightaway the darkness in and outside filled us. I flicked the headlight beam onto full and it picked out the winding dry-stone walls either side up ahead as we carved through the bleak Pennine countryside, and even though the moon was still just about a full one, its illumination was swallowed by the dark never-ending vastness. Streetlights seemed unheard of and even cat's eyes were absent from this swelling and dipping and twisting and turning road.

I thought hard to make sure the knife that the 'jacker had used on me was tucked away. I'd put it under my seat for now when the 'jacker had slept, but we had to be careful; with Gran on board he could perk up and try something. He knew what was in the boot, maybe he'd finally worked out that he could take it all and get a lot richer. He'd have to face the gang of course, but we hadn't seen them for a while, so maybe he'd figured they were gone. I knew they weren't.

PITTER PATTER PATER BATTER

'SHOOT THEM!' HE ORDERED ME. Gran had broken the silence, her voice echoing from the darkness in the back, unwittingly bringing back the violent memories to me when she'd asked me if I remembered playing in the Pennines. Gran must have realised it wasn't a decent question to ask as soon as she'd said it. She knew what I was thinking about now; not about running through the fields with a happy family when we'd visited her in the summer, but about my stepfather cuffing me for not wanting to shoot rabbits.

He'd make me stand to attention for half an hour while he continued shooting or get me to take my shoes off and walk through the baked fields if I didn't. He had been bitter, bitter about having to leave the army, angry with me for him getting old, angry that he'd been trained to kill people, but never been anywhere he'd been given the chance to use the only 'skill' he'd acquired in life.

Also he just had violence in him, like many people on this island: as it's been conquered and then settled on by so many warring invaders, and then divided into class, it's no surprise that the make-up of Britain's inhabitants causes many to be prone to aggression, especially when the upper class is discreetly happy to see that their working-class defenders are still fit to fight. See the universal upper-class condemnation but lack of action when the English hooligans kick it off abroad. Of course the upper classes condemn it, but secretly they're fucking relieved to see their working-class soldiers are still territorial and angry enough to protect this island that the upper class own.

He never said a word about why he'd had to leave the army, and once when I'd asked him was the only time I saw him display another emotion than anger. Afterwards he'd beaten me, not the worst he'd beaten me: a thick lip and bruises. He'd beaten me much worse than that. So it was that wild animals got it and when he wanted someone to bully, if it wasn't Mum it was me. It was just as well that Mum had been a nurse on a casualty ward and had taught me how to stem the flow of blood from wounds. She put up with him for so long in that way that some people do, just for the love of their children and for the memories of how it had been, and also because she didn't know any other life.

'I dorn't supporse tha does remember mutch,' said Gran. She could tell what I was thinking and she regretted setting me off on that track of thought. She knew her son had been a bastard, maybe he still was. Wherever he was.

'Sor, tha just along fort ride?' she asked big Bruce, taking away the bitter poison that was frothing round both of our mouths.

'I'm going to see my soulmate, Granny Gron,' answered Bruce, his voice tightening at the thought.

I saw Gran's puzzled expression. 'His girlfriend, Gran,' I explained.

'Orrr, smashen chuck. A Lankeh?'

He nodded. 'From near Hollingworth Lake.'

'Sling thee 'ook! Nearby Rochdale.'

'Yep,' he replied drawing out the 'yep'. 'I'm meeting at old stones near lake.'

'Holy Grail storns?'

'Yeah!' He was excited at the confirmation that someone else knew they were there. 'I can't believe I've met two people who have heard of them. You know them?'

'Never seen 'em, butt ah've 'eard 'bout 'em since ah were... koh, farv or six. Int Beloved Wood they are.'

'Yeah,' said Bruce breathlessly. 'You call it Beloved Wood as well?'

'Aye pet. Allus. They're called that as special things 'appen up there. An' sum raht queer things anall.'

'You're telling me!'

'Like thinking you met the love of your life up there ten years ago!' spouted the carjacker from the front laughing falsely out loud at his own comment.

'What *has* happened up there Granny Gron?' asked Bruce.

'Nowt.'

'Nowt what?' There was pleading in Bruce's voice as his face took on a worried look.

'Folk seeen things an' that,' Gran answered, her voice a hush. 'Little people and daft things lahk that. Dark things...' Her voice trailed off and then just as quickly she piped up, her tone one of optimism. 'Butt folk tell meh et's raht luvleh up there anall. Lahk 'eaven ont earth.'

'But what else has happened?'

'Oh, nowt else. Now stop getten sor nesh. Et's raht parky – is windor orpen?'

I shut my window fully up for Gran. Bruce shifted a bit. He wanted to push Gran for more, but she'd told him that that was that. No more. He sounded nervy when he spoke. 'Put your foot down man. Please, let's get there as quickly as we can.'

'So ya can meet a fuckin' little person at the woods!' The carjacker was definitely pushing it because Gran had arrived, but almost as soon as he'd finished he received a cuff from behind and I shot him a glare that I doubt he could see in the darkness. He'd felt Bruce's cuff all right though.

'*Fuck you!* What was that for?'

'For swearing in front of Granny Gron. Don't be so ignorant and don't do it again. Understand?'

'I don't understand anything about you. Crustie loser.'

'Dorn't fret chuck,' said Gran, soothing the situation once more. She didn't give a damn about swearing, but Bruce wasn't to know. Gran realised she'd left Bruce worried and had sought to reassure him about the wood.

'It's okay Granny Gron,' acknowledged Bruce. 'I'm cool.'

'Aye, is that windor up, Patrick?'

I told Gran that it was as we carried on speeding through the countryside. I knew the way back to the major road. Now I sought to reassure Bruce as well. 'I'll get us as near to the stones as we can, then we'll have to book in somewhere for the night. We won't be able to find them in the dark. Tomorrow's the date, so we'll get up early and walk with you until we find them and then me and, erm, Tom, can do some work together.'

'What tha doen?' For an old lady she didn't half ask a lot of questions.

'Oh, we've got to shift that weedkiller. Will you be all right waiting in the hotel while we do it? Should only take an hour.'

'Aye, should be. Deliveren it?'

'That's right Gran.'

I breathed a gasp of relief. At this stage my mind was crushing me: how do we deal with the carjacker if he does wrong again or tries to run off, what if Bruce goes off the rails, what if Bruce's girl doesn't show up, what if Dead does?

'Anybodeh 'ave raht tahm?' asked Gran, bringing me back to the real world.

'Never trust a hippy with a watch, Granny Gron,' laughed Bruce holding up his bare wrists.

I looked at the digital clock on the dashboard and wiped some dirt that was on the hour. 'It's around nine I think Gran.' The real world was beginning to seem weird, like I wasn't in it, like nothing was real.

'Bugger et! Fust tahm ah've missed *Corrie* in yures!' Gran turned her attention to the carjacker. 'Does tha live en Lundun then, tha int frunt?'

'Who me?'

'Aye.'

'Yeah. I told you that.'

'Whereabout? Not that ah've 'eard of anywhere mutch.'

'North London.'

'Tha follor football then?'

'Yeah.'

'Which team?'

'Manchester.'

'Eh? Citeh or Unahted?'

'United of course!'

'Been to see 'em mutch? Ah thought tha would follor Lundun team.'

'Nearest team to me is Tottenham, but they're crap. I watch Manchester on TV sometimes. Last match I saw Manchester was two-zero up, the other team had scored one. Did you see that on TV? We won again.'

'Two-one then. Who againrst?'

'I dunno. But they won.'

Gran nodded wisely. 'Sor where's Tottnum, anywhere near Sorhor? Ah went there one tahm when ah were mutch yunger, when our Albeh were still alahv Patrick, butt ah dorn't think tha were born then.'

'No, I don't remember you ever being down south, Gran. He lives quite near Soho anyway. Have you really been there?' I was amazed.

'Ah've onleh been there once. Morst folk were raht mardy and citeh were loppy anall. Ah went to Buckinem Palace and Sorhor and that's enough for me,' she said bluntly. She liked it where she was. I could see Gran in Soho though, come to think of it. It's the only unique part of London; other cities have got their equivalents of Chelsea and Islington and even

Camden to some extent, but nowhere's got a place like Soho with it's mix of prostitutes, party-goers, Soho villagers and the street stench of sex and excitement in the air. Yeah, no wonder Gran had been there. Buckingham Palace must have been such a great disappointment.

She continued speaking to the carjacker. 'Tha bin en Lundun long?'

'Long enough to remember bins and smoking on the Underground.'

'Ah've lived int village long enough to 'ave lords of dead folk int address booke. Any rords, et's just job for tha oop 'ere?'

'Yeah.'

'Well, as folk sair orver Pennines, "Where there's muck there's brass".'

'I 'ope so. Ain't no other reason bring me up 'ere.' He really wasn't listening.

'Ah'm glad ah'm not starten out these days with amount of folk chasen after one job and there's nor securiteh offered by bosses. Ah did little bit en cotton mill en Mappelthripp, butt en them days lasses didn't work outside 'ome mutch. We ornleh 'ad one babeh to bring upp. Little bastad putt us off 'aven anehmore.'

It sounded awkward, Gran cussing her own son like this, not to me as I'd heard it all my life, but Bruce noticed it. 'What's this for you then, Granny Gron?' he asked, breaking the silence that was otherwise ready to snap itself. 'Just little holiday?'

'Aye Bruce,' she replied. 'Our Patrick's promised meh little brerk for munths. 'E's morst probbleh torld tha that doc told meh ah'm goen blarnd. Ah'd better looke while ah'm able.' I noticed her glance bravely at Bruce. 'Ah've lived a long lahf thus far an' ah've lived it 'ow ah've wanted. Ah've nor regrets. What ah do knor now is that there is a God or summit waiten for meh, waiten for us all. 'E's gonna give us review of our lahves when 'e takes us upp there, an' 'e'll tell us what fun 'e's 'ad watching us. Ah mean, 'e's made it worse for you yung folk. Now they're sayen everythen that's good is bad for tha. Dorn't gor int sun, dorn't eat tasteh grub, dorn't drink too mutch, even dorn't 'ave sex. Sor if tha dorn't do all this, what's point? Tha may as well be dead.'

Gran looked up, a mischievous twinkle in her eyes. 'An' that's why ah knor there's a God and 'e's got sense o' humour. 'E wants to see which lahf we choose. Ah'm looking forward to mah review as ah've dunn it just as ah pleased an' never 'urt a soul.'

'What if God's a she?' I asked Gran.

'Nor, God's defnetleh a blorke. If God were a she, world would be better than it bluddy well is!'

'You're not scared of dying then Granny Gron?' Bruce asked softly, tugging his beard as he spoke.

'Scared? Ah can't wert to see what bugger's got to sair to meh when 'e drags meh upp. Ah've lived a fur lahf, sor ah reckon ah'll be looked after.'

She paused to look at us all, one by one with those telling and knowing but fading eyes. 'Ah see it lahk this. Tha's 'ad night out and drunk and smorked ciggehs. At sum time, tha may be ont deathbed and remember one naht as top naht, then ont deathbed tha may think and recall that drink and that ciggeh – and now ah knor that seems so far awer for tha three, lahk it did for meh, not long since, butt stay with meh. Sor, if a friend gets tha a parnt of beer and gives tha sum ciggehs, are ther contributing to tha lahf or are they contributing to tha death? When tha lay dying, lahk ah might do soon, tha may be of two marnds which is only when tha realise who tha were. Some might think, thank God ah enjoyed lahf or others might think ah wish ah 'adn't 'ad all thorse drinks and ciggehs as now ah've got less lahf left. An' we worn't knor until that tahm comes. We worn't really knor who we are until we were.'

Gran looked at Bruce through her specs, before she blinked and leaned back keeping her eyes shut with the blink.

MEDIA IS HYSTERIA

T HE YELLOW LIGHT from streetlamps showed Gran's wrinkled face in the mirror, the lines around her mouth from forty-plus years of smoking and smiling, those on her forehead from a lifetime of struggle and strife. Next to her, big Bruce stared out at the road, twiddling his beard while he no doubt thought of tomorrow. Everyone was quiet, exhausted and hungry. We followed signs for Manchester, then Rochdale, and finally Littleborough which according to Bruce was the closest town to the Beloved Wood.

We slowed up outside The Angling Tavern, a pub that advertised rooms on a handpainted sign hanging by a hedge, and I quietly swung the motor into a small empty car park at the side that led to a further space round the back where I parked. It was an oldish white building, about a hundred years old, illuminated at the front by eerie white floodlights.

As we went for the door I looked back at the dark lake and had an uneasy feeling; Dead and his men weren't the sort of chaps that would give up. Not only would the deaths of three lads they'd been chasing uphold their fearsome reputation, it would enhance it. I wondered if they'd kill my gran too.

'Folk sair at bottom of watter is village that were fludded,' Gran whispered as we entered the pub and our eyes adjusted to the new brightness and fresh surroundings. There was a smell of sticky beer from the patterned carpet, a few framed old pictures of local streets and a non-descript cream wallpaper, so you could neither love it or loathe it. An open door led to the bar room and in front of us was a deserted reception.

'Ah don't know if owt's true,' Gran continued. ''Eard et when ah were just little. These days ah dorn't knor what to believe though. One day et's int 'papers that et's bad for tha to eat eggs and next a different 'paper says et's good.'

'Don't believe anything you see in media Granny Gron,' said Bruce. 'I used to be journalist and, believe me, if there's not a story to be had there's one to be made up.'

'So what's to do?' asked Gran, looking at Bruce.

'I suppose, just be aware of it,' he replied.

'Eh?' questioned Gran. '*Speak up chuck.*'

'Just be aware of it Granny Gron,' repeated Bruce, louder.

'*Eh, ah still can't 'ear tha,*' said Gran, rubbing an ear to try to clear it.

I leaned right up to her. 'Put your hearing aid in Gran, *like the doctors told you.*'

'*Well ah can 'ear tha now, can't ah.*'

'*Course you can Gran!*' I exclaimed. '*I'm practically putting my tongue in your ear. Try your hearing aid.*'

'*Ah left et en 'ouse,*' she shouted back.

'*Well you won't be able to hear us then,*' I said, loudly.

'Eh?' she said staring blankly at me, then Bruce.

'He said, *"You won't be able to hear us"*,' Bruce repeated, even louder.

'*Eh? Why does everyone speak sor quietleh these days?*'

'Forget it,' I said to Bruce as he made to speak again. 'She has these turns when she's tired.' I shrugged at Gran who stared back glumly.

We reached the reception desk, empty except for a blue A4-sized signing-in book, a yellow Cancer Research charity box and opposite a large mirror showing us what a strange sight we were. The only sign of life was the noise coming from a far corner of the bar room where a one-arm bandit was being played by someone grunting with the exertion.

'I thought you were a gardener,' I said to Bruce in a hushed tone while leaning over the counter to see if I could see anyone.

'That was before I became a journalist,' he replied, leaning over the counter too.

'Who'd you write for?' I asked him.

'Loads of newspapers and magazines, some television,' said Bruce. 'Freelance. But I had to leave media in end.'

I was interested, but distracted by the urgency for us to reach the safety of a locked room. 'Hold on,' I said to Bruce as I stepped away from the reception desk and went past Gran and the carjacker to look through to the bar room where I saw an old northern man wearing a flat cap and a beer belly kept in by braces. He was playing an old-style one-arm bandit, the ones actually with an arm.

'Hello,' I called out to him. He peered through what were clearly drunken eyes as he cranked the arm down.

'*Get lost lad!*' he bellowed, turning his attention back to the spinning oranges and lemons. 'Ah'm on flippin' winnin' streak. They can't throw me out *and neither can you*! Now bugger off!'

I returned to the desk. 'I thought northerners were supposed to be a friendly lot,' I said to Bruce.

'Well she seems to be,' he replied nodding to a white door marked 'Office'. 'It's just started. Listen.'

I cocked an ear and heard the unmistakable murmurs and moans of passionate sex.

'Sounds like people are having fun,' he said, grinning. 'Pennines have come alive.'

'This is fuckin' bullshit,' said the carjacker, stepping close behind me. I kept my eye on him in the mirror.

'You're lucky that Granny Gron can't hear a thing at moment or I'd have given you another cuff lad,' said Bruce, his smile fading and his voice rising to carry above the grunting old northern man and the groaning lovers as they started to get more frantic.

'Getting a bit nervous about tomorrow are we?' teased the carjacker, displaying his foolishly arrogant manner. He carried on baiting. 'Can't handle it, like you couldn't handle a job.'

'I could handle a job,' replied Bruce. 'But I didn't want anything to do with media. And I'll tell you why – if it'll get through your thick head, you'll understand why.' He looked threateningly at the carjacker who was fidgeting behind me. 'Everything in life, every action, every spoken word, every appearance, every decision, every thought can be reported,' announced Bruce sounding exasperated, even agitated. 'And also distorted. That's why I got out of media and dropped out from West. For me it was more like dropping in than dropping out. I dropped in to somewhere where I could walk around without having to hang head in shame at what I saw around me.'

The groaning from beyond the office door took on more of a yelping now and we could hear a table banging briskly to the lovers' beat. 'We're force-fed a diet of media fodder,' continued Bruce, looking even more threateningly at the carjacker. 'And journalists are under pressure from ad agencies, global pharmaceutical companies, PRs, marketing campaigns, political parties, weighted surveys, biased vox pops and old moneyed families through their editors to write what people read. People have forgotten how to think for themselves. They're no longer themselves. They're somebody else's self and most people are working against each other rather than for each other.'

'It's natural selection 'ippy,' snapped the carjacker. 'Survival of the fittest. You just can't handle the system. That's why you're such a drop-out.'

'There's nowt natural about system we live in,' counteracted Bruce, twisting to face the carjacker full on, but unaware of the carjacker's hand I watched in the mirror creeping behind my back towards the charity box. 'It serves a particular elite. It destroys potential of majority. Newspapers play a major part in this. Intrusion, inaccuracy, refusal to admit mistakes, under-representation of minorities, neglect of community by faceless companies, incitement to hate and tabloidisation of events.'

All of a sudden there came a loud thud from the bar room. '*Bugger it!*' yelled the old northern man as he hurriedly slotted in several coins and yanked the handle time after time; the banging and breathless yelps from the office now going ten times as fast as the yanking.

'Television, radio and newspapers can't wait for another OJ, Monica, Diana, Kosovo, or another random mass shooting,' continued Bruce his voice continuing to rise with the noise around us. 'Your mind has been produced by media and media is hysteria. In your mind's eye you have a media-created image of yourself and that combined with your inherent badness is why you are fucking scum that you are.'

The office sex was urgent now and those having it were getting turned on by the spontaneity of it, the girl's yelps being replaced by her deep-throated yells of 'Bastard!'. In the mirror I noticed Gran looking up at the ceiling blissfully unaware of the goings-on and from the carjacker's face next to her I saw he wasn't listening to Bruce at all. He was just throwing in comments to wind Bruce up and to distract us, but I was watching his fingers slowly grasp the charity box, which was unusually – as he'd obviously spotted – not chained down.

'It's known as free speech mate,' said the carjacker,

wrapping his slimy hand round the box. I got ready to grab him as soon as he started to slide it away.

'But free speech includes blatant lies,' Bruce said loudly. 'One journalist writes a rumour and rest follow. It's laziness. No-one can be bothered to check. If it's been written once and got away with, then why not? Then that rumour becomes reality. There's no law to it. I'll tell you why. Because owners of media make all laws now, bludgeoning both judge and jury to injustice. I call it "journlawism".'

By now, the old northern man was in a frenzy as he pulled the one-arm bandit's lever over and over followed by an aggressive curse of '*Bugger!*'. I saw a brass bell on the counter and started to ding it above the shrill sounds of pain and pleasure. Noises of the Pennine night started to take on a pattern of crank, whirr, ding! '*bugger!*', bang, 'bastard!' crank, whirr, ding! '*bugger!*', bang, 'bastard!' Soon the cries became so frequent and loud that they filled the air with just the sweet utterances of 'Bastard!' '*Bugger!*' 'Bastard!' '*Bugger!*' 'Bastard!' '*Bugger!*' 'Bastard!' '*Bugger!*'

'Before almost every story there's a rumour,' Bruce continued, having to shout now. 'After every scoop there's another rumour, wrapped in a fable inside a conspiracy theory. Media brings those rumours to life, makes them real. That's the rumour-fuelled society.' With that he stepped forward and punched the carjacker clean in the face, knocking his hand from the charity box and pole-axing him like a tall tree being felled. At that same moment the old northern man shouted with delirious delight as coin after coin was coughed up and simultaneously the girl was climaxing. '*Jackpot! Jackpot! Jackpot!*' the old northern man shouted. '*Bastard! Bastard! Bastard!*' the girl cried.

'Sounds like she's coming,' I said to Bruce, as I bashed a final loud ding which echoed away into the post-climax quietness.

'Bloody well hope so,' Bruce said as he stared down at the unconscious carjacker.

'Me anall,' said Gran, not changing her vacant look into thin air. 'Ah want to get *sum* sleep tonaht. At this rate that robben bastard on floor'll be onleh one who 'as aneh shut eye.'

LISTEN UP

THE GIRL, aged about twenty-five, and as red in the face as she was in the hair wandered into view from the office door which she locked behind her. She was smoothing a denim skirt and then pulling down her white shirt. Finally, just before she reached her side of the reception desk and allowed herself to look up she ran her fingers through her ruffled hair. She looked at me with the sexiest big blue eyes I could imagine before asking if she could help in a grating Liverpudlian accent, her throat obviously hoarse from her cries.

'Sore throat?' asked Bruce with a cheeky grin and she coyly nodded. Bruce leaned towards her, winking. 'Must be a bastard locked in that office, eh?'

Quickly she pushed the signing-in book towards us. 'Just the three of you is it?' she asked and we all enthusiastically nodded while discreetly glancing at each other and the knocked-out 'jacker who lay out of sight from the girl on our side of the desk.

We went through the procedure of signing false names and minutes later, after Gran had hankered for an unobtainable half of lager, she was tucked away. I went with Bruce who hoisted the carjacker over his shoulder to my room where I locked the door. We were on the ground floor which was not ideal, but it was the only rooms they had and I imagined waking up to Dead's scarred face pressed flat against the window...

'Same arrangements again Bruce?' I said, shaking the shivers from my back. He nodded wearily. 'Do you want to kip first or shall I?'

He opted first, so I asked if he'd mind if I went for five minutes. I had to call Ged. I walked down the corridor from our rooms, past reception and went outside. There was not a soul about in this isolated little place. Just a few hundred metres down the unlit road we'd arrived on I'd noticed a phone box, so I went inside, slipped a phone card in, dialled Ged's club office number and waited.

One ring, two rings, three rings... someone picked it up.

I spoke quickly. 'Hello Ge...' But shit, it was an answer machine. '*All right people. It's Ged's machine here at Penelope. Leave your greetings. Cheers!*' Beeeeeeeep.

'Ged, it's Pat. You there man? Ged! *Ged!* If you're there pick up the phone. It's urgent.' I listened, pressing the receiver to my ear, gripping the phone tightly as though it would somehow bring him to me. 'Okay Ged, I've got to be quick. It's Pat and I'm here at a pub called the Angling Tavern by Hollingworth Lake, near Rochdale. I'm in Room Two. Give us a call. Tonight. Now, if you can! Get the number from the operator. Otherwise... Cheers. Ged...'

I couldn't think what else I could say, so I pressed the next call button. My head went heavy and I leaned it forward, putting the phone receiver to my forehead, asking myself question after question: Who could I call? Who else is there? Is there any way we can save our lives? Who's out there who can help us? No-one, Ged's the only one who knows this mess, he's the only one who could act quickly enough and he doesn't even have a home phone – he virtually lives underground at that club. He was down there so often he was going to turn albino. The journey was getting sticky now, but hang on in there, there had to be something… Ged's mobile. Maybe, just maybe he's stood on the door of the club for once.

One ring, straight onto answer mode. '*Hi, this is Ged's streetphone. Leave a message and we'll speak soon.*' He must be downstairs as I suspected and out of reach of the signal. '*Leave your message now.*'

'Ged, it's Pat. I need some help. I'm at the Angling Tavern, near Rochdale. I need you to call me there as soon as you hear this. It's important. I'm in trouble. I'm going to Manchester Airport tomorrow, hopefully by noon. There's me and my Gran and another couple of passengers but they'll be all right. Gran and me need enough cash to fly to Dublin, get some space until this mess is sorted out. And I need someone to take your Saab back and all that's in it, so you can get rid of that fucking "weedkiller" and my life can get back to near-normal in a couple of months.' I listened for a few seconds in case he suddenly popped upstairs or something else came into my mind to say. But nothing did and I slowly put the receiver down.

My walk back to the Angling Tavern was grimly quiet.

When I got back to the room I rapped the three knocks we'd agreed on the door and Bruce opened it. A waft of sweet smoke hit me. Bruce was intently smoking a spliff and looking at the torn map of Beloved Wood he'd drawn. We didn't speak, we were too exhausted to talk.

Face down, fully clothed, on top of a bed, the carjacker was crashed out. There was another single next to him and about ten seconds later my head was on a pillow. I collapsed there sweating, wondering if Ged would get the message before praying myself into some sort of a clumsy slumber.

KNOCK KNOCK

I T WAS STRANGE thought Ged. The last people had left, including Sophie, hours ago, the club wasn't open tonight and yet someone was ringing the main door. He looked at the flyer for Purple Rinsed that he was about to work on until his wiredness led to tiredness and he could finally get some sleep.

It had been some after-show party, going on all day and the rest, or so he thought, but it was difficult to work out times with the state his head was in. The main door rang again and Ged placed the laptop out of harm's way under the chaise longue before going to see who was there, making a mental note to get the security camera fixed later.

He had to go up anyway to turn the lights off and set the alarms. It had been a good night, he thought, not just in love life and party terms but also in takings. Anyway, it was probably another late-night blagger who didn't know the club was shut tonight or even someone from the party who'd left something, sometimes someone.

He smirked to himself as he climbed the steps to the door recalling the couple of times that people had crashed out in strange places around the club only for their mates to return to retrieve them a few hours later when they'd realised they were missing someone. What a funny job he did. Still, he thought, it was better than a real one.

The ringing had stopped, now they were banging and knocking on the door. Ged got to the top of the steps and peered through the peephole: it was one of Dead's men, big lump with a crew-cut atop a head and neck the same width and dressed in a dark blue Burberry trenchcoat, but Ged couldn't quite remember his name; maybe it was Damon or something like that he thought. He'd have to tell him the after-show party was over. Then he thought again, his brain recovering a moment of reality. Shit, this is probably about Patrick he realised and there was no ducking out especially when you're talking about your best friend. His legs and head still felt hollow and weightless from the pill he dropped a while back, but the caller outside looked friendly enough. He undid the various bolts and turned a few locks.

'Hello,' Ged said in his usual amicable manner. 'It's Damon isn't it – how can I help you?'

The reply came not verbally but in the form of a barrel poking out through a hole in the visitor's trenchcoat pocket. The after-show party was just beginning for Dead's man judging by the expectant look on his twisted face. As Ged spotted the gun, he instinctively took a step backwards allowing the felon plus two more in dark suits who came from either side of the door frame – and were about the same width as it – to step inside.

The one with the gun motioned Ged down the steps which he carefully took backwards, not moving his eyes from those of the lump with the gun. At the bottom, Dead's man continued to usher Ged towards his office. The other two followed behind him.

'You should get that camera fixed outside. Now get in there,' he said, pointing to Ged's office. Ged pushed the door open and went inside. He was thinking on his feet but what could he do here? Nothing much and he realised this was the calling card of one angry man. One of the three slammed the heavy office door shut and, keeping the barrel pointed at Ged, the leader spoke in a harsh London voice that snarled and coughed violence. 'He who owes, where is he?'

Ged shrugged. It came so quickly the first thing he knew about it was the crunching noise on the side of his jaw. From down on the floor he looked up to the perpetrator, one of the lumps who stood towering above, the knuckleduster still on his clenched fist.

Ged rubbed his aching jaw. He must have just turned away in time or it would have been broken. Or more likely he thought, the punch hadn't been intended to bust his jaw or he wouldn't have been able to speak: these chaps could target hits more accurately than a guided missile – but with what felt like the same force. Ged managed to move his stiff jaw enough to mouth back to the three men that he didn't know Patrick's whereabouts.

'Have a good look around,' commanded the leader before looking down at Ged, the gun now on full view and pointing towards Ged's knee. 'And you, you cunt,' he spat, prodding Ged's knee and pressing his face in close. 'The name's Demon, not fuckin' Damon.'

Ged stayed on the floor keeping one eye on the gangster who rose up above him, still keeping the gun pointed at his knee, and another on his office which was getting ripped apart.

'My full name to you is Demon Ian,' stated the boss thug. 'You won't forget it this time.'

Ged watched as Demon's two beefcakes opened drawer after drawer scattering and looking at every piece of paper and flyer. He watched as they came across the night's takings still stuffed in an opened tin box in a drawer. The one who had found it looked over to Demon Ian and raised a queried eyebrow as he held some of the notes up. Demon Ian firmly shook his head at his man.

'Don't be so fuckin' stupid,' Demon Ian cussed at the one holding the money, before turning his attention back to Ged on the floor. He seemed smarter than the average meathead. 'You see,' he carried on, 'it's all logical. If Dead doesn't get what he asks for, he don't like it and he won't like us and he may cause us some hurt, either financial or physical and ain't a lot we can do about that. He's the big boss. So it's better we give you some hurt and get Dead what he wants. It's all logical in this business. Stand up.'

Ged edgily stood up, half expecting to be knocked straight back down again. Instead the leader nodded for both his men to go forward and Ged suddenly found himself with his nose slammed against the wall while his arms were held tightly behind his back. Demon Ian addressed his two men. 'That's enough of our time spent on a speculative search. Let's do our deed for Dead the proper way.'

Ged felt a tight coldness surround his wrists and heard the click of the handcuffs, then his ankles were pushed together before they were secured with a thick rope. Suddenly he was span round and shoved over the edge of the chaise longue so that he was on his arms, facing Dead's three men.

Demon Ian pressed the gun to his crotch.

'Now we hear this Patrick geezer is your best friend from school,' said Demon Ian, his manner becoming very vexed now. 'I mean, I know where my best friend from school is. Most people do. Do you?' He looked to the thug on his left, who nodded and then repeated the same procedure with the one on his right. 'See, everyone knows where their best friend from school is. You don't lose that friendship. You get invited to their engagement party, stag night, their wedding, even their funeral if they go first. You don't lose touch with a best friend from school. It's a lifetime thing. That's what a best friend from school is about. So tell us where yours is.'

'I wouldn't tell you even if I did know,' said Ged, feeling his fear start to be overtaken by anger. 'I'd rather he came to my funeral than I went to his. *That's* what a best friend from school is about.' Ged grimaced as Dead's crony pressed the barrel of the gun into his balls, turning it slightly so that it really twisted and dug in. They were already tender from the humping he'd been doing. Now he was in agony.

'Okay, tell Dead to give me a day or two. I can try to find him,' Ged hissed through gritted teeth. 'All I know is that he's on the road somewhere. But I don't know where. I haven't heard from him for a couple of days. He could be anywhere in Britain. Believe me.' Ged felt the barrel being twisted further, so much that it caused him to groan in sheer pain. He felt like he was going to pass out.

'Supposing I told you,' said Demon Ian, starting to relish his job now, 'that I'm going to kill you with this gun if you don't come up with something better than that. And what would you think if I told you there aren't any bullets in this gun.' Ged cried out loudly when a sharp pain hit him between his legs as the barrel was dug even more powerfully and deeply into his crotch crushing one of his balls against his inner thigh. Suddenly the agony eased slightly and Ged was able to look up through the tears of pain that had been brought to his eyes at Demon Ian and the other two big blurred figures before him.

'Oh,' said Demon Ian in mock surprise. 'Look, here's a bullet I've just found.' He held it out between thumb and forefinger in front of Ged's face. 'Take a good look at it. Nice craftmanship, it'll be the death of you. Take a good look at it.'

Ged closed his eyes. This was it. So far he'd avoided all this heavy shit in a business renowned for it, but now…

Suddenly all four of them were looking around and staring at the ringing phone. 'Who's that then calling at this time?' asked Demon Ian. 'Don't get it. Let's see. It might just be the man we're looking for.' Ged cringed; if it was Patrick he prayed, just don't say where you are, just don't…

'Ged, it's Pat. You there man? Ged! Ged! If you're there

pick up the phone. It's urgent.' Everyone listened, leaning their ears to the answer machine. *'Okay Ged, I've got to be quick. It's Pat and I'm here at a pub called the Angling Tavern by Hollingworth Lake, near Rochdale. I'm in Room Two. Give us a call. Tonight. Now, if you can! Get the number from the operator. Otherwise... Cheers. Ged...'*

'Classic timing,' said Demon Ian, with a smile at Ged before slotting the bullet into the gun and pointing it back at Ged's testicles. 'You boys, take that answer machine and smash the phone up. Do it quick, we need to get on the case and let Dead know.'

He looked over his shoulder as he watched them go to do as he said, but his face turned to dismay as one of the two lumps picked up Ged's mobile and threw it across the floor.

'No, not that you brainless moron,' he cursed. 'It won't even work down here. Fuck me, you idiot, don't you know a thing? Come on, let's go. Leave that where it is and smash the land phone up. That one!'

This time they got it right and one of them ripped out the answer machine while the other put the phone on the floor and clomped his size elevens on top leaving a pile of cracked plastic. 'Now, get outside you two,' ordered Demon Ian. 'Let's get the good news back to Dead.'

Demon watched the two thugs leave the room and pull the solid door shut, all the time pressing the barrel into Ged's sore spot. 'It's been good fun, hasn't it,' declared Demon Ian when the two of them were alone. 'When I heard you say that you didn't know where that friend of yours was do you know what my first thought was? Bollocks!' He sniggered at his pun. 'But that phone ringing and that message, well, you were saved by the bell. Saved by the bell.' He pulled the gun away and slipped it into his trenchcoat.

'You're lucky. Dead don't mind you,' he continued. 'In fact he quite likes you and your club which is why he told me to kill you only if we didn't find out where your mate is. I'm going to lock this door behind me and don't think about trying to get out.'

With that Demon Ian went to the door, switching the light off and sending the office into total darkness. He opened the door letting a shaft of light in and span around so his voice carried clearly to Ged. 'Make sure I'm on the guest list,' he said, adding just before he banged the door shut: 'I quite like it here.'

VICIOUS LONDON GANGSTERS PLAN MURDER ATTACK

DEAD CLOUTNER got into the motor. He sat in the front passenger seat staring ahead not saying anything. He shook his crew-cut ever so slightly. 'What's up Dead?' said another of the gang, a gangly sort in a dark suit, who was sat in the back.

'Heaven, that's what's up. And them boys're going to be at the Pearly Gates tryin' to persuade Peter to let them in when we see them,' grated Dead Cloutner matter-of-factly. 'That's what's up. I feel for them lads now. They ain't got long left. An' you know that.'

'Do we know where they are Dead?'

Dead just stared ahead. 'Too fuckin' right.'

The gang member in the back had been working for Dead for years now. He knew this mood, the quiet before the storm: Dead was thinking, building himself up for the kill, the veins on his thick neck pulsing up and down, his temples clenching and unclenching, the scarlet scars on his scalp positively throbbing.

'Where are we going Dead?' asked Double-barrelled Dan from under his moustache in a broad east Eton accent. Dead took a deep breath before putting his mobile on the dash and smoothing down his jacket.

'We 'ad a stroke of luck, lads,' he announced slowly, before pausing to wet his dry, cracked lips. 'Demon Ian 'as followed up my request to 'ave a word with Ged Nealson, the black geezer who owns that club by the bridge. Ged said he knew nothin' of where that prick with my Charlie was, which he dint at the time.'

He paused again, jutting his jaw out into the distance of the passing scenery. He wet his lips once again before continuing. 'But Demon Ian's on for a pay rise cos he checks out Nealson's answer machine and finds there's only a message from pretty boy blue saying that he's staying in Room Two at the Angling Tavern, a boozer by a lake called Hollingworth, near to Manchester.'

He paused again, his villains hanging on every theatrical word. 'I'm worried for the lad now. I'm worried for all three of them. I dunno what I might get up to when I see 'em. You remember that slag what run off with a bit of my Charlie for 'is personal. He ain't running anywhere anymore.' His front teeth clenched as he gobbed out through bitter lips. 'It's difficult to run when you've 'ad your feet bashed for an hour with my brass hearing aid. Toes really fuckin' crunch.'

Double-barrelled Dan, the BMW's driver, looked at Dead smiling to himself, before choosing his words carefully. 'This lot, they're going to end up dead, Dead. I can sense your feelings.'

'Too fuckin' right. I'm going to work that ugly fucker so much he'll end up lookin' fuckin' handsome!'

'Are we going to use tools Dead?' asked Double-barrelled Dan, relishing the thought of a spot of shooting.

Dead nodded slightly with his teeth still clenched in a maniac's smile and his eyes wild like a dog's going in for the kill. 'You know that. I'm gonna blast him so fuckin' much that his whistle'll end up looking like it's been worn by Robinson fuckin' Crusoe.'

One of the men in the back pointed to a spot on a map. 'Got

it, Dead. If Double-barrelled Dan puts 'is foot darn we can be there in a couple of 'ours.'

'D'you 'ear that DB?'

'Yes Dead. Loud and clear.'

'We should be there at dawn. The cocks are gonna be crowin',' Dead grated his huge rough and ready palms together at the same time as grinding his teeth.

'How we gonna play it Dead?' asked Double-barrelled Dan as he switched on the ignition, still thinking of getting his hands on his shotgun and blasting away.

Dead Cloutner pulled out his Beretta. He looked down the barrel before slipping it into his outside right jacket pocket, his hand fondling the trigger. 'Like I said, I dunno what I might get up to when I see 'em. All of a sudden,' he said bolting upright and butting his head forward, 'Dead is alive. An' you know that.'

THE MEN WHO WOULD KILL US

I WAS SCARED NOW. As night became day I knew there was little chance of Ged calling back. There were no phones in our rooms, but I'd been straining to hear the slightest noise and I'd have heard the reception's phone ringing. I hoped Ged was okay.

We were away later than I'd wanted. I didn't realise that Gran wouldn't be able to hear us knocking – deaf when it suits her and a lay-in suited her – but we'd eventually managed to get her up and us out of the place without paying. I'd realised Gran obviously wouldn't be able to stay at the hotel while we did our business up at the stones, so she'd have to wait in the car.

We were still yawning, stretching and peering into the early-morning light when I started the engine and quietly edged the car out of its parking space at the back. Gran, who had been given the privilege of sitting in the front now, was the first to wake to the day.

'Eeeeh, et were ever so exsahten doen runner,' she croaked, her vocal chords still wishing they were in bed. 'Ah wish ah'd dun more exsahten things like that when ah were nipper. Morst exsahten thing ah did after ah were married were catch buzz to shops. Et were so easeh to get awer wi'it anall.'

'We're not away yet Gran,' I said sleepily. 'Let's wait until we're at least out of the car park before we start talking about getting away with it.'

'Can we 'ave classical music on?' she asked, leaning towards me. 'Ah love et first thing int morning.' I reached forward to press the stereo's tuner until it came across the classical station and we were rewarded with a bit of Friedrich Witt. Apart from his mumbled quip about loving it first thing in the morning, Bruce was quiet, wrapped in thoughts, which was not surprising considering what the day would reveal, whether years of waiting had been a waste. I had my doubts by now, but didn't want to let him know. I didn't fancy his chances, but we were going to give him the chance to find out, so long as the gang didn't rear their ugly heads or the petrol didn't run out on us. Or both.

The 'jacker was hunched sulkily, occasionally cupping and gently touching his red and purple eye. I cocked an ear to Witt's meanderings. I knew my classical composers. Mostly, it's what I'd listened to in the flower shop as punky stuff and that didn't go down so well with most of my customers. Then I see them.

Or to be precise, I see their red BMW first and then the four big bastards in the car for just as we turn out left, they're pulling up and now we sit facing each other.

Dead Cloutner looks up from the front passenger seat where he's directly opposite me, his right hand tucked in his outside right jacket pocket, his eyes wide as though he's been hypnotised and his lips snarling like a murderer's, which he is. To his right, Double-barrelled Dan, also in a suit jacket, but slimmer and younger with thick swept jet-black hair and his moustache almost curling at the edges stares back in bewilderment at Gran. Behind them, two other cronies lean to get a look at us, as startled as we are.

I hear the carjacker curse behind. Well man, too late now. We gotta go, go like the wind, get past these barking mad dogs, just get round them and away. I'm having a fit of the mind like stones vibrating under a fast-moving inter-city train, my thoughts flailing around my head like a man trying to wriggle from a hangman's noose.

Bruce shouts through the noise of the straining engine: 'Turn around and go! They'll shoot if we don't go now! *Now!*' It's a rough call. There's no way that we can go fast enough in reverse to get away, and yet the time it takes to turn around will slow us down even more. The road's narrow and penned in on the left side by a high dry-stone wall and to our other side after a narrow grassy verge is the icy-cold lake lapping at our edges. But there's no other choice. We have to risk it. If we don't move off in five seconds we won't have a fucking chance. Five seconds or we're dead.

I swing out sharply to the right, angling into a frantic, backwards U-turn as I shift into reverse, then first. The gears make a hideous, grinding noise, the boot clatters into the dry-stone wall while the back wheels jump to the edge of the road, and hit some gravel, and then we're spinning, revving without traction as the car groans and shakes.

It takes a second or two before the tyres catch hold again, and when we roar away with our noses pointing in the right direction, their guns are coughing behind us. One bullet snags my wing mirror, cracking my face right between the eyes as I look back at them. Steering like a maniac, I'm already shifting into third when – chicckoooooooo! – another bullet bounces off the bonnet. The carjacker lets out a howl and my hands fly off the steering wheel in shock. The car bucks off the road, careering out of control, bouncing into a bushy hedge only to bounce back again allowing me to get a grip and get us back on track.

Straight behind me, the carjacker and then Bruce next to him are curled and next to me Gran is hunched down, her hands at the end of a rigid pair of arms grip the seat edge so tightly that her fingernails are tearing into the material. We're being hunted again, chased like a wild horse as we gallop along the road round the lake.

In my rear-view I see their motor suddenly screech to a halt and one of them jump out from the back before it's off after us again, two silencer barrels pointing out the windows. The one who's jumped out turns back and runs – it looks like the hotel is about to get some enquiries. Dead's head pops out the front passenger side window and he takes aim behind the barrel. Now I'm waking up.

I spot a red and white flag of England fluttering atop a wooden scout hall. Lucky for us, there's no other people on the roads at this early hours' time as we complete a lap of the lake, motoring it past the pub where we've just met our pursuers. We're making space on them, this Saab shifting superbly, but our fuel is low and I have to make sure we turn off when we reach the one road that leads from the lake to the Beloved Wood.

Bruce is peering over the top, intrigued by the silence of the shooting, but the carjacker remains curled as tight as he can and Gran remains hunched. She's the first to speak up. 'What's rush chuck?' she asks, underplaying the morning's near-death experience.

'Being followed,' I reply, keeping my look firmly out front.

'Ah'm not bluddy blarnd yet!'

'We're being followed, Gran' I repeat, concentrating hard on the road and the turn-off we cannot miss. 'There's some guys after us for something we didn't do. I thought we'd lost them, but it appears we haven't. Sorry Gran, we're going to have a bit of an adventure. I'll explain it all later.'

'Oooooh, 'ow raht exsahten. Ah won't put mah nose int other folk's business, so ah dorn't care what tha's been playen at. Ah know tha's a decent lad, so ah know tha never do folk wrong.' She leans back and slowly clicks her seatbelt in and around her. 'Ah sumtahms feel like ah missed out on lahf by spenden all tahm int village. Et remarnds me of wartahm, this does pet, all this shooten. Mind tha dorn't crash though. Eh chuck?' She looks back behind her, her frowns folding on her old face like a wet sponge being squeezed.

It's typical of Gran that she's the calmest of the lot. 'Keep wick. Looks lahk we're losen them, Patrick,' she says before quickly changing the subject. 'Bah way, does tha ever 'ear from Julia?'

'Only in my head, Gran,' I reply after I've screeched the tyres into the sharp right that will take us, if we can keep far enough ahead, to the woods.

'What about Ged?'

'I hope to see him very soon Gran. I hope we all do.'

'Luvleh blorke 'e is,' notes Gran to me. I wondered if he'd heard my message and if he was all right. I had an uneasy feeling...

I look out in front, my eyes are watching our route as carefully as if we are climbing a winding mountain path. 'We're heading the way you told me earlier,' I shout to Bruce through the straining noise of the engine, constantly checking my cracked wing mirror through the shards to see how far the BMW is behind. 'There's the hill up there Bruce,' I continue, indicating through the windscreen at a rise in the landscape looking like the profile of a giant green sleeping goddess with a thick cluster of trees growing and stretching back from the head, growing in such a way that it appears as though her mouth is slightly agape. Welcome to the Beloved Wood.

As we swerve round a tight curving bend, I check behind again, expecting to see the red BMW loom into sight behind us, but it doesn't. I glance down at the petrol gauge: in the red. I put my eyes up ahead, concentrating, just glancing in the mirror as we come out of the bends that run through this hilly road.

The new day's brightness was getting to my tired eyes now and I checked the sky, the same sky that Julia had taught me to see. It was an all-encompassing cloud pulled over our heads like a colossal dome-shaped grey cover. I got my sunglasses, mirrored Oakleys, from the pocket in the side of the door next to me and slipped them on, then directed my sight to Bruce, realising that now he couldn't see my eyes in the rear-view mirror, instead seeing a reflection back of himself.

There was silence in the car, a kind of aftershock I suspect, although the carjacker had finally come out from his protective ball, while Bruce looked between where the BMW might appear and the ever-nearing Beloved Wood. Gran just sat still, dealing calmly with the situation as older people do and looking all the while at her picture-postcard Pennines scenery.

So we motored on for a couple of miles further and further into the lonely Pennines like this and still there seemed to be no sign of the red BMW. I couldn't think why, unless they had crashed. Or knew where we were going.

'The gang seem to have gone now, disappeared into thin air,' noted Bruce, looking out the back and then gazing at the massive hill that we had to climb to reach the Beloved Wood and all that it held for us up there. Gran looked up at it too and touched my arm with her old hand. It felt cold as she gently squeezed my forearm and let go, still directing her gaze to the large clump of trees. The carjacker just stared out of the back window now, not letting his pinky eyes from the twisted route that his life was taking.

I put my foot down some more as Mozart blared out from the radio, blared out as though he'd written that tune for us to speed-drive to along those small winding roads being pursued by the men who would kill us.

'Aye, that's Beloved Wood, upp there,' said Gran pointing as we drew closer and looking to each of us in turn, her voice a combination of awe and fear.

'I think you should stay in the car while we go up,' I said to her. 'It looks a bit far Gran. We'll only be gone for half an hour.'

'Gi'ower chuck! Ah could manage et. Butt ah'm not goren upp there aneh rords. Tha wouldn't get meh upp there if tha told meh ah'd get yung again. There's summit queer upp that 'ill.'

'Okay Gran, we'll be quick anyway.'

She looked at me through her watery blue eyes in the mirror. 'An' tha beware anall. Just beware.'

Gran's words reverberated round my head. What could we find up there? What *would* we find up there? Would we ever come back from the Beloved Wood?

FROM USA TO THC

'A BAD OMEN, perhaps we shouldn't go up there,' I thought. But no, we're in this together. That's me, you, hippy Bruce, Gran and *him*. Gran had been sitting thoughtfully. 'Were ther real guns them blorks 'ad?' she asked, and I nodded sagely.

'Were ther Ammurcans?' she asked, frowning between her slight eyebrows.

'No Granny Gron. They're from London,' Bruce explained soothingly. 'Unfortunately, guns are everywhere these days if you want them.'

'Not in mah village! When et comes to ey lads ey, et's Ammurca's fault isn't it?' Gran said, looking round to Bruce for confirmation of her belief.

'Possibly. Parts of Britain's like a small America now,' he answered. 'And there's certainly a lot of guns out there. I've been to New York, Miami, LA, Dallas and Washington, and yeah, there's guns everywhere. It's in their constitution, right to have guns. We have to remember though that it was British and other Europeans that went over there in first place with guns. But it's become worse and yeah, Granny Gron, what's bad over there often comes over here.'

'And what's good anall?' asked Gran. Of course, she had her own opinions, but I think she was interested in hearing our modern views on the world. I checked the shards: as the hill loomed larger up ahead, there was still no sign of the red BMW behind. Where were they? I knew they wouldn't have just given up like that, not when Dead had come this far away from London in person. Oh, he wanted the prize now. He wanted to kill us badly, me first.

'Coke,' piped up the carjacker, smirking.

'Coke?' asked Bruce despairingly. 'You're mad man! I'm going to –'

'Coke,' the carjacker loudly repeated. 'Coca-Cola. In my opinion, it's the best thing to come out of America.'

'You're entitled to opinion,' said Bruce, while looking at him with perplexed anger. 'No-one can say an opinion's wrong. Misguided perhaps. I'm sure some of their medical developments, in treatment of HIV or cancer for instance, are more beneficial than Coca-Cola.'

'You telling me you've never drank Coke then?' retorted the carjacker.

'Only when I were in Latin America and couldn't drink unpurified water. Only when I had no choice.'

'See then, they got Coke everywhere, all over the world.'

I was edgy here – just the mention of the word, even in a different context, setting me on full alert – but Bruce was already diffusing any potential trouble. 'In Guatemala City they sell you Coke in clear plastic bags with a straw,' he said.

The carjacker sat up, actually excited at something. 'You're joking!'

'It's only bottles of Coke out there,' continued Bruce. 'You get money back on bottle like they used to do here years ago. But people are so poor they miss out need to bring bottle back. They knock deposit price off and serve it in these little plastic bags with straws in.'

'Must be lords of cancer then from plat-stic,' commented Gran glumly.

'Don't know about that Granny Gron.'

'What about Pepsi?' asked the 'jacker, still extremely excited.

'Pepsi comes in goldfish bowls,' Bruce said seriously. 'It's only way they'll serve it so air can get at it. It contains ingredient that Coca-Cola doesn't that's against both Mayan Indian and Catholic religions, two religions that make up city.'

'You're joking!' The 'jacker was sat upright and staring in wonder at Bruce. 'How do people carry Pepsi then without spilling it then?'

'You see loads of people walking around with goldfish bowls balanced on their heads. Full of Pepsi.' I looked in the rear-view mirror and caught Bruce stifling a smile as he pretended to look out of his side window.

'You're joking ain't you 'ippy?'

Bruce turned to face the carjacker. 'Of course I am,' he said matter-of-factly. 'It's all rubbish except that Mayans and Catholics do make up city's religions. It's just a rumour I made up.'

Stung by his own stupidity, the carjacker mumbled some curses aimed at us three as we chuckled at him before he slumped back in the seat.

'Don't worry 'ippy. I've already got you back,' the 'jacker said, before turning to stare out of the window, a satisfied smugness about himself.

We were just a couple of minutes away from the nearest point to park before we climbed the hill. We had to find a secluded spot so that Gran was safe enough while she waited. There was only about an hour or so until Bruce was due to meet his ex. Gran could keep an eye out for her down at the bottom of the hill, but there looked like there were hundreds of ways to get up to the top, so we'd have to get up there quickly.

'You be all right in the car Gran?' I asked.

'Aye course I will,' she'd replied. 'Daft bugger!'

Well, I laughed at that. I remember thinking: 'She's right. Dead Cloutner, from the old school of gangsterism, would never touch a granny.'

As the day grew lighter, we passed a disused canal with

some cows sitting down in a field by the side of it. We were quite far into the Pennines now and they were stunning, a small blackened church with a twenty-plot graveyard and dry-stone walls surrounding it the only sign that humans had ever lived in this part of the world. Half a dozen white sheep ate grass in the next field, and I recalled Gran telling me how even the Pennine sheep's creamy white coats had been blackened from the polluting mills of yesteryear.

Then, as we swing another left-handed corner I ask Bruce if he's got his map. 'We're nearly there Bruce, get it ready.'

'I'm just… just looking for it man,' he answers, worry in his warbling voice. 'I'm sure I put it back in my pocket, this one. It's been there all along.' I glance in the mirror and see Bruce going through each pocket, then looking round on the floor, the sweepingly loud classical music from the radio matching his frantic searching. He's the most worried I've seen him, almost as though he's a different person; his eyes dart about, and he bites his lip as he frantically pats all his pockets, before, finally, he looks up. 'It's gone. It must have dropped somewhere.'

'Are you sure?' I ask urgently.

'No, hold on!' Bruce says, perking up. 'I definitely put it back there, in my back pocket, first thing this morning. I remember because it finally started to tear where crease has been folded so often. Are you sure you didn't take a look at it, Patrick?'

'Never once had it in my hands,' I reply, still checking for the BMW in my mirror. We really seemed to have shaken them off for sure now, but still I couldn't figure out what they were planning. I knew something was wrong and I was about to find out just how bad things were for us.

Bruce turns his attention to the carjacker who's still sulking. 'What about you?' *He* just shakes his head and rubs his nose with his grubby fingernails.

'Are you sure?' asks Bruce accusingly.

'Ah saw 'im wi' scrap of pairper this morn,' croaks Gran from beside me, her old voice still taking its time to wake up to the new day. 'What were that then?'

Suddenly, Bruce grabs the carjacker, his huge palm entirely surrounding the carjacker's skinny neck. 'If you've f... if you've taken it, I'll squeeze the life out of you.' Bruce puts an extra squeeze on, joining his huge hands together to throttle the carjacker even more.

The carjacker's choking and puts a hand up trying to pull Bruce's mass of hands from his neck, his weak fingers clawing at Bruce's strong thumbs, trying to bring them down. They don't budge. The terrified 'jacker puts his other hand up trying to signal something while spluttering.

'Www...w... ait,' he chokes. Bruce slackens his grip, then looking at Gran, pulls his hands away. Gran sits unfazed, staring ahead at the Beloved Wood, swirling her tongue around her dentures as though nothing has happened.

'Okay,' says the carjacker, glaring at Bruce with all the considerable hatred he can muster. 'Okay 'ippy.' He's taunting Bruce, a new confidence found in his voice and body posturing: he knows Bruce shouldn't have made those moves in front of Gran and won't make them again. 'I took it,' continues the 'jacker. 'I left it on the reception this morning. That's when the old bag in front saw me with it. I told you you'd pay for hitting me, 'ippy.' I flash a dirty look at him, but he's too happy with himself to notice.

'Go on,' coaxes Bruce, returning to his usual calm now. I check the mirror again. Still no sign of the BMW, but I'm worried about our fuel situation. I've never driven this car before Ged lent it to me, so I don't know if the red on the fuel indicator means it has a few miles left, no miles or loads of miles. I have a disturbing feeling that we are going to find out: the Saab doesn't feel to be firing on all four, something's not letting it fly as it should, like something is dragging us back.

The carjacker continues, getting cockier. 'It wasn't an

accident. I took it and left it cos I'm fed up with all this. I reckon Dead Cloutner is my best chance now. I want him to find it. I was praying for them to show up and they did and I reckon the one that got out will be finding that map about now. Dead Cloutner and his gang will be on their way to meet us. And when I meet them, I'll offer them a deal on the cargo. I'll get a cut and tell them what really happened to me. I'm like one of them really. Now you can't meet your bird. Or you can, but they might meet her first, ha ha! See, it doesn't work out if you mess with me.'

'You're a fool,' states Bruce, keeping his cucumber and echoing my sentiments. 'Only cut they'll do with you will be across your rib cage. And in any case, I can remember where stones are. I've looked at map for so long.'

Then Bruce takes hold of the carjacker's skinny shoulders in his huge hands, and leaning right up to his shocked face whispers something in the carjacker's ear.

I couldn't hear what Bruce said at the time, but all I know is that I will never forget how that carjacking cat turned white and froze, almost like he'd been told he was dead.

Bruce moved away from him, then spoke again. 'Don't be scared of "What if?", just be scared of "What is". Understand me now?'

The carjacker just looked at me with a face of fear.

'What's goen on?' Gran asked, staring at the carjacker.

'I'll tell you later Gran,' I answered. 'Just stay with us.' I didn't have a clue what was going on between those two.

'Not fussed aneh rords,' she shrugged. 'Ah trust tha.'

All along it had seemed out of character for Bruce to be so aggressive towards the carjacker. But then everyone who is capable of love – so that is everyone – is capable of hate too. For some, having hate for someone or something reinforces what they love and enhances the identity they have created for themselves. So an Indian may hate a Pakistani, a Scotsman an Englishman, a capitalist a communist, a Celtic fan a Rangers supporter, and vice versa. So Bruce, brimming with love, hated the carjacker who was consumed with hate. And how the 'jacker hated that hippy.

Bruce leaned forward. 'Does anyone have light?'

I pressed the car lighter in.

'Is that only light we've got?' he asked and I nodded before shifting down to second for a turning, and then back to fourth when we were pointing straight in the new direction. The air around was awkward.

'I need some spliff,' sighed Bruce. 'If that's only light we've got it will have to be a grass one. And I've only got super-skunk left. Do you mind if I smoke Granny Gron?'

Gran shrugged from the front, not knowing what Bruce was going to smoke. 'Do as tha pleases,' she answered.

I noticed in the mirror that the red BMW was still not around. Then I saw Gran looking back at Bruce's rolling operation. She watched as he put his legs together before placing a king-size Rizla skin in the trough created between his giant thighs. He reached in his front left jeans' pocket to get a blue pouch containing his tobacco and a plastic cash bag of lime green and red skunk buds.

'Ah had an idea once,' chuckled Gran. 'Ah were goen to sell disporsable lahters, through mail order. Folk'd send meh fifteh pence for twenteh disporsable lahters. When ah received money ah'd send them out twenteh matches – well, they're disporsable lahters! Dorn't suppors ah'll be able tado scam now ah've told everyone. Et were just joke really.' She shyly chuckled to herself, causing a cough to jump forward in her throat, cleared it, then looked up and smiled, before staring back at the cone-shaped joint which Bruce was just finishing off with a filter.

Then Gran realised that Bruce's roll-up was no normal roll-up.

'Can ah try sum?' she asked Bruce, looking at the joint he held. 'Et's that marrehwanna stuff int et? Ah 'ear about et on wireless all tahm.'

Bruce looked back at Gran as he took the light from me, then he looked to me in the rear-view with a question on his expression. I simply looked at the road turning in front of us. Gran was in her eighties and I wasn't about to make any decisions on her behalf. I glanced back in the rear-view mirror to see Bruce nodding to her as he lit it up and took a couple of deep drags that made the embers glow red-orange.

'Here are,' he said, passing the spliff to Gran after a few tokes which filled the car with a thick cloud of strong-smelling smoke like that of burning damp nettles.

Even the carjacker looked to see what Gran did. And as Bach blared from the radio and we roared, at the age of eighty-four Granny Gron had her first drag on a joint thus taking a step into our modern Western world's culture. She continued taking small clandestine tokes at its filter as though she was sipping a hot cup of tea through a delicate china cup with the smoke fuming off like thick steam curling upwards from the end of a boiled kettle's spout.

'Ah packed en smorken about twenteh year agor,' she croaked as she let the smoke out through her nostrils. 'An' that feels bluddy t'riffic.' She took another couple of drags, a bit deeper this time and then flustered off into a spluttering cough. She held the joint back out to Bruce while still coughing.

'You all right Gran?' I asked.

'Aye,' she replied as the splutters died down. 'Ah'm raht as rairn. So what's that supporsed...' she grinned. Then giggled. 'What's that... eeeh ah can't bluddy remember what ah were sayen.' She stopped giggling and moulded her tiny frame into the seat, a vacant look spreading on her wrinkled face.

Bruce leaned back as he inhaled, a smile, then a huge grin spreading across his face. Outside it had been windy for a few minutes now, the light had gone gloomier and shadows darker as stormy-looking clouds built up. At the top of the hill I could see the Beloved Wood's trees swaying like a packed terrace of footie fans surging forward, then back again, with the excitement of the whirlwind action.

The first few drops of rain landed on the windscreen, small streaks at first, but soon replaced by larger drops and more and more of them. I put the windscreen wipers on and took a left up a small mud track. We wound and bumped along the track as I looked for a place to park the car out of sight. Up above, on top of the hill, the Beloved Wood was lashing about so much now that it looked like some of the trees would break free from their roots and fly off jerkily into the stormy skies, like umbrellas tearing from someone's grip on a stormy day in town.

'Ah feel bit laht-'eaded,' whispered Gran, her words and eyes both turned lazy.

'It's all right Granny Gron. It's normal,' Bruce stated calmly. 'But we need classical music off. We need something a bit mellow and full of bass for Granny Gron to get full-on THC effects. Got any reggae?'

'What's THC?' asked Gran, alarmed.

'Tetrahydrocannabinol.' It rolled off Bruce's tongue.

'Eh?' startled Gran, a touch of paranoia creeping from behind her ears.

'Don't worry. It's more natural than most food that people eat these days. It's the stuff in cannabis that's making you feel relaxed,' explained Bruce. 'That's got quite a lot in.' She seemed satisfied enough and the stuff they were smoking did smell extremely strong. 'I know,' grinned Bruce, sinking deeper into his seat. 'At start of that ambient tape there's a track by Scientist. Then there's a bit of Love from *Forever Changes*. Best album ever made and it's my lucky tape.'

'Do you think she's going to show?' I asked, trying to disguise my doubts.

'We'll see,' replied Bruce before shooting a daggers look at the carjacker who had been very quiet since Bruce had had a word in his ear. I was intrigued as to what he'd said, but didn't feel it was something I could ask in front of Gran. Whatever it was it had scared that clueless Cool Cat witless, not that he'd had much wits about him in the first place.

'I had a dream last night,' said Bruce, his eyes focussed on something beyond the end of his nose. 'Us four were driving along, and on edge of road was a naked woman. Hitchhiking, without a stitch on. Her body were tanned and curved and she held her right arm casually out with thumb sticking up. We went by her. We went right by, without even slowing. A minute later further down road, she were there again. But each time we just went straight past her. I woke up sweating like an old sock, man.'

'What do you reckon it meant?' I asked him.

'Not sure.'

'She's dream that tha's goen to miss,' said Gran, slightly anxiously. 'She were there, exporsed, and tha just couldn't stop to help lass. Ah'm sorry chuck, butt that weren't good dream. Et were bad dream.'

Bruce focussed away from the spot where he'd been staring and looked over to firstly the carjacker and then Gran. 'You're right Granny Gron, maybe she were just a dream.' Gran knowingly nodded at Bruce.

I rewound Bruce's tape and pressed play. I checked Gran and noticed that she was having a bit of trouble with her false teeth. She was pushing them back in, but they didn't seem to be sitting on her gums, then she started to giggle to herself and this made the task even more difficult. Bruce, who'd seen her struggling as well, leaned forward.

'Let me help Granny Gron,' he said, after he'd stubbed the joint out in the door's ashtray. Leaning forward through the gap in the seats, Bruce put his thick forefinger on her front teeth and pushed them back in. Gran opened her smiling mouth and they stayed there.

They started to laugh to each other as Scientist's deep, dubby bass vibrated from the speakers. Bruce leaned back and rocked his head to the beat. Soon it moved even more loosely on his shoulders because the car was bumping from side to side as we crossed an uneven grassy field. I'd turned off the mud track and headed towards what looked like an old shepherd's hut, now dilapidated with only three weathered walls standing. The rain was lashing down even harder now, the wipers on full speed not clearing it at all properly for a full vision out front. The carjacker just stared out the side of his window, his face still frozen in terror like someone who had got in the way of the lava. Gran was rocking in time to the reggae's bassline as well now.

'This music sounds lahk best music ah've ever 'eard,' she bellowed, her face a mixture of bemusement and bewilderment. Bruce's eyes shut as he was carried away on some jointy journey, a spliffy sojourn, a blunted beano, a THC trip through the mind fantastic. Who knows what thoughts ran through Bruce's head, but they certainly kept him occupied and full of enthusiasm for life. With his eyes still shut and his head still rocking and rolling, Bruce drawled a question to Gran about her courting days.

'How did you used to date in your day Granny Gron?' he asked her.

'We used to 'ave dances in orld 'all by church,' answered Gran, eyes shut as her memory took her back sixty or seventy years. 'Started int afternoon and were finished by eight, narn int summer. So we 'ad to act quickleh if we were courten'. They were grand, butt ah don't get out that mutch these days.' A great big smile formed on her face. 'When ah were yunger mind, ah were a laht rooker, radishing even if ah ser sor meself and ah 'ad my morments, but there's 'ardleh nowt to get thrilled for now. Before ah met Patrick's grandad, our Albeh, ah lived a bit though ah can tell tha.'

Gran was off, back decades, her imagination enhanced by the skunk, but her concentration suffering a bit. 'Ah remember meeten this raht educated blorke once. 'E 'ad raht decent professional job, ah think 'e were sum sort of financial annihilist or summit. Aneh rords, 'e... where were ah? Oh aye, 'is celery were flippen massive. 'E were from Manchester and called... eeeh ah can't think now. Ah think et were 'arold or summit. 'E were from Manchester. 'E were raht posh, ever sor extinguished. Any rords he used to buy meh lords of gifts, on impulse, nuthen planned. Ah called 'em "splurchases". 'E used to get meh corsets and brassieres, stockens with line upp back, all sort of neurotic underwear. An' ah remember 'e were raht sexeh, a real bed-rodied lover. 'E were from Manchester. Can't think what 'is name were.'

Bruce was in stitches behind me, a combination of his absurd highness and Gran's malapropisms.

'Gran, stop getting carried away now,' I said as we pulled up round the side of the old stone hut, the rain pelting down even heavier than before. 'I think you might be a bit affected. You keep getting your words mixed up.'

I turned off the engine and immediately as the wipers stopped, the windscreen was awash with water flowing down it like we were under a car wash. 'Looks like this is the end of the road,' I said, turning to the carjacker. 'Do you like the Pennines then?'

He ignored me, but couldn't ignore Gran as she turned to laugh at him and mimic me, almost singing in a high-pitched voice like a batty witch: 'Lookes lahk this is end of rord for tha,' she wailed. 'Lookes lahk this is end of rord for tha. Et lookes lahk this is end of rord for tha, lookes lahk this is end of rord for tha.'

The carjacker was mesmerised by her, but it was putting the frighteners into me. 'Ssshhhh Gran, please,' I urged and she said it once more before turning to face the front and laughing her head off to herself. We'd reached cracking point, we were one step away from one of us going totally crazed – Bruce had lost the map, the carjacker was a lost cause, I'd lost our way a few times and Gran had simply lost it.

'Et were our densiteh to be together. Ah might 'ave married 'im 'cept for our different classes,' smiled Gran, simply talking out loud in her stoned state. 'An' 'e were already married. When ah found that out ah were raht shocked - et were a tapestry of justice, ah tell tha. If we'd bin caught out, in them days we'd borth've bin in sheepdip. Ludicrous. Aneh rord, ah were too young to get 'itched. Ah mean, ah were ornleh sixteen! Eeeh, when tha gets orlder tha has sor maneh good memorehs et can make tha sad.'

There was no stopping Gran now: she was out of her tree. 'Then there were that raht funny one ah met at Christmas naiveteh play. This were when ah were int late teens, just after Mum 'ad passed away an' ah wanted to knor what was int future for meh sor ah'd bin to see side-kick – that's even what this side-kick had on CD for job applehcairtions sor ah knew et were genuine. We ended up 'aving raht wild affur, just for few week. Sheh were raht boozer an' ah 'eard sheh died int beginning of Seventehs, just before munneh were caramilised. Dropped dead one day from psoriasis of liver. Eeeeh, this music is raht grert, why dorn't they ever play it on Radior Four?'

I knew I should have been concentrating on the task ahead, but I'd never heard the old lady go on so much and all the time with a great big grin across her wise, wrinkled little kind face. She'd been with a woman as well, which was news to me. Just then the reggae stopped to be quickly replaced by some melodic hippyish guitar music.

'Love,' announced Bruce from behind his shut eyes as he played absent-mindedly with his Swiss Army knife, running the edge of it around his throat as though he was shaving.

'Nor, et were more lahk lust,' chuckled Gran, before leaning her head to one side and slowly, slowly... slowly drifting into a stoned slumber, a half-grin still remaining on her face. I think she was enjoying the journey.

I eyed Bruce in the mirror play with his little sharp knife

some more and then flip it closed and slip it away into his pants. Abruptly he opened his eyes and they were right on me in the mirror like he'd sensed me watching. He smiled at me and I knew we had to make a move, it was getting too mad in there and I felt that the drug had got into me too. The music was resonant and the lashing rain was whipping like a million cat-o'-nine-tails on a million blood-soaked backs, while the wind swirled it around outside in a forbidding way. But, despite the weather, despite the gang, despite the car's fuel nearly being gone, despite the madness creeping up on us all, and despite Gran's hushed warning of the woods, we had to get to the top of that hill, even if it killed us.

EVIL GANG AND THE 'HILL OF HATE'

DEAD COMMANDED his troops. 'Let that Scouse bird out now. You get out with 'er and make sure she don't say a thing.' Dead paused while one of his men; a really stupid-looking giant dimwit with a pudding-bowl haircut, a nose that was almost at right angles halfway down, and dressed in the gang's trademark dark tight suit got out, dragging out the Liverpudlian girl from the pub hotel with him.

Dead looked straight ahead, out the front up to the hill and the wood at the top, ignoring the slaps and screams that came from outside the car. Then he ignored the silence, only speaking when the giant dimwit clambered back in causing the BMW to sink even further on its suspension.

'It was nice of 'er to show us the way. I 'ope you thanked 'er Frank and told 'er 'ow important it is to us that she tells no-one how lucky she was to meet us.' His tone was mono, his mind one-track now.

'She won't say any more Dead,' said Frank the dimwit.

'I 'ope she ain't in pain,' added Dead.

Frank the dimwit put his hands up defensively. 'She won't be feelin' no pain Dead.'

Dead Cloutner wasn't even thinking about her now. 'Let's park up be'ind that wall an' get up that fuckin' hill. That's the wood, we can just see the tops of the trees from 'ere. Who's got the map? I don't wanna be fuckin' walkin' all fuckin' day lookin' for these fuckin' kids an' their granny.'

He turned round and snatched the map from the other gang member in the back. Frank looked to Dead for some sort of acknowledgement. Dead gave him a quick backhander. 'You weren't supposed to touch her, you stupid cunt. I'll see to you later,' he said calmly as he unflapped the map.

'Beloved Wood,' he sneered, staring at the simple words scrawled in Bruce's unlevel handwriting. 'It ain't gonna be beloved today. An' someone gimme a fuckin' umbrella. It's like we're gonna find fuckin' Moses up there. I 'ope those fuckin' boys are praying. They oughtta.' He snorted, then announced to himself. 'An' you know that, Dead. You know that.'

GED OR DEAD

GED HAD HEARD the door being locked up and that was the last he could recall until now, the pain from his balls sending him semiconscious. How long had he been out? He had no idea. What if...? He couldn't bring himself to think about Patrick. He needed to know the time, to see if it was all too late. Even if he'd had a watch on, he wouldn't have been able to see it in the bludgeoning darkness of his underground office.

He looked around to see if his eyes adjusted. Nothing, it was as though he was blind. He felt his hands still cuffed and his feet still tied up. It was hopeless thought Ged. He didn't even have a lamp he could switch on if he hopped over to it or a lighter he could flick on for a few seconds. The air was getting stale in the room and he had to do something.

'Okay Ged, I've got to be quick. It's Pat and I'm here at a pub called the Angling Tavern by Hollingworth Lake, near Rochdale. I'm in Room Two. Give us a call. Tonight. Now, if you can! Get the number from the operator. Otherwise...'

Patrick's message echoed round his head. He remembered Patrick when they'd first met, there by the bus stop in his school uniform. Ged was being picked on by a couple of older lads, racists, until Patrick arrived. Pat was not what you'd call 'hard', but he had such a self-assured sense of right and wrong that if he knew something was not good he'd sort it out ahead of anyone, not physically, but verbally battering a wrongdoer down until they crumpled. Such was his confidence when he knew he was doing something right that it would take a foolish person to have a go back. Everyone Ged had seen had backed down and that was how he'd met Patrick back in the day.

Ged would gladly die for him now. After all, he'd got him into this trouble in the first place; without him Patrick would have lost his business, but not his life. His brain started searching, using parts of itself that can only be found in a life or death situation like this. If he could get out, then maybe… the spare office key, he had a spare office key and unless he was mistaken it was still where he always kept it: inside the leather case on his mobile.

Ged dropped off the chaise longue with a thud and ignoring any pain rolled along the floor to where one of the cronies had thrown his mobile and sure enough he soon rolled his leg onto it. A bit of manoeuvring and Ged held the phone in his hands behind his back, feeling the outline of the key through the stretched leather and rolled over to the door. He wriggled the key out with his fingers and standing up, unlocked the door.

It was still pitch-dark. He needed to know the time. Suddenly something else clicked: the time was on his mobile and if he could just roll through the club to the base of the steps, then get through the fire door and up the steps to the front door he'd be able to get a signal to enable him to listen to his messages. Maybe, just maybe there was something from Patrick on there that could help to save him.

Ged rolled across the club, sending some bottles from the after-show party that still lay on the floor scattering across it. So the cleaners hadn't been in yet. Maybe he hadn't been semi-conscious for as long as he thought. Or maybe they weren't due in until tomorrow. He just wasn't sure. He got to the base of the steps and stood up, using his stomach muscles to stand from a cross-legged sitting position. He nudged the fire door with his shoulder. It was locked from the other side, as he'd suspected. There was only one thing for it, so Ged took a couple of hops back and bounced towards the door putting his full weight behind the shoulder barge. To his complete surprise, the door smashed open, leaving splintered wood hanging from the frame by the lock and Ged in a heap on the base of the steps. Without having free arms to put out and cushion his landing he'd fallen clumsily on his side, but for now the pain was secondary.

He sat on his arse facing the door he'd just busted and went up the steps on his bum. At the top he caught his breath and pressed the phone on behind his back, feeling his way on its keypad to tap in his security number. Leaving it on the floor and edging away from it he looked at the time in its green illumination. He'd been out of it all night; nothing unusual there then except the manner in which he'd got there.

He vainly tried the front door. Locked solid. He looked back at the phone, his only hope of reaching the world outside clubland. The signal was at its lowest. He just hoped it wouldn't cut out. He edged closer again to dial for his 'Messages' and as he did so he heard a blip. Shit thought Ged, the battery is low and he had no charger in the club. Sliding slightly away from the mobile he managed to put his ear down to the ear piece. A female machine voice told him he had six new messages.

Agonisingly slowly, it then told him to wait. The first message was Tomb, garbled celebratory nonsense and Ged skipped as quickly as he could to the second: Sophie, skip; third: someone who he didn't know trying to blag the club, skip; and then the voice he'd wanted to hear: '*Ged, it's Pat. I need some help. I'm at the Angling Tavern, near Rochdale. I need you to call me there as soon as you hear this. It's important. I'm in trouble. I'm going to Manchester Airport tomorrow, hopefully by noon. There's me and my Gran and another couple of passengers but they'll be all right. Gran and me need enough cash to fly to Dublin, get some space until this mess is sorted out. And I need someone to take your Saab back and all that's in it, so you can get rid of that fucking "weedkiller" and my life can get back to near-normal in a couple of months.'*

Ged acted quickly. He slid his hands up to the phone and feeling out the large button pressed it once to get to 'Phone Book'. With a weird twist of his head worthy of a circus contortionist, and ignoring the extreme pain emanating from his crotch area, Ged searched for the name he wanted and hit dial. There were a couple of minor gangsters he knew in Manchester, more like nightclub gang-stars really now, but who could still get hold of what he needed to help Patrick and his Gran.

He twisted his head down to the phone and heard it ringing, once, twice, three, blip! Ged shot up and stared at the mobile's screen. The battery was dead, as dead as his best friend was going to be if he couldn't quickly figure something out. He rolled over and groaned, the pain really hitting him now, in his balls and in his brain. His best friend was going to get murdered and he was trapped in the club.

Ged scanned around in the darkness trying to think of anything that could stop it. He groaned to himself again, this time louder, and felt a sickly taste coming up from his stomach into his mouth. This was the worst possible comedown.

STONES IMMACULATE

OUR SENSES WERE ON FULL ALERT as we slipped up the side of the hill, drenched from the moment we stepped out of the Saab. Bruce strode in front, silent, praying and wishing in his mind no doubt. I looked back at how far we'd walked, easing the spade I'd brought from the boot further up under my arm.

We were making good distance and the car was out of sight behind the ever smaller hut, even from up high as we were. I hoped Gran was okay asleep back there.

'When we get to the clearing,' I shouted to the carjacker who was in front of me walking up with head bent down and hands on knees, cowering from the howling wind and sheets of rain it blew into us, sheet after sheet after sheet, 'if you can dig a hole for the coke that's worth ten grand of the stuff to you. When Bruce has met his girl, or not, I'll go back down and bring the first lot of coke up.' My voice was carried away with the wind which whirled up and over and back down the hill, but he heard me.

'You're fucked up!' he shouted back through the gale at me. 'Why don't we just hide it down there where the car is? It's gonna take about two or three journeys to bring all them bags up here.'

I caught up with him. 'Exactly. That's why no-one would ever think of looking up here.' We eyeballed each other as we carried on up.

'Well, I hope they've found that map,' he snapped back at

me, pausing his step to flick a look of loathing at me, 'and if they come I'm gonna land you right in it.'

Then he faced me squarely, the rain dripping from the end of his nose. 'You might be fucked up,' he said pointing at me, 'but,' he continued switching his point to Bruce striding up ahead, 'you're nowhere near as fucked up as he is. You don't scare me, but he does.' There was real terror in his voice. What had Bruce said to him? What had put the fear into him?

All of a sudden though, the carjacker put his head back and shouted up towards the endlessly teeming sky. 'We're here! Come for us. *We're here!* Here we are Dead! Come and get us Dead. *Come and get us!!* I'm with you. *I'm one of your lot. We're here!* What are you waiting for? *Dead, Dead, Dead!*' I barged past him, knocking him slightly and he stopped as suddenly as he'd started his pathetic behaviour. His voice echoed around us as I carried on. Bruce and I didn't care. If the gang were here and we were killed that was how it was to be.

I looked round at the carjacker, until he came alongside me and then I let him walk in front, between Bruce and myself. He looked at me as he went by and mouthed 'Fucking mad' to me pointing at his head. I didn't know which one of us three he meant, we were all altered by the cabin fever and cannabis fervour that had set in.

The big hippy continued to stride several paces in front now, just pausing at the edge of the woods, his footsteps crunching on the ground below with each rhythmic step. The sound of falling rain hissed like a forest of adders and magnified on the thick shelter of leaves as we stepped into the Beloved Wood, but it was so heavy that large drips fell all around, causing the ground underneath to mud up in the mush of dead leaves and ferny undergrowth. Bruce waited for us to fully catch up before continuing at a pace, a little slower now as he dodged round trees.

At least it was slightly easier to walk with the relative

dryness underfoot, although it was darker under the roof of leaves and sometimes looked impenetrable up ahead. Old, mashed leaves stuck to our soles and the land smelt fresh, a clearer atmosphere to aid our tired and muddled minds, but there was still thick evil hanging in the air.

We walked further and further into the Beloved Wood, the trees' branches and bent twigs seeming to reach out to pull us further and further in. Shafts of light and water cascaded through breaks in nature's overhead cover and ran down the side of giant green mossy tree trunks that looked like they'd stood on their commanding position on top of this part of the Pennines for centuries. They most probably had. They seemed to watch the strangers in their midst, coaxing us in, coaxing us in.

We walked on in silence, drying out a little, listening to the thunderous sound of the stormy rains. Underfoot twigs snapped and in the distance thunder rumbled after the flash and crackle of lightning. I kept my luggies sharp and my glazzies peeled, constantly checking behind as it was highly likely that this wood hadn't had so many visitors at one time for years and years and years.

Even more so now, I had my doubts about Bruce's girl showing, especially as our walk continued on and on, deeper and deeper. I had no doubts the gang weren't far away. Their perseverance was admirable, but then again they had a lot to gain and their fearsome reputations to uphold. For them, this had ceased merely being about money. Now this was men's business.

The more we walked and the more I thought, I realised what strangeness had started back there at the traffic lights in Tottenham High Road. Now, in the Beloved Wood I could see the wood from the trees and that. This walk was a deathwish, but it was excitement as well, an escape from the cancer-causing drudgery of normal life. If you're still here, then that must be the same for you too.

At this point, I realised I didn't care if I lived or died. I wanted a special life, like we all do, but I didn't want a life at all among those like the carjacker. Nazty bastards such as him destroy it for the rest of us. In madness lies freedom. I couldn't get Bruce's words to leave my head… they were bombarding my tired, aching mind… in madness lies freedom… going right to the end of our journey… in madness lies freedom… becoming in tune with my body… in madness lies freedom… he was right and those words and his voice followed my every step, my every heartbeat and breath… in madness lies freedom. They span round my head a thousand times… in madness lies freedom… step by step, getting closer… in madness lies freedom… striding with purpose… in madness lies –

'There they are. We're here!' Bruce's exclamation of sheer delight brought my mind back to where we were.

I looked and saw a small immaculate circle of stones in the most beautiful small clearing ahead. Before me was a paradise with soft grass and mossy bumps, almost like lime-green velvet cushions to sit on, and around the edges grew fuchsias and wild roses of all colours and there, right in the middle of the clearing, were the stones. They were about waist-high to Bruce and sunken firmly in the ground in a small circle, just about a pace across, just there as though – like the trees – they'd always been there, greyish beige but showing brightly and just beyond them an ancient yew tree's branches hung low towards them, as they probably had for close to two thousand years.

The rain had slowed to a fine mist and I stood and trembled as I shut my eyes. There was a smell, a stirring smell of the fuchsias, and roses, the smell of their petals filled my nostrils, and swirled around my body with their heady delicious scents. I stood there feeling the energy and memories flowing through me, Julia was there too and Mum and all friends I'd loved. And you, of course, who are this far. I saw the clouds in the sky drift by inside my eyes speeded up in motion, so that days of clouds passed in seconds. The clearing was exactly as Bruce had described to me when we'd first met and it felt like I'd been plugged in and tingles ran up, then down my spine. I opened my eyes and for a brief second everyone was there, smiling and laughing; and then they were gone.

'Fuck this!' cussed the carjacker as he grabbed the spade from my loose grasp. 'This place is shit!' I stepped back expecting him to hit me with it, but Bruce had taken a step towards him and any thoughts of that quickly left the 'jacker. Instead he swiped the edge of the spade through a bunch of fuchsias and chopped their sweet-smelling heads off, just snapped their necks, as easily as that. The headless stalks quivered. I stared at them, dismayed, until they stopped moving – that Cool Cat character hadn't changed at all. Whichever way you look at it, a thorn is not a rose, even though it grows from the same place. There was no way to change him.

I found myself telling him to dig a hole the same size as the car's boot, but it didn't sound as though I'd said it. Bruce's voice came into my head once again, louder this time. I tried to shake those words out, but back they came, squirming and forcing their way inside my very self... in madness lies freedom. Now they're getting into you too, you know these words... in madness lies freedom and you know that's right... in madness lies freedom... for right at that moment... in madness lies freedom. In madness lies freedom. In madness lies freedom. In madness lies freedom. In madness lies freedom... I shook my head to clear it, and the words lifted for a while, but my mind was still clogged heavy.

The carjacker was digging furiously, his cap thrown on the floor, with Bruce forlornly looking over him. I could hear Bruce saying something about the public school where he'd known the carjacker from, where Bruce had been the one doing the digging and he was saying something to that effect, that the roles had reversed now. I looked to Bruce and he looked back to me; his eyes were watering. He lifted his chin slightly, indicating for me to go.

'It's all right,' he said, his words echoing in the clearing and sending more tingles through me. 'I'm going to look for my lost love in wood. You go and when you come back it will all be sorted.' My hair stood on end and I turned without looking back. I marched through the wood, the Beloved Wood, not caring if I saw the gang...

Bruce's voice and his words came back into my head and wouldn't leave me as I marched back through the wood, faster and faster. They weren't haunting me, just encircling me, covering me in the same way that the cloud covers the land and then comes down, and hangs there like the heaviest fog. I couldn't push his words out, it was all there was. In madness lies freedom. They were back... In madness lies freedom. Spinning around in my head like a fairground carousel... taking giant powerful steps... my legs spanning the forest floor... moving onward, onward, onward... in madness lies freedom... these words and Bruce's voice swamping me, coating me, infecting me... in madness lies freedom. I knew the way forward... *in madness lies freedom*... I paced and paced around in the wood, not heading anywhere, the rain running down me in small streams, dripping everywhere and soaking through my clothes so that they clung to my damp, shivering skin. I'm out of my mind by now and yet in my mind I knew exactly what to do. I'm going to move the world one step on.

HOLE

AS I STOOD THERE in the depth of the Beloved Wood, with the high heavens opened above, I knew exactly what was going through *his* evil and untrustworthy mind, and it was at that very point that I knew how to play it.

I'll just dig this hole. Make sure the shovel's always in my hand. When that wanker comes back with some of the coke I'll smack him round the head. Catch him clean with this shovel in his face. Bam! And he'll go down. Same if that hippy gets in my way. Then I can get back down there, knock the old dear out, throw her out the car and return to London. I'll get rid of the coke and retire, ha, ha! He's madder than I thought if he thinks I've come up here to bury half a million quids worth of cocaine for just ten grand! Even if I see the gang I'll tell them what's what. I could even leave a couple of bags of the coke up here, so I could give them all of it back from the car and still have some. No, I want it all! What's this? Some old dish. How the hell did that get up here? So what, who cares, I'll just get rid of that and dig some more. There it goes. Maybe I can get in with this gang. Get some respect. Get known around the manor. My parents would be proud of me, ha! They did nothing except give me orders and plan my life out so that it was good for them to boast about. Wonder what they'd tell their friends now? Ha! They deserve all they got after leaving me at that fucking terrible school with its strict rules while they went off and lived it up with all the other diplomats. Abandoned me and left me to fend for myself. Well, that's what I'm doing and I'll have more riches than even Jake had. Jake, my darling little brother, Jake, big in the City. Such a wanker. This hole's probably big enough now. Just stay here and wait... God, am I going to be rich. Personalised number plate, the lot. Get some Johnny big-shot clothes. Buy a swanky flat down in the Docklands. Buy some property up in north London. Shitholes and rent them out to a bunch of wanky students who wouldn't know how to fend for themselves if they had someone wiping their precious little arses. I'm going to have so much power. I'll get a new knife, carry on scaring people with my tricks. Work, work, work, that's all my fucking parents could say to me. That's when they could manage it between parties at this embassy or that state building. How about them once asking how I was, or even who I was? Well, this is my work and this is me going to work. I'm quids in! Look at me now. And why should I work for someone else. I'm smarter than that. I can make a living without having a boss telling me *what to do. I will pick my own hours and no-one will order me what to do ever again. That'll do on the digging. You could fit the whole fucking car in there! I'm really tired. When I'm back home I'm going to spend. I'm going – what's that noise?*

There it is again. Definitely someone. Who? That hippy fucked off – it must be him coming back. That nutter the hippy. Get ready Thomas. It sounds like there's two of them. The hippy and is it, is it him? *Maybe there's three. even, maybe it's the gang. Shit, what do I do? Can't see anyone. What the hell do I say? I saw something like this on TV, what was it, what did they do? The gang have got guns! Fucking hell, I don't want them shooting me. Guns, guns... fuck! Hole, got to get into... got to get... into the, into the hole.*

Keep your head down. Just keep your head down Thomas. Where are they? Where the hell are they? Who is it? It's the gang, it's the gang with guns. Don't want to... head down! *Where the hell are they? Oh shit. Don't even look. Closer. They're here, close. Very close. No, no, please, urrrgh, no. Look up, shit, look up.*

'Oh no, oh no. Please… please…'

REAR-VIEW

I FELT LIKE I KNEW, like I knew this wood, as though it were embracing me and sending me through, its twigs scraping me like skeletal fingers to see me on my way, its leaves soft and cold like Gran's old hands brushing my face.

We're still in this together. We *can* go forward, there is no turning back. What needs to be done will be done. Now theory and action are the same and that's how it is.

I am marching, faster and faster at this point. Wet clothes brush together, twigs snag and scratch as I brush past them and duck under low branches. I slip on wet roots, but haul myself quickly up. Straight, I am only going one way, straight to those stones, straight to see how Bruce has got on, straight to the hole the carjacker has duggy-dug digged. I'm marching quickly, back to where it's at.

Will alone is taking me there, making me do it, keeping me on track, keeping us on the straight and narrow. The noise of the rain up above is a hiss, a buzz, loud and inside my head like a thousand wasps have flown into my brain. Buzzing, flying, all trying to escape from the enclosed space, but too many, too many and… I shake my head trying to clear the noise and it changes note, goes higher pitched while I shake, but as soon as I stop it comes back louder. I shake again, and again the buzzing wasps are there, angrier, stinging inside my skull and stinging each other until the rage is utter and complete.

I stop dead in my tracks.

He is just stood there, stood without expression. And he is motionless, as still as the trees around. For an age we stare at each other, my arms have dropped to my side and my breathing is heavy, so heavy that I have to open my mouth. I'm panting like a dog. My mouth is dry, my head is wasping still, then, with a nod of his head, a nod that says it all, there comes a silent intensity inside my brain that feels good, like a cool shower on a sweaty body. Suddenly, there is peace. Even the teeming rain seems to stop hissing. I walk quickly, the noise slowly creeping up again. He walks slowly just ahead until I am right behind him. Then he turns round to face me again.

'We need,' he says, holding my elbows in his mighty hands, his long, lank hair dripping with water and plastered to his scalp, 'to do something, don't we.'

I look into, I mean really into, his eyes. His pupils enlarge and I see them grow. I nod. He squeezes my arms and looks back, his eyeballs flickering, taking in my eyes, and my soul beyond, like there is a thin shaft of laser beam going in through my eyes from his pupils, connecting us, putting our minds together, synchronising our every step. He lets go of my arms and turns to walk towards the clearing that we can see, bright and alight and glowing.

At the edge, where wood becomes space we stand. We can see *him*, we watch him as he spins around, looking, looking for where the noise, the footsteps, the breathing, the voices, are coming. The light is brilliant on him, illuminating and causing his dark eyes and skinny white face to flash like a long-ago lived-in skull. We watch him scurry and dart, we watch him stoop and stand on his tiptoes. We watch him panic like a scared cat and then cower in the hole he's dug.

'She didn't show,' I say to Bruce, 'did she?'

'She never was,' he says looking sadly at me, rain running down his face for a thousand tears. 'She never was anything more than a dream, a wanting of my mind. It was what I told that carjacker tosser in car when he needed to be told. Freaks me out now I realise how powerful mind can be, man. All she was, she was all I ever wanted. She is all I ever want. I want the love of my life, it's all I'm searching for: love. But she never was, man. When I was reading a book and became one of the characters she was one of the book's leading ladies. I must've made it up here one summer. I don't even remember which book, maybe I'd taken something; whatever man, she never was, she never will be...' He looks down, really sad, his face the entire picture of woe. 'I will have to keep searching, remain on the road. I need to find my lost love.'

'And one day...' I say to him, my voice echoing inside my head.

'It's okay,' he says to me, his normally deep voice just a light breath. 'I noticed you have "love" tattooed onto your skin. Perhaps I found it when I hitched a lift with you. Perhaps together we can show love.' He looks up at me, a shaft of light quivering through the branches catches his handsome features.

'So madness brought us here,' he breathes, 'and so it shall free us.'

The sound is back, twice as loud, so loud, and I clamp my ears to try to lessen it, but it doubles again as I walk out into the opening, trying to shake the noise away, trying to rid myself of the heaviness in my head. I walk to the edge of the hole where I unclasp my head, the cacophony of sound now so intense, *loud, loud, loud*. A million wasps are inside my skull stinging my brain, sticking their horny poisons into my mind, jabbing me and swarming, growing in numbers until there's only room for them to just vibrate on the spot and sting, sting out at anything. I look down at *him* whimpering, pleading, his whimpers vibrating within the noise inside. The hissing stays loud, but louder over the top I hear her. I hear Mum clearly.

Patrick, I'm always watching you son, always here… Patrick, go on, I urge you. Go with the surge son. He is as kin Patrick, he is a skin. He is as you, but he's not good… Go with the surge son. He is not good for this earth, send him back, send him into the ground, into the earth, send him to where the flowers grow from. Let them push up through him. I urge you, I err you on. Go with the surge, go with the surge…

Her voice dissipates into another noise inside my head. Unbearable, unbearable. Why my mother, why my mother urging me? I grasp my face, pushing my fingers into my eyeballs, screwing my eyes tightly, I push at my forehead, pressing my fingers deeply, and sweep my hands back through my crop, trying to force the sound out. Then I open my eyes and just for a moment I see them again and there's peace and the sound of summer laughter, here on this hillside, in this clearing: I can see Mum just there and Julia's with her and some friends and people from the flower shop and there's Ged dancing in a trance frenzy and there's Bruce and Julia's radiant and so's Mum and then from behind Mum steps her mum. It's Gran, she's up here and she's holding a big reefer in one hand. In the other she's got a pistol, a great old-fashioned Western-type silver pistol with an exquisitely carved white bone handle that she's spinning around on her trigger finger. She's wearing a long Twenties shimmering purple dress, one width all the way down from the narrow straps hanging from her bony shoulders to her ankles. Her black heels don't sink into the mud of the clearing, they just seem to hover above it. Then Gran's young again and she looks beautiful, the most beautiful woman in the world. She looks like Julia and like my mum when she was young.

I start to laugh. Laugh! Oh it's hysterical. 'Go on,' I urge Gran. 'Kill him!' She brushes past Mum and turns to smile at her and at Julia, and they both put their heads back as they laugh with me. Oh everyone's so happy. Just so happy, like Christmas, like birthdays, like sunny days. And Gran walks to the carjacker who's snivelling and whining and she points the gun to his head and just shoots him. Bam!

She leans forward a little to put the gun to his cracked, bleeding head again, as he slumps to the floor of the grave he's duggy-dug digged and pulls that trigger. Then she shoots him again, shoots his head again and again and again, six times in total, each time making his dead limp body jerk until his head is not a head, just a shattered large mess of blood and brains and skull. We're all laughing and Gran looks at us, a seriousness on her face. She's the oldest, she's the wisest. Gran knows best. ''E's raht baddun 'e is, raht baddun,' she says, dropping the gun on top of his lifeless, limp body. ''E deserved ta dar, 'e's devil 'imself.' Then abruptly, everyone is gone. They've no need to be here any more now that the carjacker's no longer with us, now that the good has been performed and the bad done. He was devil himself.

The unbearable hissing returns to me and I turn my attention back to *him*. When he finally finds some courage, some courage from within his cowardly bones, he looks up. I am stood above him, the gun pointing righteously towards his head. There is a terror like I've never seen in a man's eyes before. His expressions and breathing cross between laughter, tears, panic and fear in each second. His emotions are out of his control.

'Oh no, oh no. Please… please…'

His eyes plead with me and momentarily dart beyond to the edge of the wood and to the centre of the clearing. He starts to shake, his shoulders all jiggy up and down, his breathing rapid and shallow, his bottom lip all quivering, and I look at what makes him shake, what makes him shake more than the gun: there, in the centre of the stones where he looks, lays Bruce with his huge arms outstretched either side of him, a look of peace and contentment on his face. I look back at the carjacker, at Thomas, his whole body shaking with fear. He tries to say something, but his terror has lost him his language.

He tries to raise his hands; he manages a little bit and starts attempting to stand up, rising from his pit.

'Stay there,' I say to him, a silence once more descended inside me, an utter silence upon the clearing. 'You've dug your own hole Cool Cat...'

He slumps back down and almost cries except he has no tears. He's never had any tears. I'm glad you're still here to witness a couple of days in the life of a Tottenham carjacker. 'Drive round to the street there fucker...' I think back to the angst-looking suit guy rushing down Tottenham High Road, and the Union Jack fluttering and the pretty girls just outside Enfield '... or I'll cut your fuckin' head off with this blade, I ain't scared'.

I look to Bruce, rolling in the mud now and laughing, curling up in the foetus position and then stretching and all the while laughing and splashing. I remember the villages we've passed through on our trip, the conversations about drugs, our families, media, sex, the b'n'b, dodging Dead's bullets, introducing Gran, seeing their red BMW for the first time, the carjacker's terrible racism, his general hatred...

'Put both hands out in front of you,' I tell the 'jacker. 'Palms down.'

He does as I say and I walk round the hole, pacing like a tiger let loose from a cage and encircling its prey, all the while keeping the gun pointed at him as I do my lap; his eyes try to follow me but as I go round a second time, his fear overwhelms him and he can no longer bring himself to look.

I pace round that hole four or five times, my step quickening with each lap and I look at the useless lump of inhumanity in the hole from all angles and whichever way I see it, I know I have to do this. I bring the gun across my chest and check the silencer is on firmly.

Here, don't go thinking I'm the evil one again or feeling sorry for him. Remember, he's the bad one, he brought this upon himself with his thoughtless lack of compassion. I know

I should forgive those that trespass against us, but he and his kind will be trespassing and bringing bad upon good people like you and I for all their years. Unless... well, unless the good people like us do something about it.

His hands are palms down on the muddy woodland floor before us. His head is bowed. His fingers claw into the earth like he's gripping on, as though when I shoot him his clutching fingers will stop him from slipping backwards into the grave he's dug for himself, but when I shoot him there will be no chance of that, that is one certainty. He looks up at me and his mouth opens, but no sound will come out.

He tries again. 'Leave... please, please leave me,' he whimpers. 'Please don't... please just leave me. I don't want to, oh, oh, I don't want anything. Take all the coke. Just don't, just don't. Please. Don't kill me...' and off he goes wailing.

I bring the gun down to his splayed right hand and place it on the first knuckle on his index finger. As the cold metal touches his skin he jumps and then freezes, even his breathing stops.

I change my mind, lift the gun up and move the barrel to press against the middle knuckle on his little finger. This should stop him using it for no good, this should stop him from gripping any more weapons.

Kapooooo!

I feel light, as though a massive boil that has been filling the inside of my skull has been burst. There is silence for a moment. Bruce briefly looks over and sits up from where he's been rolling in the muddy middle of the stones. The earth has blown up back into my face and some of the carjacker's dark crimson blood has spurted lengthways out and beyond where his finger was.

His blood looks to me as beautiful as the red rose, and what I see before me is life itself. A small crater is under his bloodied hand and bits of flesh and dirt that have been blown into the air drift back down. I wipe my face with my other hand and feel wetness and dusty particles swipe across, covering my dry lips. I spit out.

Then he starts crying, like a big babby.

LOVE IS ALL YOU NEED

I MOVE THE GUN to his other index finger where I place it on his middle knuckle again. He stops sniffling for a moment, bracing himself and sure enough I squeeze the trigger, *kapoooo*! This time he screams in pain, a deep scream from within his whole body and as he screams he stares at his hands and the bloody mess. At least they still look like hands.

I stare down at his newly severed finger a little way from his hand, this one I can see. It's slightly twitching. He's in so much pain he can hardly breathe, but I hope he's taking it all in. It's just like on a plant where you have to pull the bad leaves off, so the rest of the plant and other plants around can grow. It's just the same. I'm pruning him, that's all.

He can't bring himself to look at me and I'm only doing it for the good of him, for the good of us. Does he really think I want to be up here in the pissing rain? He chose to get in my car. This was his risk, his choice. None of us can tell what will happen when we set out on a journey. But no, he won't look at me with any sort of gratitude or understanding. He's too evil to understand anything good. Instead he's just whimpering and trying to get his breath as he stares at his bloodied stumps.

Well, the good news is that I haven't finished yet. I am the driver all right. Put that in your newspaper reports, but they wouldn't and Bruce can vouch for that. They just pick out the evil and spread it to all of us. Here's the news today: we are all evil and watch out for your neighbour, and don't trust that person sat next to you. We are all evil. Yet I can see in my mind who's thankful to me for doing this and for you being in on it. Yeah, the little boy with the long hair and flares on the yellow Chopper bicycle is grateful; so are the boy scouts at the hut down the road and the friendly woman at the newsagents; so's Kevin Keegan and the man selling seafood from a stall; the old boy on the prom, him sat there in the deckchair with a vest on, he's grateful. So's Paul McCartney, George Harrison and Ringo Starr, and the Durham woman in curlers washing down her steps and so's the waiter in the Leicester curry shop.

Those wonderful men in their flying machines fighting the Battle of Britain up above us in the heavens, they'd be ever so grateful and so their widows and best friends are; the football-mad teenager tells his mum who came to this country from Kingston, Jamaica a few decades ago that he's glad for what we've done and she's proud of her son for telling her so; there's an old woman waiting at the bus stop, she's thankful, and so's the young lady in a Barbour coat walking her big black dog across the common with her children of three running in front of her. Mick Jagger, The Clash and Paul Weller are happy for our actions as well as all the characters from *Coronation Street* who are raising a toast to us in the Rover's Return. Prodigy, Manics, The Smiths and The Cure are all playing an encore for this; and Manchester United are relieved and Arsenal and Liverpool too; the farmer on his tractor, he's the happiest he's ever been, even smiling at the occasion, and all the mothers and fathers waiting at the primary-school gates at home-time are joyous for all we've done; Richard E Grant's grinning and the vicar leading the hymns at Christmas, he's singing with extra gusto, so's Noddy

Holder and Noel Gallagher. Old Trevor McDonald just can't stop smiling as he does a little celebrity dance with Robbie Williams, and don't be at all surprised that Myra Hyndley, Rosemary West and Peter Sutcliffe, scum, are not.

I can smell the metallic smoke from the hot work the Browning has been doing. It holds ten bullets which is enough for each digit on his hands, but I'm not going to use every bullet. I'm just going to shoot each knuckle of his fingers, so leaving a couple of bullets and his thumbs over. And there's you thinking I'd lost it, no not at all, this is as rational as it gets – this is for pure love: L-O-V-E-love. That's love of people and humankind and the world and for love to overcome hate. Otherwise we have nothing.

So I go at it. L's already been done, so it's O-kapoooo!-V-kapoooo!-E-kapoooo!-LOVE. And back onto his left hand, the one that held the blade to my throat, the one that held other people up, the one that would yet hold people up – someone like you – unless I go about my duty. L's around somewhere on the ground, so it's O-kapoooo!-V-kapoooo!-E-kapoooo!-LOVE.

'Aaaaaaaaaaarrrrrrrrrrrrrrrrrrrrrggh!' he cries out hoarsely. '*Aaaaaaaaarrrrrrrrrrrrrrggh!*'

There's another silence now. Even the wind and rain seem to have dropped and Bruce has stopped rolling around; he's raised on his knees in the middle of the stones and I put back my head to take a deep breath of fresh country air. When there is this much blood it actually smells. Blood smells like life; pure, which it is. It's an irony, in that during a bloody death we can smell our life. It tingles the hairs in the inside of the nostrils and it causes the adrenaline to run.

I tell the carjacker, Thomas, to look at the sky, the sky that Julia taught me to notice, the very same sky that we all look up and see. I tell him to look up to our sky. Up there, there's bits of dirt and flakes of skin drifting around, floating gently back down. Some of his bigger pieces of flesh are stuck on my hands and sleeves, a couple have even stuck on my face, one's at the corner of my lips and I can taste his blood. It's sweet. Then I turn my attention back to his hands. Not each finger came off with each shot really, a part of the palm was taken sometimes, depending on how the bullet went in during my good deed and how his pasty flesh and bone ripped apart, how each finger mashed up and lacerated with each shot. Pot luck really.

Then I notice his breath starts to catch up, rapid short breaths and he raises his bloodied, ragged palms up towards his face and stares at them, then at me with a wide-eyed terror and then stares back at the messy, red stumps at the end of his arms, his dark crimson blood dripping down his sleeves, turning the cream cuffs and sky-blue sleeves to claret and trickling from the end of his elbows onto the woodland floor below where it sinks into the damp earth. Still, he just looks fixedly at his bloodied palms, his breathing like someone having a convulsion.

'Oh no, Jesus,' he groans and then raises his voice again. *'Aaaaaaaaaaarrrrrrrrrrrrrrrrrggh! What have you done? What... have... you... done? Oh my God. Oh my God, please. Please...'*

If they are close, the gang will hear his screams, maybe they heard the eight shots fired if they are really nearby and it will trouble them. They'll have heard that the shots were controlled, not fire of fury, or panic, but eight controlled shots. They'll be worried. They know the sound of shots; for someone to shoot with coolness, my friend, is rare. I don't know if they'll come and I don't think they'll be running if they do. Perhaps if they've heard his cries, real screams, man's deafening screams from deep inside, from his stomach and chest and from his soul, they'll edge in.

I stare at him as he cries out. A pool of blood is covering his stumps now and the blood I see is my blood too, and yours and yet I don't feel any of his pain. Do you? Perhaps you do now, but what if it had been you in my position? It's difficult for you to know without experiencing what happened to me, but I'm certain that even if you're denying it, there's a little voice inside your head, it's your voice, and every so often you're saying: 'Yes. Yes, I would have given it to him as well. It's all he deserves.' See what I'm doing here is letting my badness flow with that red-rouge blood, I'm letting all my evil out, all the horrors, all the disgusting evil in this world, all the sins of man and woman, all the filth-infested thoughts we've ever had. His blood is my blood is your blood and his badness is my badness is your badness. Do you know why? Yes, because everyone comes from the same source and will end up together, so we may as well get used to each other's company. He squeezes his eyes tightly shut.

I look away from Thomas into the sky, the sky that Julia taught me to look at, and feel Bruce at my side. I hear his heavy breathing in my ears, the sound of the buzzing gone now, the sound of the still air only filled with the sobbing of Thomas from north London. I can see from the corner of my eye that Bruce is running his sharp knife around his face and throat as though he's shaving again. A whisper of wind ripples through the surrounding tree's leaves, like gentle applause, then louder as the winds picks up and the rain falls more heavily once again.

Everything is slow-motion silence now and I look over to the circle of stones that are still, like the smooth heads of million-year-old dinosaurs popping out of a lime-green velvet sea, puddles around being churned by raindrops, with shadows from the sun that breaks through a gap in the dark clouds casting from them the shapes of old men's faces in the Beloved Wood.

Suddenly I hear Thomas's sobbing increase and then equally abruptly stop and I look down at him knelt in the hole. Bruce is behind him, in the hole as well and has his Swiss Army knife at Thomas's throat, held tightly in his left hand, his other arm behind his back, the little razor-sharp blade pressing tightly to the left of the victim's Adam's apple, so tightly that it cuts him and Bruce's face creases up, and he laughs. Bruce stares at me, and even Thomas unscrews his squeezed-shut eyes to look at me, to plead with me, then Bruce swiftly pulls his right arm out from behind his back and brings Thomas's big diggy-dagger that he's holding in that hand to rest on the other side of his throat, so that the blades press into both Thomas's jugulars. Bruce must have swiped up his big blade when we left the car, thoughts of revenge sweeping his mind.

Bruce has the look of a sheer madman, someone about to turn into a werewolf, someone about to become the devil, a man possessed with a mission, his teeth are gritted into a maniac's grin, a ravenous man about to eat meat, his eyebrows arch and his eyes are on the living flesh he is about to slice, his thoughts on the warm blood that will pour forth.

For a moment, what seems like days, nobody says anything, and Bruce looks at me with a smile, one of the most alluring smiles I've seen. He nods his head at me jerkily to tell me he's going to do it, that he's going to end the show of a couple of days in the life of Thomas.

I point the gun at the middle of my forehead. '*Stop! I've got two bullets left!*' I shout to Bruce, and for the first time since we've been in the Beloved Wood it sounds just like me.

SYMBOLIC GESTURE

BRUCE'S EYES are on mine, so are Thomas's in the hole, his harmless bleeding hands out in front of him on the wet earth. I press the gun deeper into my forehead and the muscles of my forearm tense as I start my squeeze on the trigger.

'*Stop!*' This time it's Bruce who shouts, his knives still pressing at the throat of Thomas.

'This is mine,' I say, bringing the gun down from my forehead, and down slowly past Bruce's head and then down some more to stop at Thomas, the barrel pointing at the border of his scalp and hair, hard in the middle of his yin-yang symbol, using it as a target. For a moment, everything freezes. We all stop breathing and even the weather seems to pause again; the clearing is as still as a picture, Bruce standing there with Thomas's long blade pressing on one side of the Cool Cat's throat and blood dribbling from another little cut on him caused by Bruce's sharp Swiss blade pushing on the other side – and me with the Browning pointing resolutely at his head. Thomas gently closes his eyes.

For a moment it stays like this, then Bruce withdraws the knives, flipping the Swiss Army blade inside its red handle and dropping Thomas's into the hole. He takes a step back and then clambers out.

'See you afterwards,' he says looking down at the floor, before turning with a glance that says it all, that says: 'Do it man'. Then he steps off into the wood.

'Thomas,' I say a moment later. 'Open your eyes and look at me.'

Slowly his eyelids let the light in and he stares at me, like a dead man would look at you, without blinking, eyes jammed open. I want to get this over with quickly, so I start talking straightaway. 'Yin-yang: in all things bad there is good.' Somehow, through his pain, he was listening for the first time, perhaps the first time in his life. I continued. 'And in all things good there is bad.'

His eyes remain jammed open.

'Everyone changes throughout their life Thomas, through experiences, good and bad. Even on this journey we've all changed and I have fought the good fight with all my might. We have come to this because of your greed. When we put our own interest before those of others in the way you do we are most likely to do wrong.'

He really seems to be listening, so I carry on. 'From a child nicking sweets in a shop to a country's leader ordering genocide – in both, their gratification matters more than the distress that is caused to others. Human history is greater now than at any other time and will continue to be so. No wonder we feel more insignificant. Our grandchildren will think it strange we never left the planet. They will find our "modern" names old-fashioned.'

My finger starts to squeeze the trigger. He closes his eyes. I don't feel any pity for him and it's so tempting, almost irresistible to shoot that bullet through his skull. I pull the gun away from his head, fire the shot and drop it in front of his shaking fingerless hands.

It lands with a soft thud, the barrel slightly digging into the soft ground that is being softened further as the increasing rain thins his blood down and seeps into the earth. His arms instinctively move for the gun and then he suddenly stops, his subconscious will for survival overtaken by the reality that crashes into his thoughts, and the sobs come back.

'I'm leaving you with a chance,' I say, stooping down to be

close to his tear-streaked face. He opens his cloggy eyes to look at me. 'You will realise why if you look to the sky and think about it. I would have killed myself if Bruce had cut your throat. Then he'd have been as bad as you and I would have been as bad as you too for letting him. So you see, I'm with you. If you're good, I'm on your side.' He puts his head down and starts to sob ever more loudly.

'I didn't want the gun, never,' I continue, still by this nazty figure. 'My mate Ged put it in the car. He'd told me I might need it if Dead Cloutner got onto me. But I was always going to dump it when I got out of London. That was when you got in. You're here from your own actions. It's down to you if the gang find you, from Bruce's map you stole and left for them. It's all up to you now. Whatever happens next is because of your previous actions. That's how it is in life.'

He looks up at me through his tears and for a moment we stare at each other. Still I see no compassion in his ways, I think he feels regret, but only for what is happening to him, not for what he's done in his violent, spiteful life.

'This will hurt,' I say swiftly picking up the gun and digging a couple of times with the handle into the soft soil in front of each hand. 'Sorry,' I say dropping the gun before grabbing both his bloodied wrists and shoving the stubs of his fingers into the earth and scooping the loose soil on top of his hands. He screams and his head is writhing from the agony.

I have never heard such a cry. It jolts my stomach and makes me feel sick. I stand up quickly and step backwards, a sticky sweat enveloping my entire body. I check my jacket pockets, then take it off, wipe my face and hands clear of his blood and the dirt and sweat and place it round Thomas's shoulders to keep him warm.

I hear his screams and curses continue as I step into the depth of the wood, but at least he hasn't tried to get up and fight me, punch at me with those little bloodied stumps. I am pleased to see as I take one last look back at Thomas that he remains exactly where he is, with his hands stuck in the earth to stem the flow of blood. Sometimes you have to be cruel to be kind and perhaps he is finding some sense already.

The last noise I hear from him is like… I have never heard such a cry.

THE WOOD

I T FEELS LIKE AUTUMN as I cross through the wood, the rain falling even more and the leaves drop and swirl around me in the ferocious winds. His shouts are out of earshot by now. At least I hope they are because I can no longer hear them.

I hear some new noises – deep, angry voices wafting through the sounds of the weather and the rustle of the thrashing trees. They become louder and louder with each step forward, soon almost on top of me. I look towards where they come from – it's the gang, but it isn't going to stop my stride in the slightest. I keep on regardless.

I am walking within a hundred metres of Dead Cloutner and the three other hard thugs. I can see them quite clearly arguing among themselves through the dense wood as they tread down the bluebells. One look my way and they'll see me. Luckily they are so wrapped up in their disorganisation that I feel untroubled.

'Let's cut our losses Dead,' says the one they call Double-barrelled Dan, not quite with his usual upper-class calm. 'Go and see that Ged character. He's all right, but if he can't come up with our cash, I'll shoot him.'

'Yeah we'll do him, Dead,' adds Frank the dimwit, obviously scared dimwitless.

'*Shut it will ya!*' Dead yells hysterically and begins clubbing Frank with the long folded black umbrella he's carrying. After a few crisp whacks he immediately calms down again. 'We're findin' those bastards. This is not about drugs or money. This is about some fuckin' florist leading us to an unfamiliar battleground. Talk about fuckin' flower power. But I do battle anywhere. You wanna argue you come face me. I ain't 'aving this shit from my men. Since when 'as Dead Cloutner backed off?'

'It's just that it's a bit creepy up here Dead,' shudders Frank the dimwit.

'I agree Dead,' agrees Double-barrelled Dan. 'This is the sort of place where years of dark history gather to spook one out.'

Cloutner turns to look at them, his arms spread wide from his body with his fists tightly clenched, one gripping the umbrella, and I watch as Frank the dimwit edges away from him and falls backwards on a slippery root. Double-barrelled Dan and the other one of his men run to help him up, two of them bumping into each other as they do. They stand and square up to each other.

'If you don't stop behaving like Laurel and fuckin' Hardy, I'll kill you,' says Cloutner, calm as a lake at dawn. 'You're like a fuckin' bunch of pissed baboons.'

'Dead,' says Frank the dimwit as he gathers himself. 'I'll be frank.'

'You are Frank, you fuckin' lemon!' jokes Cloutner, but he isn't really laughing.

'Yeah Dead, like I was sayin' I don't like it up here in the country. There's fuckin' shadows and things. I half expect a fuckin' witch to jump out from behind a tree. Listen. I can hear noises. I'm out of here.'

'Me as well Dead,' agrees his other man. 'I don't mind admitting that I'm shit-scared up here. I'd rather be between a load of Yardies and Triads. At least I'd know what the fuck to do. This place gives me the fuckin' creeps. It ain't the city is it? I'll catch you later.'

'That's what the Old Bill 'ave been saying to me for years,' replies Dead with a smile on his face but the look of a madman in his eyes.

'Listen Dead,' says Frank the dimwit, terrified. 'I can hear wails. *What the fuck's that?* I'll –' It's me that makes him stop mid-sentence. Watching them so intently I stumble and crash into a dried bush. They all look up in my direction. I stay still.

These criminal kings of the concrete jungle are as scared as men can be, like little children lost in a city centre crowd. Except Dead Cloutner.

'Over there,' says Dead pointing straight at me, not a flicker of fear on his brutal face. 'By that bush. That's your fuckin' witch.'

I can do nothing. I remain motionless and stop breathing. Dead pulls out his gun. His men are still peering, trying to make out where I am. But Dead already has me in his sights.

'Where is he?' asks Double-barrelled Dan. I hear some mumbled voices and stretch my neck out so that I can see where they are. The three are looking around, but Dead has his gun at the ready, poised like an outlaw of the Wild West.

'Just watch where the squeal comes from,' replies Dead, taking an accurate aim. He edges forward. I know if I don't move he's going to hit me between the eyes. But if I do move he'll still get me. I have to do something. Quickly. I roll into the bush. Dead sees me. He shimmies to his left. And pop! I don't know where the bullet ends up, but it skims one tree and ricochets off elsewhere. All I know is that I'm still alive. This is it I think, evil's going to win after all. Dead is steady now. I try to drag myself so that a tree comes momentarily between us. Maybe I can run if I just get a spare second. But I tug at my leg. It's snagged. The bush is holding me captive for Dead Cloutner to finish me off. He's a few steps ahead of his men now. His eyeballs bore into mine. He steadies his aim once more. I can see his finger start the squeeze. Dead wants to make my death an event, so he speaks as his aim stays true.

'I don't even want the coke back from you now,' he says

loudly. 'I'll make your mate Ged Nealson pay for that. I just want to see if you're a witch in the woods. Will the witch sink or float?' He smiles and almost winks at me. 'Either way she's d-.'

'*Dead!*' screams Bruce like a wild man. He's covered in mud, his white eyeballs standing out clearly as he drops down from the branch, landing smack-bang in front of Dead, shoving the knife in in the same movement. 'By name and now by nature. Dead.'

The Swiss Army knife stays in Dead's chest even as he stumbles backwards. Dead gathers his composure, regains his dignity, takes hold of the knife and tugs it out. He looks at it, examining his blood, but the red stuff is gushing too much for him to find the necessary strength to raise his gun to Bruce.

In the distance I hear the faint cries of Thomas billowing about in the wind, swirling about in the leaves and twisting round the trees. Dead's three men have stepped back and the thought of drawing their weapons has not even crossed their minds such is their fear up here.

As Dead Cloutner falls to his knees clutching his heart he looks round at his men and then back at Bruce. There's a look of acknowledgement towards Bruce from those mad eyes just before he curls over to die gracefully, like a proud lion. There's no roar, just acceptance. He almost looks to be smiling, relieved that he no longer has to battle through life. 'Whatever happened to love and peace?' croaks Dead just before his eyes shut, blood dribbling in all directions from his mouth.

Bruce turns, leaving Cloutner's men terrified and cluelessly looking at their dying leader among the bluebells. Without even glancing at them he strides away into the woods. 'Shoot hippy Bruce in the back,' he says loudly without breaking step, 'and see what happens to you three in the woods today.'

I rise up as I watch. Bruce disappears into the vast denseness of the Beloved Wood and I unsnag myself. As I quickly walk on I look back to see three gangsters stuck on the spot, absolutely frozen. From the distance another cry reaches us – a cry unlike any I've heard before – and I see the three gangsters shuffle towards dead Dead, unsure what to do without Cloutner's commanding voice.

There was compassion back in me now. I'd heard Dead Cloutner was, underneath it all, a family man these days, but he was so deep in the underworld he couldn't get out. As well as being as hard and ruthless as they come he'd been a bright man – to have organised as many men as he had he had to be. Not university degrees and that, just streetwise suss. Drop a nuclear bomb on the world and he'd have survived ahead of any professor, so who's the bright one there? I didn't kid myself that we'd outwitted him and I was still not sure that somehow Dead Cloutner – or at least some of his other men – wouldn't get to us yet. I didn't know what the reaction to his death would be, only that those three he'd had with him couldn't tell it like it had been.

I carried on walking for what seemed like days and days and as I finally walked out into the open bleakness of that exposed Pennines hill, Bruce appeared from another part of the wood in step with me as though he was my reflection and walked to my side.

'All done?' he said, looking at me as we continued in our stride, the mud slipping away from the driving rain to reveal his bronzed face once more..

'I saw what you did,' I said. He knowingly nodded. 'Thanks for saving me. But things will be different between us now. I won't mention it again. By the way, what *did* happen to love and peace?'

Bruce looked humbled for a second, then he looked at me with emotionless eyes. 'I wouldn't have killed him if he hadn't been about to kill you. Law of jungle. Did you kill other one?' He looked at me, willing the answer he wanted.

I carried on without answering. He regarded me cautiously and then glanced towards where the car was parked at the bottom of the slope through the sleeting rain. From then on, there was a silence which I took to be a thoughtful one on his part.

THE LONERS

GRAN HAD BEEN in such a deep sleep that she took some time to properly wake up and even then she stayed totally silent with the melancholic atmosphere that was in the car.

Most of the drive was in silence, even when we turned into the small garage. I put a fiver of petrol into the car before going in and telling the attendant that I'd forgotten my money and he made me fill out a form. I'd pay them back one day.

We raced for miles and miles through glorious green countryside and through grimy grey council estates, the rain still pouring and my thoughts solely on getting to Manchester Airport where I hoped we could leave this mess behind. If we didn't leave there by air, only God knows what we could do.

We ominously ogled cruising cop cars and layby watchers and finally Gran broke the silence as we turned into a road taking us closer to our answer at the airport. 'Tha's still raht soggeh. Mand, et were rernen mogs and dogs, raht silen down before weren't et. Did all work out upp thurr then?' she asked, smartening up her headscarf.

I shook my head. 'It was terrible.' Despite my company I felt alone.

'Is other one still upp thurr?'

I nodded.

'An' Bruce's lass?' she asked, looking to Bruce. He forlornly shook his lank hair in front of his face.

'Beloved Wood,' Gran uttered. 'Et's all true what folk sair

269

then about et, that things 'appen upp there.' She knew something major had gone on. 'Where we goen now chuck?'

'Hopefully to Dublin, Gran.'

'Eeh grert, ah'm ever soh thrilled. Ah'm nebby, dorn't normally stick mah neb int other folk's lahvs butt as tha's mah grandsun will tha tell me about exactly what 'appened upp thurr when weh get to airport?'

I nodded at Gran.

'What about tha, Bruce?' she asked seriously, looking ahead.

'I really don't know Granny Gron,' he replied sadly, looking at her through the middle of the two front seats. 'I may go off on my own. I'm used to it and I've got plenty left to see in world.'

I saw Gran look forlornly out of the window, for a moment, then she turned to Bruce. 'Is tha sad?' she asked.

'Yeah,' said Bruce to Gran before turning to me. 'Do you remember when we met?' He looked to the side of my face and I turned to look back at him. I nodded again, I could hardly bring myself to speak and looked back to the road as we slowed up on it in the volume of traffic. I had to keep my eyes sharp here, for any of Dead's men or the police.

'It's been great meeting you,' he continued, 'both of you. Meeting people is what life's about. Meeting someone who makes you feel great about life, like you two have, that gives you hope, it's what keeps us going. I mean, I've chosen lone travelling life, but as I go round if I didn't meet anyone decent I'd die within myself.' He gazed at me intently. 'And why did we meet? I believe we were meant to, all of us. That includes the other one, who we left behind. Without you meeting him, I wouldn't have met you or Granny Gron. Or Dead Cloutner.' He looked out of the side window at a patrol car that lazily passed us for a brief moment before continuing. 'Everyone we meet throughout our entire lives is supposed to be,' he said.

'Tha's raht tah knor anall. All folk ah've ever met en mah

lahf 'as come round full circle. Sor dorn't ignore any meeten.'

'That's what I mean,' agreed Bruce. 'We should treat each meeting as having a special significance. When we meet someone, we should not just listen to what they say and do but why they say and do those things. Even from meeting someone like Thomas, we can take some good.'

He paused and looked at Gran, then back at me. It seemed like he stared at me for ages. It was only seconds but it felt like hours, like he was regarding someone he loved. Then while still gazing at me he carried on speaking, quietly and somewhat subdued. 'I'm really glad we met,' he said. 'You're one of the special ones.' Then he stared back out of the side window.

From there on we meandered to the airport in silence and a state of shock. I felt like a different person to the one I'd been up the top and in the midst of the Beloved Wood. I couldn't admit what had happened up there, it was already pushed away as though I was trying to get it from my memory. It was like something I'd read about that happened to someone else.

From the entrance roads at the bustling airport, I steered the car into a short-stay and parked up. We all clambered out under the fluorescent lighting and still in a huge hush headed for the departure lounge. I looked to the two who walked either side of me: Bruce was deep in thought, while Gran was still feeling the after-effects of her first high.

When we finally reach that airport building it's really busy. As we walk into the roomy lounge, we're hit with a moving wall of rushing people and a loud announcement for a final call to board. I scan around for any of Dead's men, Ged, police or security watching us in among the mêlée. There's a group of security men over the other side by a shop, a Boots chemists, and just a few shops down standing outside a sandwich bar are a couple of suited-up lumps wearing shades. It reminds me and I take mine off and hang them from my shirt pocket: I don't want to look as suspicious as them although the dark rings I imagine I have under my eyes possibly look worse.

I look back at the security men. One is talking urgently into his radio. There are three of them now, and they are swiftly joined by another two. Suddenly three more come running up to them. I freeze, sensing Bruce towering beside me, also watching the commotion they are causing.

Abruptly two of the men dart into the chemists and grab hold of a couple of teenage girls. They're arresting two young female shoplifters and as the rest join them I figure they're not onto us – if it takes eight of Manchester Airport's security team to nab two girls for nicking make-up they're not after us. I cast my eye to the two thugs in sunglasses. They've disappeared.

Bruce tugs my arm and we wander off to stop under the departures board. As we look up at our imaginary flight, Gran steps in the middle and links arms with Bruce and me. She senses our worry and woe. Around us, people ferry to and fro, couples embrace and cry, tanned voyagers amble through to catch their flights, people drag too heavy suitcases, others stuff their faces with delicious-smelling food on the go, and a mother and father hug their son before wishing him a nice stay in Australia and emotionally tell him they'll look forward to seeing him in six months although I notice his younger sister looks quietly happy that he's leaving.

It's packed, but there's no sign of Ged anywhere. We are in some large trouble here. I'm thinking that I can't keep driving through Britain with Gran and Bruce, we have to settle somewhere very soon and as out of place as Dead and his merry men had looked in the woods, I am certain that Dead's men know every address in Britain where we can stay. Have they found Thomas yet? If so what's he said – he knew our plans to get away from this airport. He'll have told them in a bid to survive. If they found him they'd kill him either way.

Bruce senses the tension too and seeks to lessen it. 'I met this girl once after a flight,' he says. 'Rrrrr-ita was her name. From Finland.'

Gran and I look to him while we stand there on the edge of the travelling crowd. 'She met me at Helsinki airport,' Bruce continues. 'We'd been seeing each other a few weeks before and she'd decided it was time I met her family. I said to her, "But I can't speak Finnish" and she told me not to worry as all her family could speak English. So I arrived at this bar we'd arranged to meet at and there's dozens of relatives there.'

I keep my watch as I listen to him and pretend to check the departures board again.

'They're all sat round a large table,' Bruce says, a smile forming on his face. 'We sit down. Everyone there knows each other except for me. So I start shaking hands with these rather serious bunch of Finns. Then I feel something hot down back of my trousers. I'm on about my third handshake of twenty when it feels so hot I have to suddenly stand up.'

He pats the top of his arse to show us where he'd been burning, then continues. 'So suddenly I'm up hopping around in front of all these Finns with my girl shouting: "Take your trousers down! Get your pants off!" But I couldn't remember if I've put underpants on. She's still crying out and I'm still hopping about. Then she sticks her hand down back of my bum and brings out lighted cigarette she'd accidentally dropped down there. She puts it in her mouth and takes a drag.'

He looks at us two with that big grin across his broad face. 'That broke ice anyway.'

'What 'appened to lass?' Gran asks.

'Packed her in,' grins Bruce. 'She smoked too much.'

Gran chuckles away to herself and while it has taken my thoughts for a second I know that unless we can find... I scan around again, but it's hopeless, so crowded it's as though the whole of the north of England is going away on holiday.

How can we – 'Come with me.' The voice and the person with it comes from nowhere, just steps in front of us from the rushing crowds as though he's a camouflaged Vietcong appearing from a dense jungle. I tense up like a muscle clinging to a rock.

We look to the person who has spoken, in particular at the two indigo tears he has tattooed on his face.

LONDON MAN IS TORTURED

NICK CLARK STARED at his blank computer screen. He had two stories to write, just small stories, but he couldn't stop thinking about the editor's ultimatum and his news editor's words reverberated around his head. He had a week to get a big story and his idiot of a news editor had given him these two small stories to write.

'This is what we've got today,' he'd said. 'They've got me on sport as well, so there's a football match: one nil to Enfield last night. They were playing away and, er, that's it. That's all we've got – reporter got too drunk in the player's bar to file his copy. God, I'm surrounded by useless drunks. Knock up three pars on that. Just say they defended well and the Enfield fans went away happy, usual rubbish like that. Then when you've done that, what do you know about this local band?'

He'd thrown a photograph of three posing teenagers in front of Nick Clark. Clark shook his head at the picture. His news editor shook his head at Clark. 'They've just gone in the charts, Top Twenty. We've got to write some story about them. We're the bloody local newspaper. That's what we do. We provide local news. And there's blank pages to fill. I need some copy on them in one hour. If you can't find anything about them, make something up. And it had better be good. For your sake.'

Clark's mind was blank. No news on the carjackings and he was a lost man. What was worse was that he was expecting a call from his wife Jill's divorce lawyer. That was the man that was going to legally take his son away from him. He looked at the time on his blank computer screen and then around the small, scruffy local newspaper office at the piles of past editions of the *Independent Journal*, and not one bearing his byline on the front page. God, he needed a drink. Clark pressed a key on the keyboard and kept his finger there, hoping it would give him some inspiration, find him that spark that he'd had before he'd started to lose his marriage and got worse on the sauce. He looked at the screen filling up before his bleary eyes with the letter 'x' and that's what he was, he thought. An ex. An ex-husband, an ex-journalist, an ex-father.

The phone rang. He stared at it. Did he really want to pick it up and begin the end? He stared at it. It still rang.

'Yeah. Nick Clark. Get on with it.' He listened…'Go on… okay… yep, yep… I see. And you're calling from Manchester Police…? There is, yeah, there's a drinking club called that in Edmonton… No I'm not surprised they hadn't heard of it. People who go there tend to keep away from you lot… Yep, well it sounds like he could be from Edmonton. And you say he's just been discovered?' He grabbed a pen and holding the phone under his chin started to scribble key words in his notebook: 'Farmer. Heard shots. Found victim. Beloved Wood. Near Rochdale. Tortured.'

'Tortured you say?' Clark excitedly asked. He listened to the answer, the headline already forming in his mind.

He put the phone down and thought for a second. Here was a great story. Hold the front page! It was definitely front page unless something else major happened or he really was out of luck. They'd have to give him a big byline on this one. And the police had thanked *him* for *his* help. Clark's adrenaline was pumping. He had to get up to Manchester and find out what he could. Should he ask his news editor? No sod that, he thought, he'd probably send someone else, one of the eager new trainees or Sue bloody MacDougall, the front-page byline queen, and no wonder when they send her on all the best stories. Get this story and he could even make the nationals if the *Independent Journal* ran it as the front-page splash. This was his last chance. He'd better make it good. Nick Clark smiled for the first time since the late bar as he looked at his screen full of x after x, and he thought: 'Expert, excellent, even the *Daily Express!*'

As he walked through the office he thought of this wonderful news. A local man tortured and discovered in a wood up north. Fantastic!

'Where's that copy, Clark?' barked his news editor as he rushed to the door.

'It's on my computer screen,' replied Clark before closing the door and stepping out onto the street to head for the hills.

GONNA GO MY WAY

'COME WITH ME,' he repeats. I'm taking in details, anything that can tell me who is this stranger at the airport. He has a brown mop-toppish style of hair combed forward and a weak jaw, his skin has a few spots on and he's unshaven for several days revealing a few sprouts of white hair on his chin. He wears black jeans, some black Converse All Star sneakers and a navy-blue snorkel jacket with orange lining. His face has on it an expression that almost makes the tattooed tears appear to be flowing.

He's aware of us studying him with suspicion. 'Ged sent me,' he says in a slightly mixed-up Mancunian accent. 'Name's Mark. Come on, we'd better get on with it.'

He walks off, so we follow him to a coffee shop around the edge of the departure lounge where he sits down and places a small carrier bag with a CD in it and a folded tabloid newspaper on the table in front of him. I'm still unsure, is he something to do with the gang, sent here to lead us away to some quiet spot? Then when they've got us there, bam bam! We're dead.

'These seats okay?' he asks and we numbly sit down.

'That's yours,' he says, motioning to the bag on the table, 'in return I believe for a set of car keys.'

I nod and fish out the keys from my pocket. I keep hold of them tightly in my sweaty palms. I'm still not certain who's sent him and can't just let the car keys go without being sure.

He could easily pull out a gun and point it at us under the table and then scarper off with the car. Or he could just shoot us. In the crowds and confusion he'd escape and if he was one of Dead's men they'd look after him, see him safely out of the country.

'How's Ged?' I enquire, partly to test this tattooed character, and bracing myself for the answer.

'He's okay. He's been roughed a bit, but he's a tough lad as you know. Couple of Dead Cloutner's lot tied him up, but he's okay now. As soon as I saw his email I called another of the regular lads from the club – Tomb, you might know him. He's gone down to get him out. Off his head as usual but at least I knew he'd be awake and mad for it, you know what I'm saying, Patrick?'

'Yeah, I know Tomb,' I nod as I shake his hand with the keys still squeezed in my palm. This figures, Ged's been getting obsessed with his computer and you had to know Tomb for a while to know that he's out of it all the time, otherwise you might just think he's a bit eccentric. 'Good idea to call Tomb,' I add. 'He's always awake. Any of Cloutner's men onto us?'

'Not as far as I know.' He stops shaking hands with me and takes the keys as he pulls his hand away. Gran and Bruce sit quietly listening, but I know Bruce is ready to deal with anything that might flare up.

'Bearing in mind my identity, is this kosher, d'ye ken?' Bruce asks.

'As a cloven-hooved haggis,' I nod. 'I think we've made it.'

For this was the point when I felt the journey was over, when I first started to be able to catch my breath and look back on what had happened and realised that I needed to tell someone like you. It looked as though we'd got away from Dead Cloutner's men and that we were going to be able to get out of the country for a while, Ged was okay and I'd put the carjacker right from his wrong ways. But it was some ordeal and will be pointless unless the story of that Tottenham carjacker is told.

Bruce must have sensed my relief too. 'So after nearly getting killed by the self-styled super modern highwayman, we've been saved by the modern superhighway, man. Is that right?' he commented.

'Yeah,' I said, 'seems so.'

'They smashed Ged's office phone,' explained Mark, 'took his answer machine with your message about hotel on. Then left him locked in there and tied up. What they missed was his laptop though. Any road, I'm meeting fellow from that Amsterdam flight that should arrive just about when yours takes off, and he's coming into Salford with me where we'll do an exchange. Good news for you is that Ged's going to sort Dead Cloutner with some on top for his inconvenience. There's a bit spare in there for you.' He nodded to the carrier bag. 'Dead Cloutner'll be all right with Ged. He likes his club a lot and it's worth a fair bit of rich business to him. Knowing how Cloutner operates he'll probably make light of it.' He reassuringly nodded his tattooed tears at me.

I shook my head at him. 'Dead's dead.'

'What?' puzzled Mark. 'You serious?'

I nodded, making sure I didn't look at Bruce. 'The thing is, I don't think anyone will ever find out who did it. If the truth is told there'll be more deaths – those of the ones telling the truth. God knows what they'll come up with, but it won't be the truth. They may even have to do a country bunk themselves.' Mark was staring at me. 'If no-one finds out,' I said to him, 'do you think Ged will be safe?'

'What happened?' he asked.

'I'll fill you in when we're safely away,' I said, glancing towards Gran. 'Give me your number.'

Mark felt for a pen and scribbled his number down before looking at me earnestly. 'Make that call to me as soon as you land. If anything needs to be done, like Ged joining you, we'll sort it out. By the sound of things, it should be okay. Where there's something to cover, often no-one has to hide, you know what I mean?'

'Yeah, I think so. I hope so. What about my shop?'

'Ged's going to sort out your business. Pay your debts and that. Then he'll get it closed down, sell it and if you get in touch with me in a few weeks I'll forward you some more money.' Mark paused. 'I was going to say that Cloutner'll call chase off when he's got his cash, so long as you never see him again, or he doesn't hear from you again. Well now he definitely will. Things will quieten down I reckon while all those London crooks are suspicious of each other. And paranoid that they'll be next.' He looked up and around to see that no-one was listening into our conversation.

'But obviously stay out of Ged's club if you ever come back,' added Mark, his eyes firmly on mine to show that he was serious. 'If I were you, I wouldn't come back. We'll get the money from the "weedkiller" sorted out. Seeing as no-one's likely to claim it now, we'll split it and send some on to you. Things may have just worked out all right. He's a top one, that cockney Ged. As you'd say down there: "He's a right diamond geezer."'

He smiled at us, revealing a gold tooth in his Manchester grin. Gran was nodding in agreement.

I shuffled my chair closer into the table. 'I'll always owe Ged. That's what best friends are about. So where're we going then?'

'It were a nice picture of you and your Gran that he emailed over,' smiled Mark. He looked to Gran. 'We had to guess your birth date, so we made you 70 on the passport. I reckon you can easily get away with that.'

'Eeeh, thanks chuck, ah feel raht flattered,' said Gran, patting her headscarf to make sure it was still on straight.

We all looked up at him as he pushed his chair back and stood up. 'There's tickets in that bag. Flight leaves sharpish. When you're there a local called Frank O'Brien will meet you at airport. He'll look after you until you decide what to do next. He knows what you look like from email pics I sent him. Have a good flight – it's about eight hours I think.'

'Eight hours to Dublin!' I exclaimed. 'Are we pedalling?'

'You're not going to Dublin. You're going to Chicago.'

'Chicago!' I said and with a courteous nod our Mark affirmed. 'Dublin's too close for comfort. Ged knows a lot of people in Chicago through nightclub scene. In any case, it was the best offer that he could find on internet and he said that Gran would appreciate it.' I looked at Gran and tears were in her eyes. She leaned to Mark and pressed her cheek to his, a couple of tears trickling down her face and for a moment their tears were mirrored. Gran wiped her face and pulled away. Looking him in the eyes, she regained her composure. 'Thanks chuck. Thank Ged for us anall.'

'I will luv. Just don't send him postcard in case someone intercepts it,' said Mark. He kept looking at Gran. 'Chicago's the original home of the gangster anall, so keep Ged's Patrick out of trouble.' He touched Gran on the cheek and nodded at Bruce before turning to me and playfully poking me in the stomach. 'You look like you need a decent kip on plane. Play safe.'

With that he turned and we all watched him walk off and disappear into the crowd with the bowl that only a lad from Manchester can manage. I looked into the bag and felt Gran's and Bruce's eyes following the tickets I pulled out.

I glanced and placed them in my pocket. 'Two for Chicago. Boarding in twenty minutes.'

Bruce looked at me and then at Gran. I delved into the bag some more, and felt an envelope. I picked it out and discreetly opened it under the table.

'Two passports,' I announced as I opened them. 'Oh yeah, look Gran. It's the old picture of you in your passport that Ged wanted to use on his club flyer. For a night called Purple Rinsed.'

'Eh?' queried Gran, touching the sparse white hair that poked out at the front under her headscarf as I handed her a passport.

'Never mind that,' I said excitedly. 'There's some notes in here too, fifties.' I quickly flicked through them still keeping the envelope under the table. I looked up with my eyebrows raised and breathed out a rush of breath. All eyes were on me.

'How much?' asked Bruce.

'There's about thirty grand in here. Nice one Ged.'

'*'Ow mutch?!*' squealed Gran.

'Keep it down Gran,' I whispered, discreetly scanning around to see if anyone had heard us. 'It won't last long out there. But we'll have some really decent food first thing.'

'Eeeeh, ah'm ever sor thrilled. Ah 'orp weh can get semolina?' Gran said as she stared at her passport. 'An' ah 'orp there's not mutch plat-stic in Chicago. Dorn't lahk this passport mutch, too mutch plat-stic on this. 'Ere are, tha can hold et. Ah 'ope ah dorn't sound ungrertful. Ah'm not. Ah'm raht thrilled.'

She turned to Bruce. 'Ah've never been out of England before. What will tha do, our Bruce?' she asked, grasping one of Bruce's huge paws between both of her bony, wrinkled hands.

Bruce lifted his massive frame from under the table and stood up tall, still holding Gran's hands with her arms now outstretched before her. 'I fancy Peru,' he said. 'If you can lend me a bit, that is. There was a girl there I met called Carmen a few years back. I've still got feelings for her. I've found plenty of answers out there in world, but she's the one. She could be my one answer. If I hitch a lift from city to her village, I know where I'll find her.' I nodded bravely at him.

In the envelope I flicked through ten thousand in fifties. I pulled them out under the table and placed them on the chair where Bruce had just been sitting. I hoped it would help him find whatever it was that he was trying to find.

He leaned to kiss Gran on the top of her forehead, letting his hand slip from her grip and scooped up the wad which he then swiftly stuck into his jeans. Gran chuckled with embarrassment as he kissed her. Bruce looked to me. 'Thanks for loan and thanks for lift. I'll be on my way.' He patted his back pocket. 'Passport. I'm a traveller, you see. Keep looking to skies, and every time you see or hear a plane, think of me. Might go and buy a good book now to read for journey.'

'Yeah, well steer clear of any where there's hijackers on a plane,' I said. 'And hide that stash you've got.'

'Oh yeah,' he said casually. 'Don't worry, that comes second nature. I'm usually okay at customs. I think they figure that if I'm going to smuggle any drugs, first thing I'd do is get a haircut and dress smart.'

'Eh, butt ah feel raht as rern after smorken that stuff,' noted Gran. 'That should be allowed. Ah read int 'papers that et turned everyone into murderen robbers. Ah also read int 'papers that orld and yung folk can't get on int modern world, butt that's rubbish anall. Weh get on raht grand, dorn't weh. If they didn't print sutch rubbish, nobodeh'd even think et.'

Bruce smiled at me, that original charming grin that I'd seen back at the edge of the service station, put his hand out and I grasped it. He kept smiling as his huge palm covered mine before he unclasped and without any further hesitation turned and wandered off. In his time he must have bid farewell to so many people he'd bonded with that he knew it was painful to drag it out.

We watched that giant of a big travelling man in his long hair, scruffy T-shirt, straggly jeans and big boots head towards the booking desks until the throng of people around caused us to lose sight. I shall never forget him and who knows, maybe if I travel enough, or you travel enough, one of us might meet him.

'Tara Bruce,' whispered Gran to herself. 'Tara.'

'Come on Gran,' I said wearily. 'We've got a flight to catch. Let's go to America.'

I helped Gran up and led her on my arm through the bustling crowd of travellers and greeters and wavers bye-bye. We walked towards the departure gates and I suppose this is where we finish one journey and start another.

We hustled through the controls and checks and soon found ourselves walking across the bridge onto the plane. Gran walked in awe at the whole spectacle and only spoke when we were safely fastened in. Perhaps she knew, perhaps she was thinking like I was thinking that she'd never see her beloved northern England, where she'd spent nearly all her life, ever again. I'll probably be back one day, but I'll never be there with Gran. As we squeezed along the plane's aisle, Gran showed no emotion though and when we reached our seats she insisted on going by the window which left me sandwiched between her and a fidgeting overweight middle-aged businessman.

As though she'd been reading my thoughts she scanned the outside scenery. 'Better tehk et all in,' she said, still taking it all in. 'Even if ah dorn't gor blarnd, ah'll morst lahkleh never see this land again. Et's treated me well, butt ah'm glad for owning nowt now – as ah've not got mutch, ah've not got mutch to leave back en 'orm int dales.' She shrugged and turned her neck to look at something. 'Eeeeh, looke at that plairn landen,' she said pointing through the plane's window. I looked and saw a KLM flight touch down and scurry off out of our sight. It could well be that our man from the land of tulips had just landed.

As we started to taxi, Gran pulled out the airline's well-thumbed in-flight brochure and flicked through it. My mind was whirling as we swirled around on our bumpy taxiing about. Suddenly Gran turned to me. 'There's story 'ere about blorke en Middle East who got his 'ands chopped off en public because 'e got caught stealen.' She blinked at me through her glasses. 'That's terrible, ah wouldn't want to live en a societeh lahk that, would tha?'

The jet engines whooshed into action and we were pressed back in our seats as the plane got speed up along the runway.

Gran looked up from the magazine and out of the plane's window before turning her wise old eyes to me. 'Well dorn't supporse 'e'll steal again. But if tha ask meh, one who chopped 'is 'ands off is just as bad because they 'ave fallen with bad deeds of thief. What does tha think?'

I closed my eyes and slowly wiped my hand down my face, gripping it as though to feel it was still me. I was sweating, and aware that something had altered since the start of our journey. I could sense Gran looking at me. It was me that had changed.

'Now tell meh exactly what 'appened upp ont Beloved Wood then?' she asked.

'I thought you already knew Gran.'

'Ah'm not blind yet an' ah knor more than tha's told meh, but ah want to 'ear et from tha. And then ah want to knor what weh plan to do in Ammurca – can weh rent car and drive to visit our Albeh?'

I nodded. 'That's a decent idea Gran.'

Just then there was a thrusting roar and the plane went to forty-five degrees as we flung off into the air, high above the Pennines, above the Beloved Wood and the ancient stones, and Thomas, and Dead Cloutner's body, and this beautiful part of the world before rounding across Ireland and the Atlantic towards the New World. I breathed a deep sigh as I prepared to tell Gran the story of a couple of days in the life of a Tottenham carjacker called Thomas.

Sit comfortably. We're in this together.